SONG OF WINGS

BOOK 2 | THE SIREN'S CALL SERIES

KRIS FARYN

NIMBUS BRANDS
PUBLISHING

～

Wow!! Where do I begin, Kris Faryn's Book two "Song of Wings" is such an amazing, exciting story. And what better way to tell a story then through myth. Ms. Faryn's writing flows with suspense, wonder, pain, heartbreak, love and every human emotion you can imagine. Her characters are so alive and I connected to each personality. Korrina, which is Greek for maiden, has grown so much since book one "Song of Destiny" and her adventures are deeper with more insight coming to her but she still has that snarky wit and indecision. In "Song of Wings" I felt a deeper soul connection to Korrina as she becomes more aware of herself. When Korrina and her friends passed through the veil and entered the other dimension, I was enwrapped in the description of the realm of the gods and goddesses. Underneath the snarky remarks from everyone during this adventure is a story of the heroine's journey, a journey for the broken and for women who are broken and anyone who has experiences loss or heart ache but there is amazing redemption in this too. Kris Faryn is an author to watch. After reading "Song of Wings" I can't even imagine where Ms. Faryn will go with book three "Song of Curses".

SHIVANI, AMAZON

～

FREE NOVELETTE

Want more of The Siren's Call world? Sign up for my newsletter and receive a free novelette!

Sign Up For Kris Faryn's Newsletter And Read A Free Novelette Today!

CHAPTER 1

The last thing we needed was to attract the attention of the Council of the Gods. Again.

I hovered over Dad's shoulder and peered out the expansive window of our RV, our four-wheeled home away from normal life. "There. See that trail? Burned on the edges. Chimera tracks."

We'd left normal a long time ago.

Rumors of a strange bear-slash-wild boar-slash-Big Foot had brought us to the foothills outside Hot Springs, Arkansas.

How anyone could mistake a chimera for Big Foot was beyond me. The beasts were an indecisive mash-up of a goat, a lion, and a serpent. The god who'd created them had a really hard time making decisions.

But until the Council sent us our next mission, this was how we spent our free time. Hunting down mythical creatures and sending them back to their side of the veil. And unless we royally screwed up, the Council left us alone. Which was better —safer—for everyone. The gods, for all their own failings, couldn't abide ours.

Dad pulled the RV over to the side of the backwoods road,

and I hopped out before he turned off the ignition. Trees towered over us, thick and shadowed, and a chill floated on the air that defied the ninety-plus degree weather everyone else was having. Perfect hunting weather.

I reached up to a charred branch, still warm to the touch, though just barely.

Dad jumped to the ground behind me and shoved his Guardian sword into the scabbard on his back. "This one's yours. We'll back you up."

He'd been telling me this day was coming. My first time to lead the hunt. But rather than nervous sweats, excitement trilled in my blood.

I'd come to love a good fight.

I darted into the deep blues of the forest and followed the chimera's trail. My song went out before me, a soft whisper, to detect any other powers nearby. A chimera didn't have magic per se, but they were mythical beings in a human world. No human weapon could take them down.

I was a weapon. But not, apparently, human.

My song stuttered.

And that was all the warning I had.

The chimera's fire sword swung at my neck, and the scent of my burnt hair caved in on me. Fires sprouted through the underbrush, but Dad and Neri would get those.

I rolled out of the way and into a crouch and patted out the spark singeing the end of my curls. My Siren song coiled in the center of my chest.

I whirled around, took the chimera in. It didn't matter how many times I encountered the mythological, their weirdness always stole my breath.

It paced a few feet away on two paws, twirling a giant, flame-breathing sword and wielding double-edged smiles. The goat head was ridiculous. The lion head…not so much. The chimera's serpent-headed tail flicked around and darted at my ankles.

I skipped over its fangs and leapt into the air. "If I've told you baddies once, I've told you a bajillion times…" I gasped, threw a throat punch, ducked, whirled around in a low, roundhouse kick, and connected with the chimera's paws. "The hair is off"—kick to its chest, dodge the serpent tail—"limits."

The look on its two faces would have been comical had it not also been about to meet its doom.

My song sprang from my chest like a supernatural jack-in-the-box, connected with the beast, and wrapped it in a ball of white energy. The ball grew to enclose the chimera's massive size, all the while singing a melody apparently only I could hear, and, with a heartbeat-like pulse, bulged out and collapsed on itself. It sent out a disc of energy like an exploding star and sent everything the chimera had brought with it—from her wooden dishes to her red cape—back behind the veil.

What was it trying to be? Little Red Riding Hood and the Big Bad Wolf all at once?

Neri flapped down from a tree branch and landed on my shoulder. "They're getting stronger."

"Noted. Thanks for the help." In addition to being a super-powered Siren, I also was a super-powered sarcastic.

She ruffled her iridescent feathers and stretched out her owl neck. For a spirit guide from behind the veil that separated our world from the mythical world, she really wasn't much help.

Dad plowed through the underbrush, using his Guardian's sword as a hatchet. Probably not how the Council had intended him to use the weapon.

"You were a little slow on your initial attack. Remember, the first attacker—"

"Has the advantage," I finished for him. Over the past six months since we'd left Brooklyn, my friends, my life, I'd heard phrases like that from morning to sunset. And since the three of us shared an RV, it's not like I could escape to my room. Nope, my room was a bed that converted to the kitchen table during the day. And my dad…wasn't my bio-dad, even though he'd pretended to be for years.

He had since embraced his unveiled role as the assigned Guardian over my life and I rarely saw him act like a dad anymore. But trainer, coach, instructor, boss—I'd seen enough of those roles to last me however long my Siren life lasted.

"Did you clear the area?" Guardian Dad sheathed his sword into the scabbard always attached to his back, folded his arms across his chest, and widened his feet into his battle stance. Looking at him, you'd think it was the time of King Arthur, not the Kardashians and Insta celebrities.

"I was a little busy." I gestured at the chimera's destroyed campsite.

"Clear the area," he spouted off and stalked back in the direction of the RV.

"What's with him?" I shrugged Neri off my shoulder.

She flapped into the air and helped me make sure none of the chimera's friends had come with her. Not that they'd still be here. My brand of Siren power had that side effect.

"He received a message from the Council this morning. There's a new mission."

My legs wobbled like someone had kicked them. Missions from the Council were never good. Once, they'd had us retrieve a black rock from an old, abandoned prison. Turned out it was a blood stone that all the criminals had dripped their blood on, ensuring that whoever held it would be cursed.

And did the Council tell us not to touch the rock? No, they did not.

That had been a fun weekend.

We joined Dad at the RV an hour later. He knelt by the campfire, elbows on knees like a wild gorilla, burning a piece of paper that let off silver sparks. All telltale signs that he was burning the gods' message.

"You look like a hangry caveman," I announced. "What's for dinner?" I asked in my best caveman voice.

Dad looked up, startled, and dropped the message into the fire. It balled up in a flame of dancing silver and slowly burned away.

Normally, Dad would have read us the mission from the paper and re-read it until he was certain we had memorized every misplaced comma—the gods weren't known for their grammar skills.

He stood and stretched out his legs, like he'd been in ape position for a while. "I haven't started it yet. Hot dogs or popcorn?"

And six months ago, I would have shifted my thoughts to dinner. Hot dogs or popcorn? But Dad was hiding something that was in the Council's message—and expecting me to trust his silence.

I'd learned how to fight, use my song as a weapon, and live in small quarters. But the most valuable skill I'd learned since *that night* was guarding my trust.

I didn't trust anyone anymore. Especially not him.

I grabbed hot dogs and popcorn out of our dwindling stash. If I was going to fight creatures who looked like they'd been pieced together by a two-year-old who'd just discovered glue...*by myself*...I was going to have a feast.

We'd have to raid a grocery store soon if we could afford it—surprisingly, being the gods lap Siren paid less than my now non-existent allowance.

We sat around the fire, roasting our hot dogs on a stick and waiting for the foil-covered popcorn to pop. Neri perched on a brass coat rack Dad had found at someone's curb back in Mississippi.

I rotated my hot dog, the skin bubbling and turning brown. "Where are the gods sending us next?"

Dad set his dog on fire. Not by accident. Because he liked the taste of ashes. Probably reminded him of the taste of his fallen enemies or some other stupid Guardian thing. "Idaho."

"What's in Idaho?" I pulled my hot dog out of the flames, dropped it onto the paper plate in my lap, and grabbed a handful of mustard packets.

Neri shuffled from side to side, waiting for Dad to relay our orders.

He hesitated. "A new weapon. We are to recover the weapon and learn how to utilize it before Phorkys can discover its location."

Another warning flag. Instead of reciting the gods' message word for word from memory, he'd paraphrased.

"Phorkys knows it exists?" As a rule, we didn't mention Phorkys's hunters, but my mind couldn't help but go there.

"He does. And Korrina?" His voice softened, falling back into rare Dad-mode.

I froze.

"Once we unlock the weapon's secrets, the Council wants you to use the weapon as bait."

He didn't look at me. He looked everywhere but at me.

I couldn't breathe. My lungs were trapped between two boulders, shifting and grinding against each other, the dust falling into my throat, making me choke.

I knew this scene. I'd been here before. Only that time had been when Jare—*don't say his name, don't think his name*—the newest Siren Hunter had been kidnapped.

And now...

"Bait for what?"

"They want you to kill the Siren Hunters."

My song fired through me, starting in the center of my chest, spreading out and burning each of my veins, my nerves, until my hands, my feet, my knees felt on fire. *Ania*, the darker half of my soul who was prophesied to destroy the world, squirmed at the back of my mind.

"That's an order?" My voice was calm, steady, emotionless. I'd become a clay statue holding fire. I'd become a hidden torch.

"Yes. That's an order." Dad's voice went whisper-serious. Regretful and firm. He held the pain I couldn't show.

The bad thing about combining fire and clay? Eventually, the fire wins. The clay explodes.

And killing the Siren Hunters? Killing *him*?

I'd never piece myself back together.

CHAPTER 2

I moved my body, one small muscle at a time, starting with my fingers to make sure they still worked, that I still worked. Neri and Dad tried to look relaxed on the other side of the campfire, but every muscle in Dad's calves was flexed, and Neri's wings were held taut against her body.

Because the last time I'd seen *him*, he'd become a Siren Hunter.

The shock of losing him had thrown my spirit from my body into the void and had almost turned me into my shadow self, *Ania*. The embodiment of sorrow.

Everyone had been a little cautious since.

The fire sent up a spark of embers as one of the logs burned through. I waited until the fire shower settled, until I could feel my toes again, until I was sure I was still attached to my body.

"Obviously, we're not doing that mission," I said. "We're not supposed to kill Ja—"—*don't say his name*—"the Siren Hunters. We're supposed to save them." Other fun family fact? My bio-dad was the *other* Siren Hunter. "The Council can't possibly expect me—us—to do this."

I ran through my self-checks. Not hyperventilating. Not

breathing erratically. Not watching the world spin. I could handle this. I could…

The memory of Jared's smile hit me in the stomach like a Superman punch. Not the smile I fell in love with, but the last one I saw. The cruel tilt of the corners of his mouth, the slight lift of his upper lip, the barely restrained killer hiding behind a boyfriend mask.

I gasped. In an instant, Neri had her wings wrapped around my shoulders and Dad knelt in front of me, holding onto my hands.

"Breathe, Korrina. Breathe." Dad's voice was low and calm, like the hypnotist he'd taken me to see in Oklahoma. Hadn't worked then, wasn't working now.

Neri pressed her beak into my neck. "Stay with us, *Elpida*. No one is killing anyone."

I nodded, breathed through my nose, tried some of the meditation techniques I'd learned on YouTube.

Dad leaned in. "I'll speak with the Council. As of right now, the only thing we're doing is finding the weapon. That's it. That's the mission."

I focused on his words, on Neri's assurances. Find the weapon. In Idaho. That was the mission. The rest didn't exist. It couldn't.

I couldn't.

"Did they mention stopping Phorkys?" I asked. "Breaking the Siren curse? Anything other than…" Than the rest of the mission that didn't exist.

Dad and Neri met each other's gaze over my head. They did that a lot, seemed to have developed a silent language where I was concerned.

"This is part of stopping Phorkys," Dad answered. "Finding this weapon and keeping it safe from Phorkys and his hunters. Learning to wield it in the upcoming war."

Because war is where we were headed. I had healed the tear

in the veil, but Phorkys was still somehow sending his monstrous sons and daughters through, along with the rest of the baddies of the mythological world. They wanted to feed on our side of the veil. Apparently, too many restrictions placed on them on their side of the veil had made them desperate.

Desperation made for desperate action.

The attacks on our world wouldn't stop until we stopped Phorkys.

I let go of Dad's hands and pushed at my eyes, tucked my hair behind my ears. "Did they give us any other clues about where to find the weapon? What it looks like?"

Dad shook his head. "Not yet. You're—we're—supposed to go to Idaho, find a big bridge over Snake River. The weapon is located in that area. That's all we know."

I pushed off my knees, made myself stand. "Okay then, let's pack up. Get on the road."

Having a plan made me feel more in control. Having a plan that excluded the rest of the Council's mission made my world feel a little safer.

I wasn't and it wasn't. But at this point, all I had to hang onto were false feelings.

Deception could be a useful tool.

DAD DROVE.

Eighteen years old and I didn't have my license yet. Typical Brooklynite. But now that we'd left the concrete jungle of Brooklyn and New York, maybe it was time to learn how to drive.

We left behind the mountains of Arkansas and entered the plains of Oklahoma. It'd be another day before we rolled into Idaho. And I'd seen it all before.

It's amazing how much you can see in six months when you live on the road.

I closed my eyes against the noon sun, itching to do something, anything, other than sit. Driving days were the worst. Too much time to think. Thinking was dangerous. Fighting was safer.

I missed my friends. I missed my school. I missed my pranks. I missed *him*.

A low, steady beat began to hum, somehow occupying two registers at once, and it traveled up my body, softly buzzed against my bones. Logic took a stroll through my head. Something wrong with the RV maybe? Not my concern.

I grabbed a pillow, turned on the small couch, and covered my face.

The world burst into verdant greens and fairytale pinks. I scrunched my eyes, my eyelashes smushing against the pillow covering my face, wiggled my toes against the table in the RV. I wasn't asleep. I wasn't behind the veil. But my mind was seeing something other than the underside of the pillow.

THE BEATS AND LOW HUMMING CONTINUED, AND MY BODY SUNK further and further away from my mind. I felt unattached…and really, really over the drama of the mythology world.

"Can we get to the point, please?" I called out to whoever was sending me this…whatever it was.

A breeze wafted through the vision and a path parted through a flower-covered meadow. Not Siren meadow, like other times I'd visited behind the veil. This was someplace else.

At the base of a rolling hill, a small pond reflected the world around, and on top of the hill was a home.

Ivy-covered and bordered by trees, the path led directly to

the front door. I followed. This was someone else's llama drama, and I was just along for the ride.

Maybe someday I'd convince myself of that lie too.

I heard voices now, raised and loud and totally at odds with the serenity of the scenery. The front door of the house grew closer, made from twisted together branches that somehow still bloomed. A curve in one of the branches formed a handle, but it wasn't needed. The powers that be of this vision pushed open the door for my bodiless self and I was inside.

A teenage girl with butt-length blonde hair—serious hair model material—stood with her hands propped on her hips, head tilted up at a woman who had to be her mother.

"I. Am. Not. Going," the girl spouted.

"You will, Persephone, and that. Is. Final." The woman seemed to grow another foot, a golden halo formed around her body, and the ground trembled.

Persephone? Nooo.

Because if that was Persephone, THE Persephone, then that scary woman was the goddess Demeter.

The same goddess who gave Phorkys and his hunters the power to curse the Sirens. Punishment for the Sirens losing Persephone to Hades.

If my boyfriend turning into a Siren Hunter was anybody's fault, it was hers.

"Mom, please. They hate me. Why can't I just stay here?" Persephone's voice turned softer, her shoulders slumped, and with her softening, Demeter lost her halo and some of her scary-goddess.

"I can't leave you alone during the harvest, you know that. It's not safe for you to be by yourself. Melpomene's daughters will protect you, keep you company. I doubt they hate you. And I thought you liked Molpe?" Demeter smoothed Persephone's hair in a familiar gesture, and the two of them sat on a large, pillow-covered hearth. Demeter waved her hand, and a steaming teapot appeared between them. She poured each of them a cup of tea, then wrapped her arm around her daughter's waist.

My heart ached. My own mother was missing. No longer thought dead, but taken, kidnapped, hidden away, her spirit torn from her body, lost in the void.

And we had no way to save her. So this? Watching Persephone with her mother? It felt like being burned from the inside out.

"Molpe's okay, but her sisters are awful. Peisinoe is the worst. She's always pulling pranks on me, twisting my hair into knots, hiding my shoes."

"You are the daughter and niece of the king of the gods and no one bullies you, my love. Remember that." She tipped Persephone's chin up. "But you must learn to fight your own battles. A gentle spirit is to be treasured, but even gentle spirits need fire."

Behind them, a fire roared to life and the vision faded. Persephone bowed her head. "Yes, mother."

Just before the vision disappeared, Persephone turned toward me, her blonde hair like her own halo, her blue eyes glowing. "Restore her, *Elpida*."

CHAPTER 3

I sat up and the pillow slid off my face. The sun hadn't moved, the clock read only a few minutes later than I'd last checked. The vision had taken mere minutes. But…

Stuck to the metal wall of our home-on-wheels, the word HELP had been spelled out with our letter magnets.

Either Neri or Dad had a buried sense of humor or I'd somehow practiced my spelling during the forced vision.

I swirled the letters around, upended the SOS, and turned my mind to more pressing matters than unconscious spelling bees.

Restore Demeter?

It seemed likely that Persephone had sent me that vision, but why restore Demeter? She was fine. Scary and powerful and vengeful and hated Sirens and fine. Persephone was the one held captive in the Underworld. She was the one who haunted my dreams, with her lifeless eyes, crown of bones…nothing like in the vision.

That girl was…alive.

And Demeter…Demeter was a mother.

A pretty good one from the little I'd seen.

"We're stopping for burritos," Dad called out from the front seat. "Everyone stay alert." His warning was one I'd started to take seriously. We'd been ambushed more than once at an enemy feeding spot disguised as a taco stand.

Taco Bell was usually safe.

My mouth watered. I'd become addicted to Taco Bell burritos while on the road. There was crack in them there beans.

"Korrina, you hungry?"

"Always. And Dad?" The three of us could put together the pieces of my vision over lunch.

He raised an eyebrow in the rearview mirror.

A flash of his reaction hit me like a wake-up slap. Neri's too. If they knew I was having visions of Demeter, they'd never let me out of their sight.

And to save *him*, to go against the Council's orders, to have a prayer at figuring out how to save Mom, I needed space. I needed them to trust I was in control of my powers.

Not being sent random visions from a faraway goddess.

"What is it?" He switched from Dad to Guardian, sniffing out my new secret like a hungry dog.

"Make it three burritos. I'm starving."

I'd tell them. Eventually. When I knew more of what it meant. When I could spin the thing as something I had chosen. Instead of something forced on me that I, once again, had no power to stop.

Dad parked down the street from the Taco Bell for many reasons.

One—the RV was too big to go under the drive-thru window.

Two—the parking lot was too small to turn the monstrosity of our home-on-the-go around for a quick getaway.

Three—Neri had to do her business and refused to do so where anyone could see.

Dad stopped on a tree-lined street with tall bushes hiding someone's backyard. Neri hopped over the bushes and did her mythological deed. While we waited, I pulled out my phone and checked social media. Cloud and Danica were getting ready for senior year, Danica having fully recovered from Luke's poisoning last year. Tula too. Tula had taken my spot in Mischief and Mayhem, learning the ropes of pranking the popular to protect the misfits.

I thumbed through recent pictures of the three of them at a concert, Danica kissing Cloud's cheek and Tula fake-gagging.

As happy as I was that they were all okay, I still wished it was me in the photos. Not Tula. I shoved my phone back into my bag before I could give in to text them.

For their safety, I'd cut them off. People around me tended to get hurt. All three of them certainly had. The further away from me everyone was, the better.

Neri fluttered over the hedge, swallowing what looked like a dragonfly. "I'll watch the R/V while you two go eat Taco Hell."

She'd come up with that one all on her own. Six months with me, and I'd corrupted an ancient, before-time-existed creature.

Dad and I took up our normal positions. Him on my left, dagger hidden up his sleeve, sword so-not-hidden on his back. Me, song at the ready, my own dagger up my own sleeve.

We went slow, cautious, assessing everyone as a threat, dismissing no one as an innocent. Living in such a high alert state all the time...if life ever did go back to some kind of normal, I'm not sure I could turn it off. It felt permanent, this constant awareness, constant tension of watching my back, my Dad's back, fighting for our lives.

Fighting for burritos.

We made it through the doors with no incident. Didn't mean we were safe.

I checked out the restaurant. Barely full and the workers looked like the human variety.

Then, I spotted it.

A shiny lure in the corner of the restaurant, one I had yet to resist.

"Korrina…"

Not even Dad's I'm-serious-don't-do-it tone could hold me back.

I sprang forward and rang the bell.

The *dong* reverberating from the Taco Bell bell wasn't strong enough to drown out Dad's groan. But the guy behind the counter let out a cheer.

We placed our order and turned as the door dinged with a new customer.

Three new customers.

Males, around my age, wearing matching forest green hoodies pulled low over their eyes with some sort of logo on the shoulder. What I could make out of their faces were piercings. A lot of piercings. Nose, eyebrows, lips, cheeks.

They walked next to us but kept their distance. I took a mental snapshot of the logo so I could draw it later. It was an image of two dark red, but almost translucent seeds, tips pointed down, a drop of blood dripping from each. One guy turned his back to us, and on the back of his hoodie was the logo again, bigger this time, with the words "Save the Mother" screenprinted underneath.

They looked like some kind of eco-friendly goth band.

"Rock on," I said to the closest guy.

He startled then turned his head toward me so slowly a sloth could have won a race. "You dare to speak to me." It wasn't a question.

"Uh, yeah. What are you, part of a band?"

He pushed back his hoodie revealing blond spiked hair with

a line of green running through the tips. "I am nothing more than a follower."

The Taco Bell dealers passed over our food with a crinkle of paper bags.

"Who's the mother?"

He stretched out his arms and his two weirdo friends did the same. "The mother is everything civilization has not yet touched. She is earth and sky, the deepest ocean, the shallowest puddle."

"Right. Well, enjoy your lunch." I followed Dad out of the restaurant and shook off the groupie heebies.

Whatever band they were followers of had to be strange. I definitely needed to check it out.

And get my own angsty hoodie. Danica would be so jealous and Jare—

Nope. Back up. End on the word jealous.

We climbed into the R/V, no enemy activity detected, but as we passed Taco Bell, the three hooded groupies stood at the window, motionless, no food in hand.

Sixteen hours later, we crossed the Idaho state line.

IDAHO'S SNAKE RIVER GLISTENED UNDER THE HIGH MORNING SUN. If I liked to fish, I would have been itching to get a line in the water. But I did not like to fish, nor did I like to swim. How Sirens and mermaids ever got confused had to be the biggest mystery in mythology.

We leaned over the railing of Idaho's highest bridge and stared at the river snaking below. Like a snake. Hence the name Snake River. They got creative naming this one.

"No hints whatsoever?" I asked Dad.

Dad shrugged. "Just one. It moves to the same place high on Snake River at noon."

"And they couldn't tell us where and what. No, that'd be too easy."

Dad grunted and Neri returned from her aerial search, soaring down to where we were and landing on the railing next to Dad.

I narrowed my eyes at the river, at the rocky and deep sides of the gorge, when something Dad had said finally hit home. "Wait, what kind of weapon moves?"

Neri and Dad both cocked their heads at me in the same manner. They were spending *way* too much time together.

Neri opened and closed her beak. Dad said "huh."

We'd spent the morning looking for a magical weapon and searching the area for evidence of a weakening of the veil.

Not evidence of something mobile.

Without discussion—and with very little time left before noon—we left the center of the bridge and found hiding spots in the brush. If the weapon was moving, us being on the bridge could make it turn back and we'd lose our chance. Right now we had the element of surprise—and a head start on Phorkys. After today, we could lose both of those advantages.

I shifted on my belly, trying to keep the bridge in sight while removing the rock from under my rib, when my stomach announced it was lunchtime. From Dad's hidden spot, where he'd totally camouflaged himself, I heard a groan.

My stomach had given us away on more than one occasion.

An answering groan sounded from the other side of the bridge. The sound grew and grumbled until a white SUV pulled off the road and parked in the brush on the opposite side of the gorge from us.

A girl hopped out of the driver's seat, and a tall guy unfolded himself from the passenger's side. They walked to the back, popped open the hatch, and threw on a pair of black backpacks. The girl locked the SUV with a beep of her keys, then tossed them at the guy, and something about the two of them shot a low throb through my stomach. They walked close together, elbows touching, laughing and joking with each other about something, oblivious to the world.

They reached the center of the bridge.

Something else began to throb inside my chest.

When I was born, the Sirens—in their ultimate wisdom—decided to attach a scepter of power that everyone wanted to my soul, effectively hiding it from the world and all their enemies and turning an innocent baby into a weapon.

That same scepter—which I'd only recently figured out how to kinda use—began to pulse.

I sat up, gasped for air, rubbed at my chest.

"Korrina, get down," Dad hissed.

"The girl"—I hissed back, in between painful pulses of the unnatural power attached to my being—"She's the weapon."

Dad sat up, a crown of leaves sticking out of his hair. "You're positive?"

I nodded and said the only thing that made sense. "She's a Siren."

Dad's eyes went wide, and I heard Neri suck in air from her hiding spot in the tree branches. "They've activated them," Dad whispered.

"Yeah, you'll have to explain that later. Right now, let's go get our weapon." I stood, checked on the Siren and her friend—boyfriend—best friend, swallowed back a deep, resonant pain.

Ugh, broken hearts hurt. *Focus.*

They checked each other's backpacks and pointed below at the river and gorge.

"Why is the weapon always a girl?" Dad muttered.

"Because we're badasses the world wants to use. Even if it can't admit it needs us."

CHAPTER 4

I had cute-boy-alert jitters in my hands, only this wasn't a boy. She was a Siren. Family, in a weird, twisted way.

I didn't know which Siren ancestor she came from. I didn't know if she knew or if she was as oblivious as I had been. I didn't know if she'd hug me or throat-punch me when I told her the truth.

What I did know was that she was getting ready to take a suicidal jump with her status-not-updated boy right here, right now.

They'd hopped onto the railing of the bridge, ten feet apart, each of them with their toes pointed away from each other, hanging over the gorge.

My power pulsed in my chest, pushing me toward her and pulling away at the same time, like a magnet that couldn't make up its mind. I gritted my teeth and focused on suppressing the scepter without using my life force, as Neri had been uselessly trying to teach me.

I stepped out of the brush and onto the bridge, my vision already starting to go fuzzy. The other end of the bridge seemed to waver, like heat waves coming off the pavement. I shook my head, remembered Neri's teachings. *Feed the scepter emotion, not blood.* I still hadn't figured out how to do that, but I pushed my worry toward the center of my chest, let out a breath.

Didn't help.

"Hey, don't do it," I called out.

They jerked their heads toward me, gripped tighter onto the railing. Her blonde dreads flowed over the small backpack strapped to her shoulders. I wanted to save both of them, but the Siren was the target. Save her, probably save the guy anyway.

The other end of the bridge seemed to rip in two, and *someone* stepped out.

My throat clamped shut, the scepter struggled to be released, my song swelled.

And my heart? Somehow, it managed to break again.

Jared. He was there.

Just. There.

My spirit arched for him, reaching toward him, needing the impossible. To touch, to kiss, to split in two so part of me would always be part of him.

Fire sparked at his fingertips.

I blinked, shook my head. Fear focused my vision, my power drilled in, my mind cleared.

"You new?" she called back, oblivious to the danger stalking closer to her.

Odd question. "Well, to you, I guess. But hey, whatever's going on, just come down. We can talk. Have coffee. Do you like coffee? I'm so in love with coffee. I saw this place back—"

"Relax." She shook a limp wrist at me. "Unwind." She rolled her shoulders back and stood, balancing on the steel pipe. "Let go and be free." She grinned a kinda stoned grin and leaned over the river, her body a thin forty-five-degree angle. She raised her arms over her head, her ratty t-shirt lifting to show off a belly ring. A breeze rushed over us, pushed against her.

Jared started running. I did too. We'd never make it. But his cursed fire might. His ability to deliver Demeter's curse, turn my Siren cousin into a feathered mythological creature, then kill her. The Siren Hunter's M.O.

The bridge shook under my feet as a semi-truck blasted passed us, whistling the air around my ears. I took a deep breath, searched for the small flame inside my mind that had come to represent my *Elpida* power, the center of my soul. I tugged on it and the blue flame brightened, warmed my blood. My aura became visible, shimmering purple around my hands, my body. My Siren song filled my lungs, my throat, brushed against my tongue, coated my mouth in sweet honey.

Suicidal Siren and her friend stretched into matching arches. Her heels lifted up, her toes left the bridge. He followed a second later.

My song left my lips, the first note more of a high-pitched, "Noooo!"

Her body twisted until she was parallel with the river, her legs spread, her feet kicked up behind her. She reached around to her backpack and pulled on a red ball.

Jared and I met in the middle. For a small second, we weren't mortal enemies. Just two people sharing a what-the-eff moment.

The Siren and her friend grew smaller and smaller. Something white exploded behind her, behind him, unwrapping into a parachute.

"She's a...base jumper." Wonder mixed with amusement filled Jared's voice as the Siren and her friend coasted through the sky, following the trail of the river as they descended lower and lower.

And, for a second, he wasn't the Siren Hunter.

For a second, he was Jared.

My Jared.

My gaze slowly turned to him, my Siren song pounding at my throat, the scepter filling my chest, begging to be released.

I was scared.

More scared than I could remember being.

I didn't want to see those eyes again. The ones that hated me. That smile.

But I couldn't stop.

He looked tired. Purple shadows lined his eyelashes, clashing with the deep scarlet of his eyes. My hand reached for him, my initial instinct to stroke his cheek, to make sure he was okay, stronger than my instinct to stay alive.

His hair was longer and dark waves curled at his cheeks. His skin had lost its healthy olive complexion, as if he were battling a long-term illness. He turned, looked me up and down, and moved out of my reach.

"Hello, *Elpida*." His mouth curled around the words.

Not Korrina, but my title. My power. The thing he lusted after, instead of the girl he used to love. The only thing he cared about controlling. Destroying. *Elpida*.

"Wut up." I jerked my head in greeting, defying the brokenness aching through me. The tendrils of my song twisted out of my mouth and covered me in a protective barrier. Neri had taught me Siren 101 well: Don't die.

The green flame in Jared's hands brightened.

"Wut. Up?" He cocked his head, as if he'd lost the usage of informal speech. "Such plebian language for such an exquisite power."

"You used to like it." I used the sharp corners of my words to cover my cracked insides. If only there were emotional super glue.

"I used to like a lot of things that weren't good for me." His gaze trailed my body, up and down.

Ouch.

"Korrina!" Dad's distant voice called out, followed by Neri's rabid screech.

"Guardian Daddy to the rescue." Jared's lips spread over his teeth. "Always a second too late."

Jared blew at the flame he held and the green fire turned into a burning vapor. A fog that floated across the few feet that separated us and settled around me. An acidic cloud sticking to my skin. My thin, weakening barrier was the only thing saving me. It wasn't enough. Jared's flames ate at my power, dissolved my strength.

I knew what I should do. Kick, punch, fight, sing. Bring the scepter out, banish him back behind the veil.

Follow the Council's orders and kill him.

I couldn't.

He wasn't just a Siren Hunter.

He was Jared. My Jared.

He leaned forward, traced my cheek, my lips.

And I kissed his fingertips.

CHAPTER 5

Jared yanked his hand away from me, as if my kiss had burned him. The world was tinted green, his flame-fog still coating my skin, eating away at my song's barrier, but for a split-second, his eyes shifted from scarlet red to normal brown.

I blinked, refocused, and Jared's eyes were as red-violet as they'd been since the moment I'd chosen to save the world and sacrifice him.

We moved closer together, and his salt-scented breath washed over my cheeks. We used to share chocolate-flavored kisses and my song would lift us both into the air, defying gravity, physics, *everything*. Because true love was powerful.

Not powerful enough.

He growled, flexed his hand. His dagger flashed in the sunlight, glinted on the downward swing.

I cringed, braced for the killing blow.

It didn't come.

Jared yanked the blade against his own skin. Black blood welled up around the cut and his eyes leapt to a deeper red. His green power grew stronger. Flame flared to life in his hands.

"You have no power here, Siren witch." His words struggled, then strengthened.

I stepped back, clenched my fists. Witch? I'd show him witch.

"Wanna bet?" My lips lifted into a snarl. I dropped low, swung my leg around, and swiped at his knees. I let my song loose. The fire flickered and died in his hands, the fog coating my skin melted away.

Jared flew back, landed on his feet. He crouched down, then launched himself into the air, fire streaming from his palms.

I didn't want to kill him. I didn't want to hurt him.

But I had to survive this fight so I could save him later.

My song blasted from my lips, swirled around us, lifted me into the air and kept Jared off his feet. The currents of our combating power pushed us together, spun us around.

We'd been here before.

From the flicker in his gaze, he remembered.

I pushed that aside, waved my left hand in the air, distracting him like a photographer distracts a crying baby, and threw an uppercut punch at his face with my right.

My knuckles crunched against his jaw, pain ouching down my wrist, but it was familiar. I focused on the familiar. I focused on the fight.

My song reached another octave and we dropped to the ground. Jared fell like a rock, dropping to his hands and knees. He wiped at his lip, his hand coming away with a smear of black blood.

Out of the corner of my eye, Dad appeared, his Guardian sword flashing high in the sky.

I wasn't going to carry out the Council's orders.

But Dad might.

I twisted, threw my song into the air like a shield, and a purple flash of light blocked Dad's sword from coming down on Jared's crouched body.

Dad deflected, I turned back to Jared. "Run," I breathed.

He looked at me, tilted his head to the side, confusion narrowing his eyes. He leapt to his feet, slashed at the air and opened a portal to his realm, and stepped inside.

I caught the tattletale of his smile too late.

Green fire exploded toward me as he closed the portal behind him.

Neri screeched. Dad roared. The fire hit my chest, wrapped around my throat, and sent the world to shadows.

I floated in darkness. Deep voices chanted, surrounded by the steady beat of a hollow drum. A starry night came into focus. An earth-splitting scream drowned everything out.

Two orange flames floated in the night. A shadow between the flames blocked the stars. I was frozen in place. Had Jared killed me? Was I dead?

Was that death creeping toward me?

A low muttering whispered through the night. "Not my daughter. Not Persephone. Not my little girl. Where's my baby? Where's my little girl?"

Fear struck my veins. Goddess Demeter was here. Oh crap.

Death would have been a friendlier god to meet.

Demeter held a torch in each hand. The flames flickered and danced over her naked body. Scratches traced the curves of her waist, her breasts, her neck. Her expression was tight, as if her muscles had all been cinched together, but her hazel eyes rolled around, not seeming to see anything, to focus on anything.

The light of her torches fell over me. "Have you seen her? My daughter? I can't find..." Emotions rocked her face, rolling across her smooth features in waves. Tightening her skin. Drooping her mouth. Her wheat-brown hair hung in limp strands. A tattered shawl the only thing covering her shoulders.

Blood dripped from her fingernails onto the handles of the torches.

"Hades." My tongue formed the answer, but my voice was a total coward. The god of the Underworld's name cracked on my lips.

Demeter passed me by as if I didn't exist, her eyes wild, unfocused. Her torchlight flickered over her bare body, showing long, skinny wounds up and down her back as if she'd whipped herself. Her long hair stuck to the wounds, dried blood caking around the strands. She stumbled into the night.

"Korrina." *Snap, snap.*

The night faded.

The ground beneath me was soft and bouncy. I opened my eyes.

Dad and Neri peered down at me. Above them was the ceiling of the RV.

I propped on my elbows. "What happened?"

Neri stuck her wings on her bird hips. "I warned you to be conscious of draining your energy. Do you listen? No."

"Did you not see the blast of fire he threw at me?"

Neri and Dad looked at one another, then back at me with narrowed eyes.

"Unfortunately"—Dad's voice dropped to you're-in-trouble low—"we were too busy fighting past the shield you threw at us to see what happened."

Oh. Right.

"You were going to kill him." As if that answered all their questions. As if it was a good enough answer for using my power against my allies.

Dad cringed. "I wasn't going to kill him. But I was going to disable him, bring him to the Council—"

"So they could kill him?" I sat up and pushed away the wave of dizziness that threatened to throw me back to my pillow.

He didn't answer.

Neri hopped closer. "If he threw fire at you, you should be cursed. Feathers sprouting everywhere. But you are whole."

I pressed my lips together. I didn't want to jinx what I was thinking—hoping—by saying it out loud. That he was fighting. That he could be saved.

That maybe he'd forgive me.

Dad and Neri exchanged another look, and that one I understood. They'd put a pin in this. For now.

"What happened to the Siren and her friend?"

"Gone. By the time we reached the river, they'd disappeared." Dad stood and made his way to the front of the RV. "We've gotta move. Find her before the Siren Hunter picks up her trail."

I followed him, grabbing a bag of cheese puffs on the way, and settled in the passenger seat. "She's a base jumper." I echoed Jared's insight. "They both are."

"You've got an idea of where they might have gone?" Dad turned the key in the ignition and the RV grumbled on.

"Crazy attracts crazy." I pointed to a billboard down the road. A billboard with a picture of a screaming person strapped to another person, falling through the sky after voluntarily jumping out of an airplane. "Let's go meet some skydivers."

CHAPTER 6

We rolled into DZone Skydiving, the local community of
skydivers and base jumpers, and climbed out of the
R.V. just as a small plane touched down outside a big metal
building. People loitered with various sizes and colors of backpacks on. Which I now knew were parachutes. High above us,
black specks fell out of the sky, then popped into different-
colored parachutes, which swooped down and skimmed the
earth, one-by-one.

"Five-minute call. This is your five-minute call.," a loudspeaker said. The loitering people lined up outside the airplane
and began to climb into the open cargo door.

We walked inside the building. Opened parachutes stretched
across the floor with skydivers rolling up the lines and folding
the material, squeezing them into tiny bags. Body odor and
cigarette smoke floated in the air.

"Hey! You!" My Siren cousin jumped up, throwing her parachute thing on her back. "You chickened out at the jump spot.
You ready to go now?"

"Huh-wha?" I managed.

"Weren't you there to jump?" She buckled her chest strap

and did a few moves to check her gear. Seemed to be all muscle memory.

"No. I don't, you know." I gestured at her. 'Cause, wow. "But it's great that you do."

She pressed her lips together, then noticed my Dad at my back, sword peeking over his shoulder.

"So why are you here? With a bodyguard?" She crossed her arms and widened her stance. A couple of the bulkier guys noticed she was in defensive pose. They stood and made their way over.

"Well…" Okay, so I couldn't drop the stink bomb that she was a Siren and I was sent here to protect her from my evil boyfriend. Especially not with those meatheads listening. I didn't know much about her, other than she was possibly more nuts than I was, but I did know how hard the whole you're-a-Siren-and-yes-Sirens-are-real-and-are-not-mermaids thing was to accept. "I'm interested in learning…" I drew out. "I saw you on the bridge and thought it was cool." Oh man. So lame.

"Great! C'mon, let's go." She hooked an arm around mine and dragged me across the building. Her bodyguard relaxed and went back to packing their parachutes.

"Where are we going?"

"See, here's the thing. I think you're lying through those pretty teeth. So you can either get out of my DZ right now, or you can go skydiving. Throw yourself out of a perfectly good airplane and I might be willing to listen to what you have to say. Otherwise, forget it."

"I'm not—"

"Nu-uh. My bullshit detector is never wrong. The jump's on me. So the only excuse you have is that you're not really here to skydive. In which case, I want nothing to do with you." She let me go and walked into a room with a sign that read Manifest.

I rolled my options around my mouth. Leave her unprotected and give Jared a chance to kill her—not happening—or jump out of a plane.

Jump. Out. Of. A. Plane.

Not gonna lie, the thought had my blood racing. In a good way. If Cloud could see me now…he'd say I was jeopardizing my mission of mischief. Not that I had my own mission anymore. My life was now dictated to me by an invisible council who didn't understand the meaning of Bite Me.

I took a deep breath and pushed through the doors of the office.

"All right. I'm in."

She turned around and rested her elbows on the counter. Two other women manned four computers, their fingers flying over keyboards, desk chairs thrown to the side and totally ignored. Behind my cousin was a wall of windows, showing off a runway and a field littered with parachutes.

Her lips ticked. Not quite a smile. But closer.

"Get my girl…" She waited for my name.

"Korrina."

"Korrina, on the next load. How about your old man?"

Dad had followed me in and was waiting at the back door.

"Him?" I thumbed over my shoulder. I could feel him cower. He might be a fearless Guardian of an even more fearless Siren —mwah—but he hated heights. "Not gonna happen."

She looked Dad up and down, then smirked. "I gotcha."

"You are not jumping out of a plane either." Dad squared his shoulders, went into Guardian pose. For a man trained in the art of war, he wasn't so great with the covert ops thing.

"Then why did you bring her here?"

Dad had no answer. But he went a shade of pale I was all too familiar with and once again, he was lying. About what? I wasn't sure yet. But he definitely had a secret.

He swallowed. "Korrina, just…be careful. Listen to the safety video. Twice."

She scheduled us on the next load. My name appeared on a large screen in the main part of the hangar, along with my instructor's name—Dave—and a cameraman. Woman. Named Amity.

My Siren cousin picked up a helmet that had a camera attached to the side and gave me a wink.

Amity it is.

I watched a quick safety video then was shoved into a tandem harness. The tall, lanky guy from the bridge, all beard, no chin, acted very excited about being strapped to my back for my first tandem.

"Five-minute call. This is your five-minute call," came the loudspeaker voice again.

My stomach folded in half, then in half again, turning itself into an origami shape. Half excited, half freaking-out.

I found my tandem instructor, Dave, and followed him onto the airplane. We sat on a long bench, straddling the person in front of us. Dave's long legs surrounded mine, while mine bumped against Amity's thighs. Dave hooked his rig to my harness, tested all the straps.

The plane took off. Okay, cool. All cool. I've been on planes before...

Amity stretched forward and lifted up the door. She wiggled down the bench seat and sat at the edge, her legs dangling out the door as the plane climbed to altitude.

Cool air rushed through the plane, waking all my senses. This was nothing like the times Neri had flown my spirit around Brooklyn.

A light above the door switched from red to green. Amity swung outside the airplane and hung onto a rail.

Dave scooted us forward. With his big, lanky legs, I had no choice but to be pushed to the edge of the plane.

"Is it too late to say screw this?" I yelled at him over the noise of the plane.

"Yup. Amity's guests don't back out."

I hated Dave.

My heart pulled a tantrum against my ribs. I was not doing this. I was not…

Dave stood us up, crouched over me, dangled me outside the plane. Amity nodded her head. With each nod, we rocked. One, two…

And we were out of the plane.

Air beat my skin. My lungs seized. As fast as we were falling, I couldn't suck in air. Dave grabbed my arms, pulled them away from my chest. The skin on my arms buffeted against my bones. Amity fell in front of us. The girl was flying upside down in a headstand. She danced around like she was breakdancing. She reached out, grabbed Dave's hand, and twisted us around.

Below, the curve of the earth spun on the horizon. Patches of green fields and puffy white clouds grew larger and larger.

Amity sped away, getting smaller and smaller. Dave jerked his arm. Something grabbed us from above. Had Jared learned to fly? Were we under attack? My feet flew in front of my face. We slowed.

"Woooo!" Dave yelped. I looked up. A large stretch of white canopy rippled in the wind and floated us through the air. "Was it everything you thought it'd be?" Dave yanked on a cord, and we dipped to the right, spiraled around the air.

"I'm just glad to be alive," I shouted back. The wind whipped around us, and the parachute rustled.

"Girl, this is living. You're heavy, you know that?"

I rolled my eyes. If Dave thought I was heavy, he must be used to dating twigs. Literal twigs. I'd lost ten pounds in the past six months. Ten pounds I needed.

"Didn't anyone ever teach you to not talk about a girl's weight?"

"No. I mean hev-ee. You seem to be carrying the world. Most people are light after their first jump. Like they've let go of whatever crap they were holding on to. Maybe it's waiting for them on the ground, but up here..." Dave pulled on another cord, and we spun again.

"I've got a lot of crap." I shrugged in my harness. My stomach did a gentle loop-de-loop with Dave's next spin.

Dave was quiet for a while. He pointed us toward the lowering sun. The sky was turning orange and yellow. Our feet skimmed the top of a cloud, and we sunk through the middle. The air grew thick and humid and cool. We passed out of the cloud a few seconds later. The green fields had grown larger. Buildings and cars driving on the street were visible, but everything looked like a Claymation village.

"None of my business, but here's the thing. Why would you want to hold onto crap? It stinks. It's gross. It can make you sick. Soul sick." He pulled hard on a cord, and we dipped sharply, descending faster toward the ground.

I didn't answer. My kind of crap wasn't the kind I chose to hang on to. It stuck around and it did stink, it was gross, and I was soul sick. But no matter what I did, I couldn't shake the mess off.

The ground rushed us. Dave yanked both cords down, and we gently touched the earth. He unhooked my harness. Amity ran up to us, carrying her parachute over her arm.

"How'd she do?"

"Calm as a lake."

"Huh." Amity looked me up and down. Her lips pursed, and she chewed on her bottom lip. "All right then. C'mon. Dave," she called over her shoulder. "Make sure her dad knows she's with me."

"You got it, babe."

"I told you to quit that." She turned to me. "I hate it when he calls me babe."

I pushed aside a smirk. Luke had called me babe—back before he'd betrayed and almost killed me. I hated it too.

"Is her your—"

"Boyfriend? He wishes." She tossed a look back at him that made me think he wasn't the only one wishing that.

Amity dropped her rig off at the packing room, helped me out of my harness, and led me upstairs. She unlocked a door and held it open. Inside was her office. A simple desk with a vase of sunflowers on the corner. A Mac desktop computer. The walls were covered with pictures of people skydiving, Amity with her arms slung around friends, all holding parachutes. A wall filled with a full life. A life that did not have room for what I was about to tell her.

She pointed at a chair in the corner while she sat behind her desk.

"Okay, Korrina. Spill."

"Wait a second…" Information dawned on me. "You're the drop zone owner?"

"Yup."

"How old are you?"

"Nineteen. Why? You think I can't—"

"No, I'm just…impressed."

She picked up a pencil and rat-tat-tatted it on the desk. "Don't be. Gramps died. Left me the business." She shrugged.

"Still…"

"Why are you here?" She leaned forward. "What do you want?"

I took a breath. "I was sent here to protect you."

Amity's expression went very still. Her head dipped slightly. She hummed under her breath. A tingling stream of air rushed around me, so quickly I almost missed it. She raised her head.

"Why?"

Okay. I did not expect her to accept that so easily.

"It's…complicated."

"Try me." She leaned back in her chair and crossed her arms, tapping her pencil against her bicep.

I bit my lip. I knew I'd have to tell her everything, but hadn't quite thought the conversation through. The one thing that had convinced me Neri was telling the truth about me being a Siren was my own struggles. Struggles only a Siren would understand. Struggles that had nothing to do with being a teenage girl or hormones or boys.

"Do you sing?" I asked.

Her sage-green eyes flicked open wider. "That's an odd question."

I leaned forward. "Is it?"

Her pencil stilled.

"Because here's the thing," I started, trying to pick the right words. "For a while, I didn't sing. I could, but when I did, things happened. People got hurt. And sometimes, I couldn't control the song. It was something inside me, but not really a part of me. Like this entity with a mind of its own."

Amity's tanned skin went computer-tan white. "What are you saying?"

"Six months ago, I found out I was the descendant of a special race of people. People who have powers. Real power."

She swallowed, hard. "What kind of people?"

Sweat slicked my palms. I wiped them off on my jeans. "Sirens."

"Sirens?" Amity's gaze narrowed and sharpened.

"Yes. And, I know it sounds crazy, but it's true. The Sirens in Greek mythology…they're real. And we're the last of their race."

"Get. Out." She stood and leaned over her desk. "Get off my DZ, now."

"Amity, please. Listen. You're in danger. There are people who want us dead. They know who you are. You need to come with me. So I can—"

"DAVE! Get in here."

"That thing you did with your voice when I first came in

here. You used some power. You hummed. I felt it. That's your lie detector, right?"

Amity's body started shaking. Footsteps pounded up the stairs.

"You know I'm telling the truth." I reached for her. She had to listen.

"What's wrong?" Dave ran into the room.

"Get this psycho and her dad off my DZ." Her hands trembled as she pointed her finger in my face.

Dave wrapped a large hand around my arm and hauled me out of her office.

"Korrina?" Dad met us at the bottom of the stairs.

"You need to leave. Now," Dave said. "I don't know what she did to Amity, but I've only seen her that pissed once and it didn't end well."

Dave escorted us back to our RV. We pulled out of the parking lot and didn't talk until Dad pulled over on the side of the road a mile later.

"So," I started, "that went well."

CHAPTER 7

We found a good camping spot with RV hookups near Amity's drop zone. I stepped outside and took a deep breath. The stars were brilliant, but I couldn't pick out any familiar constellations. Back home in Brooklyn, only the brightest stars made it through the city lights. Out here, in the middle of nowhere, the sky looked like a black sheet had been taped over a light with a million holes poked through.

A coyote yipped. Night birds twittered. I rubbed my hands up and down on my arms, exhausted. Dave's words cycled through my mind. Soul sick. It resonated. Losing Jared, moving away from all my friends, my life…and it was all my fault. I could have saved Jared. Somehow. Maybe if I'd kissed him harder, sang my healing Siren song into him longer, held onto him tighter…maybe I could have overcome the Siren Hunter brainwashing Luke and Colin had put him through.

Maybe if I'd used the oath breaker on Jared…saved him instead of saving me.

A hot tear seared my cheek, and instead of pushing it away, I lifted my face to the dark sky, focused on the spaces in between the stars, wished it could swallow me whole.

Logically, I knew the choice hadn't been me or him. It had been him or the world.

But I wasn't buying it. There had to have been a way.

There had to be a way.

He wasn't lost.

Not totally. Not yet.

"*Elpida*, are you well?" Neri seemed to float down from the stars, a star herself with her iridescent glow.

My breath shuddered in my chest. I should have known one of them was watching me. I'd be on separated-soul watch for the next twenty-four hours, maybe longer. But I wouldn't do that again. Not now that I had a goal. Save Jared. Find my mom. And now, figure out Persephone's message.

That and convince Amity to come on a Siren adventure with me.

I was a busy-busy girl. No time for breakdowns.

"Well? I'm great. Super. Superb," I threw a little French guttural sound in the the last one and hoped it covered the slight shake to my voice.

"You let the Siren Hunter defeat you." Neri parked herself on the lawn chair at my side. "And you fought against myself and your father. Why?"

I paced the ground, keeping my eyes on the shadows. "I told you why. We're saving Jared. Not killing him. Not giving him to the Council."

"Korrina," Dad's voice resounded at my back.

I jumped. He'd used his stealth-training to sneak up on me.

"We have to know we can trust you. That in a fight against the Siren Hunters, you won't betray us again."

"I didn't betray you. I was saving *him*."

Dad took a breath, linked his hands in front of his waist. "Saving him *is* betraying us. Please tell me you understand that. Until we find a way to save him, if we confront him, he's the enemy. No more, no less."

I held my breath in my chest, and my song hummed in my ears. Rising up to my defense. I didn't answer him. Couldn't.

My control was still faulty.

Dad took out one of his knives and sliced his thumb. A drop of blood welled up, ruby-red in the moonlight. Jared's had been black, black like the space between the stars, black and empty.

He held out the knife, handle first. "Swear to me, Korrina. You will not betray Neri and me again."

Something in my chest cracked. "You're asking me to take a blood oath?"

The line in his lips hardened. "I'm not asking."

"Michael, don't—"

"You don't trust me," I said, interrupting Neri. My song sparked in my mouth, and the ground around my feet began to glow purple with my aura.

"Not when it comes to Jared."

This. This was why I hadn't told them about Demeter and Persephone. This was why I'd kept mostly to myself these past six months, keeping our relationship at a surface level. Because even though I'd forgiven him for keeping secrets my entire life, I hadn't gotten over his betrayals.

Lying to me since the day I was born. Losing Jared. Forcing me to leave my home and my friends without giving me a choice. Forgetting to be a dad.

I backed away from the knife, from him. "I won't betray you and Neri. I would never do anything to hurt you. But I will not do this."

Something blazed in his eyes, some fire I'd never seen. "So you're choosing Jared over us?"

My hands balled into fists. "No. I'm choosing choice."

The knife wobbled in his hand. His blood made a trail along the blade. "Choice." He turned the word around in his mouth, as if it was new to him. As if he wasn't comfortable giving it to me.

"Yes. Choice. Like right now, I'm choosing to sleep in the

tent." I didn't have to say the alternative. My glowing aura did that for me. I headed for the back of the RV where we kept the pop-up tent and yanked it from its storage net.

Dad met me at the back of the van. "*I* will sleep in the tent." He grabbed it from my hand and stomped to the other side of our camping pad.

"Fine. Don't apologize," I muttered.

Six months ago, he would have apologized.

I'd changed in the past half a year.

So had he.

CHAPTER 8

Aplane flew low overhead, and the scent of jet fuel filled the morning air. The loudspeaker announced the next load as I hopped onto a wooden fence post near the DZ entrance and sipped my coffee. The RV roared away, kicking up a cloud of dust.

I wasn't technically *on* the drop zone, and with no ride back, Amity would have to let me stay.

"Didn't I kick you out yesterday?" Dave's voice hit me in the back.

I turned around. "I'm stubborn. Born this way. Sorry."

He walked up and sat on the fence rail next to me. "She was pretty upset after you left."

I nodded. "Yeah, I bet."

"Want to share?" His words were half-drowned by the sound of the plane landing, its turbines spinning.

"Can't. But I know what she's going through." I wrinkled my nose. "You have no reason to trust me, but I really am here to help Amity."

Dave hopped off the fence, as if he was going to leave, but something in his eyes encouraged me to try again. He'd seen something. He knew something. You couldn't be close to a Siren without noticing the inhuman differences.

"Have you ever seen her control a room? Not command it, but control it."

He froze. Looked at me more intently.

"Have you ever lost time around her? Like you've been asleep, but you weren't."

He took a step closer.

"Have you ever heard her sing?"

He swallowed. "Not in a long time." His voice was hoarse, like his throat had gone dry.

"Because things happen when she sings?" I whispered.

A slight nod of his head, and he lowered his voice, as if he was afraid of betraying a secret. "She stopped singing a long time ago."

Empathy for Amity poured through me. I knew what it was like to have a song inside you couldn't sing.

Dave tugged at his beard, sucked at his top lip. "Amity's been through hell, and hell always leaves its marks. But that's her story, and I'll leave it to her to tell it to you if she chooses. Bottom line, I've only seen her this upset one other time. She's a strong girl. But you rocked her world yesterday."

I hopped off the fence. "I understand. I'll wait here until she's ready—"

"Her world needs to be rocked. She's hard. Like granite. But inside, she's one big bruise. You punched through and hit that bruise yesterday."

Hope surged through me. "So, you'll help?"

"Yup. She's gonna hate me, though." His eyes narrowed and his lips thinned.

Poor guy had no idea a Siren was in love with him. Which meant he was in danger. I added him to my mental list of people to keep safe. "Doubt that. Is she in her office?"

"She's taking the morning off."

I gave him a look.

"Like I said, you rocked her world."

I huffed. Who knew Sirens could be such pains in the rear? "And where does Amity go when her world is rocked?"

This time, Dave grinned. "You're going to love this."

WE HOPPED OUT OF DAVE'S PATCHWORK TRUCK IN FRONT OF A magazine-ready ranch house. It looked like something a celebrity would own.

"Guess a drop zone owner banks." I propped my hands on my hips and turned in a circle.

Giant trees with thick trunks bordered the property. A white, wooden fence kept a dozen horses out of the front yard. Polished concrete led from the gravel driveway up to a grand front porch, complete with a porch swing and manicured plants.

Dave snorted. "Heck no. DZ owners rarely come out in the green. Amity's gramps was loaded. The DZ is a labor of love."

Dad and I had never been well-off. He made his living as an on-again, off-again artist whose paintings occasionally sold for big bucks. But I'd had plenty of friends who were New York rich, living in multi-million-dollar apartments.

That was nothing like this.

"What did Gramps do? Something illegal I bet."

"Music producer. So, close." Dave winked and led the way around the back of the house. "Amity won't answer the front door."

The porch wrapped around the entire house and led to a large, outdoor kitchen and lagoon-styled pool. Behind the house was a Amish-country postcard-perfect red barn. Weeds had grown up around the sides, the area left untouched, unmanicured, completely different than the rest of the property.

Dave ignored the barn, walked through the kitchen, and opened the backdoor. "Yo, Amity. I brought you a visitor."

I waited outside. After kicking me off her drop zone, I had no doubt that she'd use her power to kick my unexpected butt out of her house.

"Amity? You here?" Dave's voice trickled outside from somewhere deep in the house.

A breeze picked up across the open field behind Amity's house and a few seconds later reached my face, lifting my curls away from my forehead, and bringing with it the soft lilts of a violin.

Good music was the scent of a delicious meal to a Siren.

Great music was the scent of the most delicious, perfectly-roasted coffee beans ever.

I turned toward the barn, my feet following the music. I'm not sure, but I think I floated to the barn.

The door creaked under my hand. Up close, it was clear how little the barn had been maintained. Cobwebs sprouted in every corner, and the wood had splintered, the paint had peeled.

But the violin music. It built until something in my chest cracked. It wasn't just music. It was emotion. An overwhelming wave of sadness and grief, with threads of hot, steaming anger woven through.

If this was Amity, she was not in a mood not be messed with.

Inside, the barn was a recording studio. Acoustic panels had been installed on the walls. Instruments ranging from an electric cello to a full drum kit to a grand piano filled one room. A bank of electronics and musical manipulation tools filled another. And in the third room, closed behind thick glass, was Amity.

Her eyes closed, her blonde dreads half covering her face, she leaned into the violin, and she played.

Long, slow notes, deep and throbbing. Scaling up to higher pitches, almost a cry.

Pain. She was playing her pain.

What had happened to this girl?

She finished her song with one last note, her chest rising and falling as if she had just run a marathon, sweat glistening on her forehead.

"What do you want, Korrina?" Her voice came across muted, struggling to be heard through the thick glass. She hadn't raised her head to know it was me, to know anyone was here.

I found a switch in the control room that would let me talk to her easily. I didn't want to risk joining her in an enclosed space. Not until I knew she had her power under control. Not until I knew she wouldn't try to blast me to the state line.

"We need to talk."

She turned her back to me and carefully packed up her violin. And instead of joining me on my side of the glass, she stretched out on a gray velvet sofa.

"You want to talk about mythology. About how we're magical and a bunch of other stuff your nuthouse friends probably appreciated." She waved her hand in the air. "I don't know how you escaped or how long you've been screwing with people, but if you don't leave now, I'm calling my good sheriff friend to come pick you up."

I leaned forward and spoke into the microphone. "I don't want to talk about mythology."

She raised her eyebrows but didn't protest.

"I want to talk about how you knew I had entered your studio before you saw me."

Whatever sarcastic remark she had at the ready soured in her mouth. She sat up. "I didn't—"

"You did. I noticed in the change in your music. And another thing"—I tapped on the glass—"this is soundproof glass, right?"

She shrugged.

"Explain how I heard your music through soundproof glass all the way up on your back porch."

She opened her mouth.

"And explain how we're talking *and* able to hear each other without me turning on this little microphone."

"You don't have the microphone on?" Her eyes darted to the light in the corner of the room that should be lit up.

I softened my voice, proving my point even further. "Dave says you can do things. Things no one should be able to do." I held out my hand, hummed my song, and a purple glow effervesced through my skin.

She pushed against the couch. As if an entire room and thick, soundproof glass weren't enough distance.

A tear pushed at her lashes. She crinkled her nose, stood, and began humming as well, lifting her hand. Pale blue light, the color of a cloudless day, radiated from her.

"You're a Siren. Like me. Like our mothers, like our grand-mothers. All the way back to the time of the Muses and Demeter and Persephone. It's real, Amity. You're not crazy."

Her light faded, and she dropped to the couch with a sob.

I opened the door, sat beside her, and let her have her my-world-just-disintegrated moment. Dave appeared in the studio, surprise tightening his face. I shook my head at him, and he nodded a thin-lipped smile and left.

"When you're ready, I'll tell you everything."

She nodded, pushed back her dreads. "I'm ready."

And so, I told her everything. From our ancestral history to my childhood to Jared. Everything.

Except for the Council's plans.

If I'd learned one thing in the past six months, it was this: keep your secrets close. Keep your weapons closer.

If Amity was the weapon the Council thought she was, I wasn't leaving her side.

CHAPTER 9

We left Dave to man the drop zone in Amity's absence and hopped in her DeLorean—complete with wingaling doors. Her hands were steady on the wheel, but she didn't take her eyes off the road and she didn't speak. Not once.

We pulled up to the campsite just as the sun reached blazing noon. Amity popped her gull wing doors as Dad climbed out of the RV with Neri, on his shoulder and we made our grand entrance.

Taking Amity to our mobile home felt a little like taking a boy home to meet the parents for the first time.

"Dad, Neri, this is Amity."

Dad put on his Dad grin and Neri bowed low, her wings outstretched.

In the noon light, Neri almost looked like a normal owl.

"It's my deepest pleasure to meet you, Songwriter." She put a little shimmer into her wings as she spoke.

Amity jerked back as normal flew right out the metaphorical window.

"Th—that owl—"

"Is super annoying. Neri, her name is Amity. Don't start with this title-calling stuff like you did me." It'd taken me *forever* to get her to stop calling me the *Elpida*. English translation? The Hope.

No pressure or anything.

Neri shot me a glare and ruffled her feathers.

I turned to Amity and crossed my arms. "Songwriter, huh?"

Amity was still all wide-eyed. "How did she know that?" She scooted closer to me, as if I could somehow offer her protection from the mythical owl. Little did she know, there was no protection from obnoxious.

"She's a good guesser. Neri, tell us more."

Neri turned her head, pouting. Great, I'd hurt her feelings. I'd have to catch her a big juicy moth later.

Dad gestured to the campfire, and we all took a seat. "The four Sirens—Molpe, Peisinoe, Aglaope, and Thelxiepeia—were daughters of the Muse Melpomene, who was the Muse of Song but became the Muse of Tragedy. Each of her Siren daughters was blessed with a different gift. Molpe—Korrina's ancestor— was blessed with the ability to heal. Thelxiepeia—your ancestor, Amity—was blessed with the ability to cast words as power."

Amity seemed to sink into herself.

"Each Siren passed those powers down to her daughters and, eventually, to you."

She went pale. "It was my fault," she whispered. "Gramps dying. Everyone said it wasn't, that a song couldn't kill, but it did. It killed him."

I grabbed her hand and held it close. I wouldn't say it wasn't her fault. That had never helped me, and it wouldn't help her. All I could do was sit here and be here.

But instead of breaking apart like some other Sirens I knew —ahem—she sat straighter, let go of my hand. "How do I make sure that never happens again?"

Neri rose into the air with a giant flap of her wings.

I groaned. She was about to get dramatic.

"By mastering your power." She somehow grabbed the sunlight and pulled it into her, until the campsite was dark and she was a shining beacon.

"Wow," I breathed. "Guess we don't have to shell out for flashlight batteries anymore."

Amity gave me a look that was one-part shock and two-parts undecided. She snorted, then let out a giant laugh, one that was unhindered, one that kept going on, and on, and on.

I was funny, but not that funny.

She wiped at her eyes. "I'm sorry—I'm sorry. This is all—oh man—how can any of this"—she gasped for air and turned to me—"be true? It's true. This is real. I'm—you're—"

"Yes. And you're handling it really well."

She pressed her lips together, and we both started laughing.

Neri floated to the ground and muttered something that sounded a lot like, "Irreverent Sirens. Never changes."

Amity and I pulled ourselves together. As much fun as uncontrollable laughing was, we had work to do.

"The Council wants us to train and get used to working together," I lied, implementing the first part of my undiscussed plan.

Dad leaned in, as if trying to figure out this person that he raised, and Neri rose into the air, about to spill all the beans. This wasn't our plan. This wasn't our mission.

But if the Council wanted to use Amity as a weapon, I'd learn how to first. I'd make myself so important to her power, they'd have to let us stay together.

Amity sobered up. "What Council?"

I positioned myself so she had to turn her back to Dad and Neri to focus on my words.

"The Council of the Gods. A tribunal of the Greek gods, led by the three Fates, who determine how the mythic world should interact with the real world." Over Amity's shoulder, Neri puffed with pride that her many lectures about the Council had finally sunk in. "They also tell our little band of awesomeness what to do, but usually in riddles that are no help whatsoever."

Neri deflated. "Decorum is so close and yet so far."

"Greek gods. You're talking Zeus and Hades and Poseidon and…" Amity trailed off, looking faint.

I grabbed her hand again. "Let's just focus on what we've got to deal with right here. All of that is behind the veil. Not close. But you know what is close?"

She shook her head.

"Coffee and Taco Bell."

Amity moaned. "Now you're speaking my language."

"Neri"—*snap, snap*—"fetch."

For future reference, forty pounds of interdimensional owl packs a punch.

AFTER WE GAVE AMITY A DOSE OF *NORMAL*, WE MOVED OUR campsite to her front yard. Her view was better. Plus, it allowed us to keep watch around her while we trained her powers and waited for our next mission from the Council.

Neri sneaked off and sent a message to her contact on the Council—she still wouldn't tell us his or her or its identity—and Dad and I got to know Amity. The Council's weapon.

I knew that's how they thought of me. An object to be used instead of a life to be valued.

Amity insisted we sleep in the guest bedrooms, of which she had many. Dad refused, claiming he wanted to keep an eye on the property.

She led me into a room at the back of the house. Long halls decorated with signed pictures of famous singers and framed gold albums. I stopped in front of the last one at the end of the hall, a platinum record with a singer's name I recognized, and Amity's name on the gold tag beneath the record.

She'd won a Grammy.

My nineteen-year-old, drop-zone-owning Siren cousin had won a Grammy for one of her songs.

"Amity...I had no idea..."

She took a couple of steps back. "I never wanted my name on that. The artist thought he was doing something nice, but all I want is to forget those words."

"Well, you may not think it's your best work, but the world disagrees."

Amity turned her back to me, her shoulders lifted and tense.

"We are but mountains, and we crumble, we crumble. We are but mountains, be gentle, be gentle." Her soft voice whispered over me, and it felt like the wind, pushing at stone. *"We all break, we all break, we all break. You think I'm strong, but I'll crumble, I'll crumble, for you."*

She turned back to me. "I've only ever sung that song one time. One time to record a sample for the artist. At the same time I was singing those words, Gramps was driving home. Flat road on top of a plateau. The road went out, crumbled all around him. The investigator said there was no way it should have happened. Freak accident." She met my gaze, tears in her eyes. "No one considered that I was the freak."

I didn't protest. A Siren knows when her power has used her. Even when no one else believes her.

"This is your room." She pushed open a door, closing the conversation. "You have a kitchenette, en suite, and the cupboard is stocked with my favorite coffee. Enjoy, and I'll see you in the morning."

She shut the door behind me before I could suggest popcorn and Buffy.

"Good night to you too," I muttered, then took in Amity's so-called guest room.

This was a guest house. I turned in a circle. A high domed ceiling arched over a four-poster canopy bed. Large wooden doors with big, clean windows peered out onto a private terrace. The "kitchenette" was more of a gourmet kitchen than I'd ever seen, and the fridge was stocked with all kinds of treats. And the bathroom. Dear God, the bathroom.

I squealed, turned on the faucet of the three-person-sized claw-footed tub, and squeezed a bunch of bath bubbles over the running water. I sank into the bubbles, and that's all the cue whoever-it-was needed to send me to Demeter.

CHAPTER 10

We were underwater.

Blue light wavered around the room, and windows above us, around us, below us, kept out the ocean. At the front of the room, Demeter sat in a throne, and a grotesque figure knelt beside her.

Long tentacles stretched out from his waist and where his hands should be snapped giant claws.

"You called me to your domain with news of my daughter, Phorkys, and I have heard nothing from you but platitudes. Speak, creature, or regret my invitation." She drilled her nails against the throne—Phorkys's throne.

Talk about emasculation.

"The Sirens plot against you, goddess. I have proof."

"Of what? The Sirens have been Persephone's friends since childhood." She waved at him, but her words growled. No longer were her clothes torn, her face haggard, but also, no longer was her expression relaxed, her eyes soft.

This was the Demeter that inspired my nightmares.

If I were Phorkys, I'd be coming up with some really good words right about now.

He straightened, and I caught the gleam in his eyes. "Ask yourself how Persephone was lost. Are not the Sirens attuned to their very environment? From the cool touch of the shadows to the taste of the wind? How then did they not sense him approach, with his the coolest of touches and the most sensual of tastes?"

Demeter leaned forward, her fingers curled tight around the throne. "Who? Who has my daughter?"

"Hermes sees much in his travels, but he only sees what happens above the surface. He has whispered a tale most chilling indeed, perhaps surpassed by my own witness."

The throne room shook, and a crack ran along one of the many windows. Demeter half rose from her seat. "I will bring this pathetic excuse for a kingdom down if you do not tell me what has happened to my daught—"

"Hades has taken her."

The room stilled, and Demeter fell back onto the throne. She paled, seemed to collapse.

"Hermes witnessed the kidnapping from the surface, but the earth crawled in shadows so he could not be sure. But I, master of the deep, have seen what happened to fair Persephone. Even now, Hades seeks to make her his bride."

Demeter was silent for a long time. Where I'd imagine most mothers would scream and grieve and panic, she became thoughtful. Calculating. "I will appeal to Zeus to force Hades to release her."

Phorkys nodded. "And the Sirens?"

"What is your obsession with those girls?" She rubbed at her forehead.

Phorkys scooted closer, his clawed hands pressed together. "They stole something from me. I want it back. I want them to pay."

That something being the scepter that was ziptied and superglued to my soul.

Demeter stood, and it seemed as if she drained all color from the room and drew it into herself. She glowed, looked every inch the scary goddess I knew. "Make no mistake. If the Sirens are responsible for my daughter's fate, they will pay. They will most certainly pay."

She disappeared in a crack of light. The room dimmed, and Phorkys limped to his throne. He took his seat, dusted off the areas that Demeter's nails had scratched. "You will all pay, *goddess*." No longer was his tone reverent, no longer his posture submissive.

Phorkys had the look of someone who had laid his trap, and already caught his prey.

CHAPTER 11

I woke to the sound of a man's voice calling out Amity's name.

At some point last night, I must have crawled out of the cold bathwater and into bed, though I didn't remember anything but the vision of Demeter. And Phorkys—the sea god after the scepter...after me. I'd read up on the guy, but seeing him in person? Man, his Tinder profile had to be interesting.

I turned my head, and something pink blurred into focus.

A flower lay on the pillow next to me, the petals limp as if it had been there all night.

And I was wrapped in a bunch of towels...something I would never have done. Fuzzy socks had been shoved on my feet, and I got the feeling that I'd had some help getting to bed last night.

Had Dad checked on me? Sure, he used to wipe my butt, but he hadn't seen said butt in years.

But then, why the flower?

"Amity?" the man's voice called out again and went panic-hued.

I pushed back the heavy comforter, changed my towels for clothes, and ran out of the room.

"Dave?" I collided with him in the hall and rubbed the sleep from my eyes. "What's going on?"

"Amity didn't show up to work this morning." He didn't stop moving but gently pushed me out of the way, the wiry hairs of his beard poking from his chin in every direction.

A sick feeling spread in my stomach. "Is that normal?"

"No." He pressed his lips together.

Flashes of Jared on the bridge, hunger in his eyes as he stalked Amity, bulleted across my vision.

And that's when I noticed the long shotgun pressed between Dave's arm and waist. My pulse beat against my throat. I hated guns. Not even Dad used guns in our fights…mainly because bullets didn't stop mythical creatures. Only old school weapons and my Siren song. But it's not like I could tell Dave that.

Besides, what had happened in Amity's life that Dave's first reaction was to grab a gun?

"If Amity's in trouble like I think she's in trouble, you're not going to need that gun."

Dave paled, his expression went wary. "Why? What's happened? What did you do?"

"My ex may be trying to kill her." I pressed my back against the wall, made Dave mimic my pose with a soccer mom press of my arm.

His breath shallowed against me, his body going still.

There's a part of the human brain reserved for survival. It's an ancient instinct, pre-fire, pre-wheel, that takes over when an external threat is near. Fight or flight. Or freeze.

Despite his shotgun, Dave froze.

"Why is your ex trying to kill Amity?" His whispered words shook at the edges.

"Remember how you said she's special?"

He tilted his chin, the slightest nod.

"She's really special. Like irreplaceable special."

His jaw clenched. "And your ex is trying to kill her?"

"You know that crap you were saying I needed to let go?" I breathed.

He nodded.

"That's the crap. We need to find her." I reached for his hand, squeezed, and took the lead.

We cleared each room in the hallway as we went, then ducked into the living room. Amity's oversized, ranch-style furniture provided perfect cover, but we didn't need it. The house looked untouched. Except for a full cup of coffee now cold on the kitchen counter.

If Amity's affection for coffee was anywhere close to mine, that was a bad sign.

Worry twisted in my chest and my song powered up. I tried to recall Neri's lessons, her attempts to teach me to use only threads of the flame, instead of one big bonfire. Every time I tried, the scepter in my soul took over, sucked my life force, and almost killed me.

But at the moment, all I could focus on was finding Amity and keeping Dave from Jared's fate.

"Amity'd never leave her coffee unfinished." Dave confirmed my guess and cocked the gun with a click that was too loud in the quiet house.

If Jared was here, I hoped his power included dodging bullets.

Dave tried to barrel past me, his mind focused on saving Amity.

I grabbed him. "She will never forgive me if I get you killed. Stay behind me."

He paused, looked me up and down. "You're special too?"

I snorted. "Yeah, you could say that. Let me lead. Deal?"

He thumbed off the safety. "Deal."

Great plan, Korrina. Let's give the unstable, lovesick puppy a gun and have him follow you.

We slipped through the back door, surveyed the area, and crept toward the barn, using various shrubs and oversized flower pots as shields. The RV looked locked up tight, the window shades drawn. Everything was quiet. No screams broke the peaceful morning, only the soft sound of birds fussing. All seemed well.

My song corkscrewed in my throat, not falling for it.

The door to the barn was wide open, and we slipped inside.

The studio was trashed.

"Amity…" Dave whispered then pushed past me. He tore through the control room, leapt over a turned over chair, dodged torn wires, and plowed through the glass door into the recording room. Empty. He ran into another part of the studio. Checking every corner. Looking under every turned table.

It was my turn to freeze.

Neri appeared at my side. Dad burst through the door, crossbow cocked at his shoulder.

"We're too late." My own words punched my gut.

From the moment I'd seen that cold coffee in the kitchen, I'd known.

Amity was cursed, or worse, dead.

Because I'd chosen Jared.

Because I'd chosen me.

CHAPTER 12

Dad turned and stomped out of the studio. Dave collapsed to his knees in the middle of the wreckage while Neri went invisible. I followed Dad outside, giving Dave a moment to process.

We all needed a moment to process.

I expected Dad to be waiting outside for me, so we could come up with a new plan.

I didn't expect him to be launching my suitcase out of the R.V.

"What are you doing?" I ran up to our home-on-the-move and picked up one of my fuzzy socks.

"Leaving." He climbed the stairs and disappeared inside.

I had a flashback of that time when I'd come home to Dad packing the RV. Dad making me leave everyone I loved.

Now, he was doing it again.

"Dad, we can't leave. Amity's been kidnapped. We have to look for clues and find her." I felt like I was talking to a child.

He appeared at the top of the stairs, keys in hand.

"You're right. And it's my fault they found her so quickly. So I'm leaving, and you're staying." He sat in the driver's seat.

"Uh no, you're not. Not without a better explanation than that." I stepped into the door and leaned against the opening. He couldn't leave without also squishing me.

He beat a fist against the steering wheel, and the effort seemed to whoosh all the strength out of him. He slumped in his seat and stared straight ahead.

"I disobeyed the Council by coming here."

I narrowed my gaze at him. "What do you mean?"

"You were supposed to do this mission by yourself. Blend in, infiltrate, retrieve the weapon. Without me. Without Neri."

Dad's behavior over the last few days finally made sense. He had been keeping secrets.

Only this time, it was his life he was playing with. Not mine.

"Dad…" Dread filled my chest. We could get away with rule-bending the Council's missions. Flat-out disobeying?

These were gods we were dealing with. Actual gods. Gods with the power to smite.

And Dad had sworn an oath to them. To protect. To obey.

Neri took that opportunity to pop in. "The Council always has good reason for their orders. Even if they don't explain them."

I couldn't be sure of the look on her face, but it was a mixture of sadness, disappointment, and fear.

"If I hadn't come, Amity would be safe." He tightened his grip on the steering wheel, and I wasn't sure who he was talking to—me, Neri, or himself.

"You can't know that—"

He tossed something at me. It was a small object. Round, metal, and cold. With a blinking green light in the middle.

"A tracking device. Found it this morning in my gear. *My* gear. That's how the Siren Hunter found us so quickly yesterday. They've been tracking me. And we led him straight to her."

I curled my fingers around the device.

"If I'd let you come on your own, I would have led them

away from her. Away from you. You'd be off-grid and safe. And now, because of me…"

"Why?" My voice sank low, and he waited for me to fill in the blank.

Why didn't he listen? Why didn't he follow orders? Why didn't he tell me?

Why didn't he trust me?

The Band-aid on his hand seemed to laugh out loud, to answer all my whys.

Dad didn't trust me.

I stepped out of the doorway, onto Amity's property, hurt radiating from my fingertips. "Don't tell the Council. I'll find her. Just go." I handed the tracking gadget back to him.

He took the device and placed it on the dashboard. "I'll make this right, Korrina. Somehow. I'll lead them away from you, so you can find her."

"And do what in the meantime?"

Dad placed his hand on the button that closed the door. His spine was straight again, and a little bit of that Guardian gleam glinted in his eyes. "I'm going to find your mom. The Council will already be after me for disobeying orders. Might as well make the run for my life count."

He knew the stakes better than I did, and that admission softened my hurting heart.

"I'm sorry, baby. I'll make this right. I will." He let me go and caressed the Band-aid on his hand. I'm not sure he even knew he was doing it, but it was enough.

Enough for me to believe he regretted what he'd asked of me. Enough for me to allow him to go.

I nodded, and Neri took up her perch next to Dad's seat. "This is where we say goodbye, *Elpida*. But I will check in from time to time. So *behave*." Her timeless gaze sliced through me, then she started humming Train's "50 Ways to Say Goodbye," complete with background mariachi music.

"I make no promises."

Dad closed the door, started the engine, and left me standing in Amity's driveway, truly on my own for the first time.

Dave joined me as the RV disappeared. "Where are they going?" His voice was raw, scratched up.

"To save my mother. C'mon. We've got to get you caught up, and then we've got some rescuing of our own to do."

DAVE TOOK THE WHOLE MYTHOLOGY-IS-REAL THING BETTER THAN I'd expected. Better than Jared had.

We sat on Amity's back porch, homemade milkshakes in coffee mugs courtesy of mwah. I wasn't sure if ice cream stirred with a splash of milk really counted as a milkshake, but whatever. We faced the barn, neither of us willing to turn our backs to the threat. Or the lack of clues.

We'd searched high. We'd searched low. We'd searched and searched again.

Whoever had taken Amity had made a lot of mess, but not a neat line of clues.

"How many Sirens are out there?"

"I'm not sure. For a while, I thought I was the only one. But then Amity was activated…" I slurped at my chocolate milkshake and ran through everything I knew. "There are four Siren families. I come from Molpe's line. Amity is part of Thelxiepeia's line. There are two others, but I don't know if the Council has activated them. Which, apparently, is how it happens. And then our power starts manifesting in scary, deadly ways."

The man I'd killed, then Chadwick, scampered across my mind's eye before I could shut that door. I held my breath until the memories scurried away. Sirens had gotten a bad rep over the years. There was no question in my mind why.

"The Council sounds like a real piece of work. So they just open the power flood lines on you, without letting you know anything about yourself or what you are?"

I shrugged. "The gods think more in terms of what they want the finish line to look like. They don't really consider how all their assets end up at the finish line."

Dave's milkshake had melted, and he'd done nothing more than spin it around in its own condensation. Not everyone processed crises through massive amounts of sugar and caffeine. I wasn't sure if we could be good friends. Not that that was the focus at the moment.

"What's going to happen to Amity?" He dragged his finger through the gathered wetness at the base of his coffee mug.

I wiped at my ice cream-stache.

"She'll be cursed," a deep voice said from behind us, and a hand gripped my shoulder, forcing me to stay seated.

Dave leapt to his feet, shotgun in hand.

And my song. My song was gone.

"Don't do anything drastic, babe. Just calm down."

My bones cringed. My blood boiled.

That voice.

That. Voice.

I hated that voice.

I may not have been able to sing. But I could punch with everything I had.

My arms went crazy. Upward thrust, and my fist connected with something solid and fleshy.

Good.

Luke let me go, gasping for air from my throat punch, and my song flooded back to life.

Because of course it was Luke.

Luke, the only guy with the ability to silence my Siren song with his touch.

Luke, the guy who'd betrayed us all.

CHAPTER 13

Luke gasped for breath on Amity's patio. Dave cocked his shotgun and shoved it into his neck. I coiled my song inside my chest, and I didn't really care how it was fueled. I would happily use my life force to make him bleed.

Luke coughed, held up a hand in surrender, and dropped to his knees, disturbing a scattering of discarded leaves.

His long hair hung in a tattered ponytail. His violet eyes were transparent. Worn thin. Overpowered by the black and green bruise covering his cheek. His Adonis-figure had shriveled to a third world version of himself.

But I had no room for pity. He'd poisoned Danica and Tula. He'd cursed Jared. He'd turned him over to Phorkys. He'd betrayed us all.

"You have ten seconds to convince us not to load you full of lead and Siren wrath." Words rasped from my throat, followed by purple tendrils of my power.

Dave looked from Luke to me and adjusted his grip on the gun.

I began the countdown on Luke's life. "Ten…Nine…"

"You…healed me." He dipped his head. "Korrina, please.

When you sang, when you healed the tear in the veil, you healed me too."

"Can't heal evil, bozo. Five…four…"

"I know where your mother is."

His words stole my song more effectively than his touch ever had.

I dropped my fists.

Luke looked up, his beaten gaze meeting mine. "Raelyn, that's her name, right?"

I studied him.

The problem with Luke is, was, and had always been that honest look in his violet eyes. It was even worse now that he was pathetic.

Most of the time, I could tell when people were lying.

But Luke had deceived me so effectively it'd almost brought the world to an end.

I tightened my throat. "You're lying. Dave, shoot him."

"Red hair, not as curly as yours. White wings. I never saw her eyes, but I'd bet they're the same brilliant blue as yours."

I held up my hand to stop Dave's trigger finger.

"She's sleeping. She was in the cell next to mine. The guards talked. No one's been able to wake her in years."

Cell? Sleeping?

I'd met my mother in the spirit void. Separated from her body, but not dead. Her spirit was very much alive.

There was a ring of truth in his words. But there was always a ring of truth to Luke's words. If only I had Amity's B.S. meter.

"I tried to leave," he continued. "After you healed me. It's like my eyes were finally opened to what I was doing, who I'd become, what my family is. I couldn't stay, but they stopped me. Colin threw me in the Grotto, and I've been there ever since."

I shook my head. "If that's true, how are you here?"

He shrugged. "Your mother saved me. Made me promise to

find you if she opened the locks. She couldn't leave herself, she can't wake up, but she thought maybe I could help reach you."

My song vibrated in my throat. "Right. While she was sleeping. Good movie, by the way. Also fiction."

"She visited my dreams, Korrina. Just like you used to."

Dave pressed his gun harder into Luke's neck. "What does any of this have to do with Amity?"

Luke shifted his focus from me to Dave, not once acknowledging the gun at his neck. I had to give him props for maintaining his cool...but it did make me wonder just what he'd been through that a gun at his neck didn't faze him.

"I don't know any Amity," he said. "Someone passed through the veil, and I slipped through after them."

"Jared," I confirmed.

Luke shook his head. "I really don't know. It wasn't the usual way Jared sneaks out."

"And you didn't see who it was?" Dave was doing his best to keep up, and, with talk of veils and another dimension, I thought he was doing a decent job.

"Not the way the veil works, man. It's more like a ripple in time. If you know how to find the weak spots in the veil and manipulate the ripples, you can take a back door from one world to the next." Luke raised his chin. "I know where the weak spots are. I just had to wait until someone caused a ripple."

Dave turned his focus to me. "Could someone have taken Amity through this ripple?"

There was a flash of movement in the corner of my vision, and the shotgun was ripped away from Dave.

Luke shot me an abused grin and flipped the gun around to point at Dave. "My turn. Who's Amity?"

Like hell I was letting Luke hold a gun.

I hummed, and Dave went still.

But I'd learned some new tricks.

I pulled my song in, concentrated the power, then used it to whip out in a strand of energy and fling the gun out of Luke's hands. It flew across the patio, through the yard, into the empty field next to the barn, and landed with a loud *crack-boom*.

We ducked, and a hole exploded in the side of the barn.

"What kind of shells you got in there?" Luke's eyes went wide.

"Buckshot." Dave crossed his arms, seemingly unaffected by my song. "Don't load a gun without intent to kill."

Dave was a little scary.

Luke's gaze went from him to me, as if he was thinking *what are you doing with this guy?*

None of your beeswax, Lukester.

I was suddenly very, very tired. "Why are you here, Luke?" I collapsed in my chair and let Dave stand as a useless guard against him.

"I want to help. I want to make things right."

"By stealing my gun?" Dave muttered.

"Dude's got a point." I pressed my fingers against my temple. Using my song had stolen a little bit of my life force and given me a migraine. My song could be a real witch.

"Old habits die hard," Luke quipped. "Look, this is mostly my fault. My family has served Phorkys for centuries. He gave us our abilities, but also used our abilities to manipulate us."

"Mind control abilities," I cleared up for Dave.

Dave started.

"Yeah, don't let him touch you. Continue."

"I heard things in the Grotto. Jared and Colin's plans, their orders, missions. And I gotta tell you, something went wrong with Jared's transformation. He's not right."

I perked up. "What do you mean?"

Luke shook his head. "He…disobeys. Not outright or where anyone can really see, but I've watched him. Colin will tell him to do something, and Jared will find every way to not do it or to do it poorly. Siren Hunters don't act like that. They're assassins. They do what they're told in the most efficient way possible."

A tiny spark lit up in my chest. I knew that spark. Had a love-hate relationship with that spark.

Hope.

Hope was a dangerous, dangerous thing.

"You want to save Jared," he said. "And I'm assuming this Amity person, right?"

"Siren," I corrected.

It was Luke's turn to be shocked. "There are more of you?"

"Apparently. Aren't you excited?"

"Scared. The world can handle only one Korrina Lore."

Ugh. He was good.

"You want to save Jared and Amity, a Siren who has been kidnapped. I can help. I know the weak spots in the veil. I know the Siren Hunters' movements. I know Phorkys's plans. I know how they find you."

"Tracking device. We found it already."

Luke crinkled his eyebrows. "No. They track your power. Each time you sing, you light up on a map like a spotlight. It's quick, and it fades quickly, but if they're paying attention, they can find you anywhere."

If the Siren Hunters could track my power, then who'd bugged Dad's gear with a tracking device?

And for that matter, who'd dragged my half-drowned butt out of the bathtub, made sure I was warm, and left a flower on my pillow last night?

"Plus, I know all about Sirens," Luke continued. "Your power, why you're tired after you sing, how you dreamwalk, your mother's power to see into the future, how you can heal injuries…I can help."

I refocused on Luke. "I can't heal injuries."

"Yes, babe. You can."

Dave and I exchanged glances. Having someone we could

mine for information would be helpful. And we had no other clues. If Luke could help us get to Amity before she was cursed or killed…

I huffed. "You'll stay on one condition."

Hope lit up his tired eyes.

"You'll wear gloves. No skin contact. And your hands will remain zip-tied unless you're peeing or eating."

He nodded, agreeing quickly. Maybe too quickly.

And just like that, I'd built a new team. A trigger-happy skydiver and a boy who'd already betrayed me once.

CHAPTER 14

The next morning, after a night of no sleeping…because of the gun-happy and betrayal-happy men in the house…I did something I'd promised myself I wouldn't do.

I called Cloud.

The line rang, went to voicemail. He was probably screening his calls, and my cheap, pay-as-you-go phone number would be new to him. Sure enough, his voice poured through my cell's speakers, like a draft of cinnamon and pumpkin spice.

Home.

"Hey Cloud. It's me. Korrina. I"—*I need you, I need about the only person I still trust. I need my best friend*—"I just needed…I wanted to say hey. Hope everything is well and full of mischief."

I hung up.

I couldn't bring him into this. Danger followed me around like a starving, stray puppy. Besides, what did I expect him to do? Hop on a plane and join me on a rescue mission to not-even-the-gods-knew-where? I thumbed through his pictures again, his happy, in-love-with-Danica pictures. They made an odd couple, but their oddness matched, made them both shine.

In the living room, Luke was sitting up in a big armchair,

sound asleep. Dave was on the couch next to him, cuddling his recovered shotgun. I really hoped that thing wasn't loaded. I gently pried it from his hands and set it safely on the kitchen counter, within reach and much safer than in Dave's sleeping hands.

I made coffee as quietly as I could, though the bean grinder didn't listen to my shushing.

"Korrina," Luke groaned.

"Do you really want to see me without caffeine in the morning?"

His eyes went wide as he shook his head, but a smirk curled at his cheeks.

Careful, Korrina.

It'd be all too easy to fall back into mine and Luke's old routines. There was nothing routine about our relationship now.

"What'd you do with Sully?" Dave sat up and wiped dried drool off his beard.

"Who's Sully?"

Luke rolled his eyes. "His shotgun."

"You named your shotgun?" I pointed at the kitchen counter so Dave could relax.

"Don't start," he growled, and Luke shook his head in the background.

Apparently this topic had already been discussed.

I shook my head and focused on more important matters. Coffee matters.

"What is *he* doing here?" a loud voice screeched through the kitchen.

Dave yelped.

I jerked, sloshed liquid gold all over the counter, and shoved the carafe back on the machine. "Neri, I swear I am going to surgically attach a bell to your neck."

"We leave for less than twenty-four hours, *Elpida,* and

already, *already*, you have found trouble." Her voice had reached a pitch I'd never heard before. I wasn't even sure if it was audible to most humans.

"That's an…an…owl," Dave stuttered. "Purple…and…wasn't here…"

"Dave meet Neri. Yes, she's magical. Yes, she's annoying. Neri, Dave. He's in love with Amity."

Dave sputtered.

I grabbed a towel, ignoring him, my spine already tensed for Neri's rebukes. "Luke's tied up. He's not going anywhere. He says he's left Phorkys's team. Wants to join ours."

"And you believe him?" If she had lips, they'd be pulled back in a snarl. As it was, her beak clipped off her words with a sharp gnash.

"No." I poured a fresh cup of coffee and joined the boys in the living room. "But since you and Dad rode off into the sunset, and since the Council put *me* in charge of this mission, I get to make all the bad decisions I want." I kicked my feet up and over the arm of the chair and inhaled my coffee.

My phone rang, and the cheap phone scrolled the number across the screen—which of course I didn't recognize.

"Maybe it's Amity." Dave sat straight, his voice relatively calm for encountering a magical creature, butt on the edge of the couch.

Amity didn't have my number, but I knew what he meant. Maybe whoever had taken Amity was contacting us with their demands.

If only.

I answered the call while Neri hopped closer to Luke.

"Hello?"

No one answered, but I could make out the distant wail of a siren in the background. The police-kind, not the feathered-kind. "Hello?"

Still no answer. But there was heavy breathing, like every movie-stalker call ever.

"Okay. Well, you stay creepy my friend." I hung up the phone.

Neri's owl shoulders puffed up around her face, hiding her neck. She waved a talon at Luke, and a golden scroll tied to her foot glinted in the light. "If you so much as breathe in a way I do not like, I will pluck your eyes from your skull."

Luke gulped, lost some of his bravado.

"You have a message to deliver?" I drew her attention back to me and my poor decision-making skills.

"Yes. One to deliver *in private*."

I groaned. "Dave. Watch him." And led Neri onto the patio.

Once I'd shut the door, she settled on the table. The morning shone with a brilliance I would not appreciate until after my second dose of coffee. I sat in a chair that protected my back and let me view the backyard and the inside of the house at the same time.

Survival was exhausting.

"What's going on, Neri? Does Dad have any leads on Mom yet?"

She ignored me. "What are you thinking, Korrina?" She no longer sounded shocked or disgusted. She sounded tired. Like she was exhausted too.

"Luke says he was imprisoned in a cell next to Mom. Some place called the Grotto."

Neri went very, very still.

"Said she's been asleep all this time, but she'd visit him in his dreams. She somehow got the locks to his cell open, made him promise to find me if he could escape."

"Are you sure he said The Grotto?" Neri's voice was raspy, hushed, church-mouse quiet.

The knot in my stomach grew heavier. Ever since Luke had

mentioned the name of his prison, it'd been growing. Some intuition, maybe a smidgen of my mother's power to see into the future, but there was something about that place. Something that wasn't friendly and something, one day, I was sure I was going to meet.

I didn't answer Neri. I didn't need to.

"Keep him close. And don't take your eyes off him."

I nodded. "Duh, Neri. Now what message do you have?"

She took the scroll off her foot and passed it over. "The Council has a mission for you."

The paper was still sealed, the power stamp unbroken. "You haven't peeked."

"It's not my mission."

I held my breath, shoved my thumb under the seal, and hesitated. "Do they know about Amity? About Dad?"

Neri shook her head. "I don't think so. I will protect him as long as I can."

"And you'll tell him about the Grotto? That Mom might be there?"

Neri nodded. "It's an impossible destination to reach, but that won't stop him."

My shoulders fell a fraction, and I tore open the scroll.

Gold lettering filled the page and seemed to wiggle on the paper, as if the text itself was excited about being read.

Find the weapon who sees, in the desert that still sings.

"Someone needs to introduce the Council to GPS coordinates," I muttered. "I'm guessing this weapon is another Siren?"

Neri shrugged. "Your guess is as good as mine. Good luck."

And with that, she raised the tips of her wings high into the air and disappeared.

BY MY COUNT, I HAD FIVE MYSTERIES TO SOLVE. ONE—WHERE WAS Amity? Two—where was Mom? Three—what was up with

Luke? Four—who was the next weapon? And five—who'd left me the flower?

Technically, Dad and Neri were on mystery numero *dos*, so I could focus on the other four. If Mom really was in the Grotto, they'd find her. Save her. Maybe even wake her.

I stalked Amity's hallways for one whole day without any big lightbulbs bursting above my head. I *did* however, successfully avoid Trigger and Lukester. They seemed to have found a balance of tolerance, which was a good thing as Dave insisted on keeping Luke zip-tied even at meal times. Turns out, stealing Dave's shotgun was not a way to make friends.

I didn't even want to know how Luke was going to the bathroom without assistance. If he *was* going without assistance.

I walked into the living room to the sight of Dave feeding Luke through a straw.

"Should I leave you two alone again?" I deadpanned.

Dave turned red. Luke took a giant slurp. "Depends. You gonna tell us what Neri wanted or are we going to have this sleepover indefinitely?"

I glared.

As much as I couldn't trust Luke, as much as I didn't know if I could trust Dave, I was also stuck.

Dave leaned away from Luke, Sully at his side. "Did the owl's message have anything to do with Amity?"

"No, I'm sorry."

Sully seemed to sag under Dave's fingers.

Luke looked between us. "Amity's priority, right?"

"Yes." Dave answered for us both.

"Okay then. You have no clues, no hints of where she could have gone. You assume the Siren Hunters took her, but for all we know, it could be anyone. Even someone *not* mythical. So it seems to me, there's only one thing you can do."

I knew where he was going. "Luke, if I dreamwalk to her, the

Hunters will find us. Phorkys will come here, and then he'll have two Sirens instead of just one."

"No, I said if you use your power they can find you. Your *Siren* power. That dreamwalking gene is all you, babe."

Dave swished his gaze between us. "Dreamwalking?"

"Korrina can walk through people's dreams and memories. She's not very good at it yet, but that's why I'm here." Luke leaned back and, if his wrists hadn't been tied together, I'm sure he would have put them behind his head. "Just call me Teach."

If Luke was right, it was possible to see what had happened to Amity. Maybe even where she was being held. If she was still alive.

If Luke was lying, we'd all be dead.

"Dave, if you hear anything you don't like, see anyone you don't like, see *anyone*, shoot him. Then shoot Luke. Then run."

I sat on Amity's big, cowskin rug—really hope it's fake— closed my eyes, and slowed my breath. Like Neri had been teaching me.

Like Luke had already taught me.

Back when I thought he was on my side.

Back when I thought I could trust him.

Back when I thought I knew who I could trust.

CHAPTER 15

Dreamwalking was a little bit like rifling through someone's underwear drawer. The better I knew them, the easier it was to find the drawer.

I didn't know Amity. Beyond her skydiving affliction, love of coffee, and Siren curse, she was a stranger.

If I had to guess, she wore boy shorts instead of thongs.

I slowed my breathing, hummed the song Amity had written. She was in there, hiding between the vowels and consonants, the choice of pitch and tone.

The darkness shifted, became gray and defined.

It was like falling asleep and waking up, all at once. In the past, I'd been able to interact with people, even if I couldn't change the outcome. I didn't know if I could do so with Amity.

My body stilled, my breathing steadied and slowed, and then, I left my body behind and stepped into the memory.

Amity was in her studio, a guitar perched on her knee, a pencil hanging from her mouth. A music stand stood in front of her with a marked-up piece of paper, and she strummed a few notes, hummed to herself, then yanked the pencil out of her mouth and scribbled something on the paper.

She was composing.

Dave said she hadn't composed since her gramps died. But learning you were a Siren, that you weren't crazy, that you were responsible for the chaos you'd caused…it was freeing.

Her dreads slid off her shoulder, and she froze. "Who's there?"

Fire snapped to a blaze behind her, but Amity didn't notice.

"Hello?"

Green fire, but not Siren Hunter green. Something less Kelly Green, more forest Green, laced with tongues of persimmon orange.

The fire darkened in the middle, as if it was burning a hole in the air, and the flames scattered. A crisp wind swirled through the studio, ruffling Amity dreadlocks and messing with my mind.

This was not how a Siren Hunter attack began.

The wind picked up, knocked over studio equipment, ripped frames from the walls. Amity ducked, covered her head, and ran for the door. Locked.

"Korrina!" Amity screamed, made eye contact, and laced her voice with her Siren power.

My heart clenched.

She saw me. But I hadn't heard. I hadn't helped. And right now, I also couldn't move. Her music stand crashed over, whipped into the air, and flew *through* me.

She went pale.

"Amity, we're coming for you. Hang in there, okay?"

She stopped fighting. Pressed her lips together.

A toneless voice whispered through the room. "Puppet, puppet on a string. Puppet, puppet, sing for me. I will be your limbs, your head. You will sing until you're dead."

Amity's arms flew above her head, as if she'd lost her bones. Her feet were swept out from underneath her and the wind became visible, full of debris, full of flame, and it carried her into the shadow heart of the fire.

I ran forward, leapt, and dove into the fire. I didn't know what I was made of in my dreamwalks. Not skin and bone, but something else. I didn't know if I could burn. I didn't know if this was cursed fire that would turn me into a monster.

But my mission was simple—find Amity. Simple missions made for easy decisions.

My fingertips went white-hot. Flames licked up my arms, curled around my neck. Fire crawled into my hair, burning without burning. Pain without destruction.

"Nice try, blood of Molpe," the toneless voice whispered, its words coming from the flame. "But she's mine."

I slammed into the wall. The fire winked out.

"Shi-crap," I screamed and slapped my hand against the wall. Amity's kidnapper knew I was here, knew who I was.

Without Amity to hold up the fabric of the memory, the trashed studio began to fade. I felt my body again, my feet tingling from falling asleep.

But I couldn't go. Not yet. I'd learned nothing new. I'd done nothing more than give myself away.

I didn't know where Amity had been taken. I didn't know who the voice belonged to. And maybe the scariest thing…I didn't know what to do when I woke up.

I wasn't leaving without my next step.

A growl vibrated in my throat.

I had one advantage. One desperate chance.

Like calls to like.

Siren calls to Siren.

I took a breath, closed my eyes, and let my Siren song out of the cage.

Amity wasn't a stranger. She was my Siren family. My power had seen hers, had searched it out, had discovered who she was on that bridge.

My voice whispered through the studio. The colors strengthened. My tingling feet disappeared.

My song grew. In the distance, Luke screamed. My voice faltered, but I shut him out and returned to singing. If Luke's warning about my power being a beacon was right, it was too late. I'd sent out the alert, and I might as well use it to find my Siren cousin.

I pushed my song against the wall where Amity had disappeared. *Let me in, let me through, I need to see you.*

The wall wavered, went transparent.

A pungent scent seeped through, and it reminded me of the farmlands we'd chased a gryphon through. Dirt, plants, manure. I threw myself into my song, begging the wall to open, to become a window. A green flame sprouted to life in front of my nose, the heat throwing me from the wall.

The flame curled and separated, thinned and stretched. Collapsed to the floor.

I spider-walked backward.

The flame slithered toward me.

I hit the glass wall of the studio.

The fire snakes caught up. They curled around my ankles, my wrists, pinning me down. The last one, the biggest one, slithered up my stomach, and whispered into my ear, "Our time together has not yet come, little Molpe. But we'll be together soon."

The snake licked my cheek, its tongue brushing pain against my skin, and everything faded.

My body surrounded me like the snake had swallowed me whole. My eyes flew open, and air rushed into my mouth as the awake-world bombarded my senses.

"No! Stop!" I screamed, before I could really make sense of what I was seeing.

Dave had Sully raised and pointed at a tall, lanky guy

wearing glasses and a girl who was wiggling her lip ring and raising her hands in the air, just outside the glass sliding doors.

Cloud and Danica had found me.

I threw myself at Dave. Sully clattered to the ground. Luke leapt out of his chair, wobbled on his zip-tied ankles, fell over...and I had a flashback to Brooklyn, back to the docks where Cloud had been the one tied up, the one who'd fallen over trying to save me, back to the night Luke had betrayed us all.

"Is Jared here?" I gasped. "Colin?"

Luke shook his head. "Maybe they didn't see it. I told you not to use your power. Way too risky."

I nodded, kept my senses on high alert. But Jared and Colin would have been here the moment they saw my power. Probably. Maybe.

Unless they already knew where we were.

Cloud and Danica knocked on the glass doors. Like they hadn't just had a gun pointed at them. Like they were two polite visitors bringing over a pot roast. Puh-lease.

I ran to the door, flung it open, and gathered both of them in one giant hug. I was sobbing. Like a lot. Snot-filled hiccup sobbing.

"What—how—why—you're here!" I finally sob-laughed out.

Danica pulled back and looked at me like I was having a mental breakdown. "'Course we're here, doofus. You call Cloud and are all 'blah blah blah I just needed to say *heeeeeey*.'" She pitched her voice high, batted her eyes, and swayed back and forth. "You forget we know what your desperate cries for help sound like."

I pursed my lips and stepped back. "Okay fine. I called because I was desperate and alone and missed my best friends. But how did you find me?"

Danica looked at Cloud, who responded by sliding his jaw back and forth.

She let out a huff. "I've been practicing." She buffed her nails on her shirt, stretched out her hand, and admired her matte black polish.

She was like one of those angler fish. Dangling a yummy treat that she knew I couldn't resist, before snatching it away and taking a big bite.

"Practicing…"

She showed me her teeth. "I hacked your phone. Was able to read all your texts, listen to your voicemails, geolocate your position, and here we are. Thankfully this place is about the only McMansion within a few miles or we'd have been going door to door."

Cloud still hadn't said a word. He wasn't even looking at me. He'd gone pale, he'd turned to stone, a gargoyle staring at a spot over my shoulder. A spot…

Oh no.

"Hey, Cloud, Dan. Long time, no see." Luke's voice stretched through the room, all casual, all everything's-fine, all I-didn't-torture-you-both.

Cloud flipped from pale to red. His hands balled into fists and he shifted so that he stood between Danica and Luke. And Danica let him.

She stopped wiggling her lip ring. She transformed back

into that girl. That girl in the hospital, who'd had her makeup stripped away. That girl who'd been forced to become vulnerable.

Because of Luke.

"Korrina, tell me why he's here." Cloud's voice dropped, lost all emotion, turned sharp and dangerous.

My insides tightened. "He showed up two days ago. Said he could help."

"With. What." The Cloud I knew still hadn't shown up. This guy was scary, about to snap.

"A girl was kidnapped. A girl related to me."

Cloud's gaze flitted to mine. He knew about my being a Siren. He knew what I meant.

"Luke's been held prisoner for the past six months. My mother helped him escape, told him to find us. He thinks he can help us find Amity."

"The girl who was kidnapped. She's...like you?" Cloud confirmed.

I nodded. "Danica knows?" From her non-reaction, I guessed Danica knew about me too.

"I know. Amazeballs." She raised her lip and nodded her approval.

"Dave knows too. We're all in the inner circle here."

"Including Luke, apparently," Cloud said. "Do *you* believe him, Korrina?" He gave me his leader-of-the-pack stare. A stare that had commanded my Mischief and Mayhem movements my entire high school career.

My spine straightened, and for the first time since we left Brooklyn, I felt like myself again.

"I think he's holding back. I think he needs us. For what, I'm not sure yet. But I know he hasn't yet given us the full truth."

"And what do we do with people who lie and mistreat others?"

I turned and looked at Luke. He scooted backwards.

"We give them mayhem."

Luke sank into the floor, his hardened swagger fell away, and he was no longer imposing Luke but prisoner Luke. His shoulders slumped. He'd already accepted whatever we were going to do him.

Despite all the shade he threw, his fight was gone.

"But we can't do that anymore," I heard myself say and faced my old leader.

I'd been his second-in-command. His most trusted.

And now, I had to take over.

I felt sick.

Cloud looked down at Luke, stretched to his full height. He'd grown. He had to be at least nine-and-a-half feet tall.

Danica's gaze darted between the two of us, and a smirk ghosted her lips. She was probably wishing she had popcorn.

"And why not, my Second?"

"Because he has surrendered. He has requested sanctuary." I pulled on my military vocabulary, words I knew would break through to him. "And I gave it to him. I will not break that faith." I took a deep breath and added, "*We* will not break that faith."

A command. To my commander. My fingers trembled, but this had to be done.

Cloud was no longer our leader.

I was.

His jaw clenched, his arms flexed, but I stood my ground. His chest pushed against his fitted shirt, showing off muscles he'd never had before, and he slowly let out a long breath.

Then he stepped aside. "As you wish."

My lungs evicted a breath I'd forgotten about.

"But Korrina, if he steps out of line…"

I didn't look at Cloud. I stared Luke down, let him know just how close he was to Cloud's wrath. "He's all yours."

~

I made coffee.

Dave positioned himself between Luke and Cloud and Danica, making himself plus Sully a pretty convincing barrier. I let them get to know each other while I gathered myself amidst the magic aroma of dark roasted comfort.

Cloud and Danica were here.

They'd found me.

And I'd found Amity.

And lost her.

I had no idea where to go from here. The mission from the Council made no sense. And now I had not one, not two, but four people to keep safe.

Two of which I'd failed before.

I Susie Homemakered the coffee, pulling out a serving tray along with five coffee mugs, cream and sugar, and carried it all into the living room.

"Wow you've changed," Danica drawled, then addressed Dave. "Used to, you could never get her to lift a finger in the kitchen, and now she's all Julia Child."

I rolled my eyes. "I made coffee, Dan. If it's that easy to impress you, we need to get you out more."

She wiggled her lip ring at me.

I sat next to her and leaned into her side. "Missed you."

She kissed my cheek. "Missed you too, boo. Brooklyn isn't the same without you."

"Nor should it be," I quipped. "Where's Tula? Saw you three had gotten close."

Cloud reached for the cream. "She's manning the mission back home. Making sure our families don't miss us."

"Your parents don't know you're here? And aren't you supposed to be in school?" I looked between them.

"Long weekend plus teacher in-service holiday," Danica answered, "means we're all yours for the next few days. I'm 'staying with Tula.'"

"I got a last-minute scholarship to a weekend space camp." Cloud turned a little red.

"You're so cool, Cloud," Luke girlied his voice and batted his eyes.

"Enough with the high school reunion." Dave rose up on his knees, dumping ice on the conversation. "Where's Amity?"

Everyone looked to me.

I sipped my coffee. Stalling.

"You're stalling," Luke pointed out.

Dammit. "I lost her."

Dave's fingers cracked against Sully's grip.

"She was in her studio, writing a song."

Dave sat on his feet, eyes wide. "She hasn't written anything since Gramps died."

"Yeah, well. She's a Siren. Can't deny her song forever. Anyways, a fire started in the corner. But it wasn't a normal fire. It didn't burn."

"Siren Hunters," Cloud said.

"Siren Hunters?" Dave echoed, his face paling.

"Yes, Siren Hunters," I said. "We aren't well liked by certain members of mythical society." I turned to Cloud. "And no, I don't think it was them. There were...odd things happening in that room. A wind rushed out of a hole in the middle of the fire, tornado'd the room, and then this voice..." That cruel, toneless voice crawled through my head. "It had power. And it made Amity go limp. I'm afraid"—*deep breaths, Korrina*—"I'm afraid whoever took Amity knows how to weaponize her. I think they're planning on using her power against her will."

Everyone went still. All of us—except for Dave—had seen me when I didn't have control of my power. They'd seen my power at its worst.

To have someone else in control of my song?

It'd be like handing over the code to the nuclear football.

"Amity has the power to make words come true," I continued. "She's the Songwriter."

Danica sucked in air. "So anything she writes…can she change the past?"

"No," Luke said from behind Dave's shoulder. Dave scooted back so we could see Luke in all his tied-up glory.

And yet, even though he was helpless, even though he had a shotgun pointed at him, Danica shrunk at my side, pressed into my arm.

I hadn't spoken to her in six months, but I had a pretty good guess at what past event she'd change.

"Thelxiepeia's line can change the state of matter as it currently exists," Luke explained. "Amity can make a volcano erupt, change the direction of a river, set off an ice age, or simply age a person from eighteen to ninety-two."

Dave paled. "How about clearing an overcast sky? Or calming a windy day?"

"As long as she writes down the words, yeah." Luke shrugged. "Those would be easy things for the Songwriter. Probably wouldn't even register."

Dave let out a huff of air. "She journaled. Every morning before the first load. Said she was manifesting how she wanted the day to go. We have had perfect weather every weekend since she took over the DZ."

"Right." Luke graced us with his signature one-eyebrow-raised look of disdain. "She has the power to change the world and she used it to have a pretty day of skydiving." He flipped that disdain to me. "Is it a Siren thing to not understand your worth?"

He might as well have slapped me. Probably would have stung less.

Cloud stiffened. "Out of line yet?" He didn't take his eyes off Luke.

Cloud had never been one to outright attack someone. He

preferred the long game. Strategize, figure out their weak spots, take them down in a way that wouldn't leave physical bruises or scars, but would change their lives forever.

Looks like that had changed too.

"Not yet," I ground out.

"So what now?" Danica tapped one of her nails against the floor. "We can't stay here."

"Not since Korrina shot out the Siren signal," Luke added.

Stupid Luke.

"We follow the Council's mission." I straightened my spine. "Whoever took Amity isn't done. The voice said we'd be together soon. If it took Amity, wants to take me, then it stands to reason—"

"It's collecting Sirens." Luke's eyes went wide.

"So we need to find the next Siren before this voice does. And odds are if we hang around long enough…"

"We'll be able to follow it back to Amity," Dave finished.

"Bingo, Dave-O."

CHAPTER 17

I unrolled the message from the Council. Like it or not, this was my team. Three mortals, an untrustworthy song-stealer, and me.

"Find the weapon who sees, in the desert that still sings."

Everyone leaned forward, as if waiting for the next line.

"Yeah, that's it. The Council isn't exactly verbose."

"That's your entire clue?" Dave sputtered. "That's the only thing we have to go on to find Amity?" He stood. "I need some air." His voice dropped about two octaves. He left the house through the back and slammed the door shut behind him.

Cloud, Danica, and I shifted to cover Dave's absence. It was a natural instinct impossible to resist. Like moving wagons around to protect the inner circle, we did the same to Luke, moving into the best position to defend ourselves while keeping our biggest threat in sight.

Luke slumped, and the purple circles under his eyes stood out even more than usual. He'd been sleeping a lot, so much so that I had to wonder if something was wrong. Then remind myself that I didn't care.

His knee bones poked at his jeans, and a memory of Luke—

half-naked in the moonlight, abs glinting as if they were made of sexy stardust—did a screen split in my mind. Luke before prison. Luke after prison. And for the first time since he showed up, I started to believe he was telling the truth.

"The weapons are Sirens, right?" Cloud asked.

"Amity was, so we're assuming this one is too."

"A weapon who sees—that's a clue about who you are looking for. What do we know about the other two Siren families?"

We all looked to Luke.

He struggled to sit up, his tied wrists not giving him enough leverage to push off the floor. No one moved to help him.

I didn't want to get close to him. Not with his power to silence my song.

But I also couldn't sit here and watch him struggle.

It was like watching a three-legged puppy trying to climb out of a mudhole.

I hummed, manifested my song, and sent a gust of power against his shoulder, helping him sit straight.

He let out a burdened breath. "Thanks."

Danica and Cloud stared at him like they were just now seeing him, seeing how badly he'd been beaten.

I nodded. "Can you tell us about the other Siren families? Did they have any special powers like mine and Amity's?"

A weak smirk toyed with his lips. "No one has powers like yours, Korrina. But yes, all the original Sirens had a special power."

Neri had talked about all this before, of course. But I hadn't had reason to really listen. They were just stories, fairy tales I was distantly related to. No one believed the rest of the Siren families had daughters alive today.

We were wrong.

"Think of the Sirens as forming a whole song when they are

together. You're the passion behind the music, the reason for the song. The emotion that lives within each note."

I batted my eyes and gave Cloud and Danica a coy shoulder.

Luke rolled his eyes. "Amity—Thelxiepeia's line—is the words of the song. Aglaope's daughters are the melody. Peisinoe's daughters are the beat."

Danica leaned forward, seeming to have forgotten her fear of Luke for the moment. "Which one of those *sees*? The melody or the beat?"

"The melody," I said, no hesitation. "The beat is present. Steady. It only sees what's right in front of it. It has to, otherwise the beat loses its timing. But the melody has to know where it's going. It knows when to swell and when to quiet."

"So we're looking for a Siren descendant of Aglaope in a desert that sings," Cloud summarized.

Danica pulled a scary-looking laptop out of her bag, opened it up, and let her fingers fly over the keys. A green light glowed behind the shape of a bull with pierced horns on the lid of the laptop.

"What..."

"Built my own baby." Danica stroked the top of the laptop, blew it a kiss, then got back to her flying finger work. "I call her Betty."

I shot a look at Cloud, but he had this goofy gaze thing going on at Danica.

Two seconds later, she spun Betty around so we could see the screen. "List of deserts that sing. Though I think that's too on-the-nose. There are lots of singing sands. But"—she twirled Betty back to face her and machine-gun typed on the keys—"there are only a few who both sing *and* are known for vortices. Vortices strengthen psychic power. If your Siren *sees*, I bet she's psychic." She do-si-doed Betty to us again, and sat back with a satisfied smile.

Towering red rocks filled Betty's bosom.

"Sedona." Luke nodded. "Makes sense. Good work, Dan."

She smiled before she remembered who he was.

I tapped my lip. "So because Aglaope's daughter is a psychic of some sort and since Sedona is a singing desert *and* a hotspot for psychic energy—"

"And a place where the veil is weak," Luke jumped in.

I acknowledged his input with a nod. "Definitely makes sense. It's as good a place as any to start looking."

The back door slammed open and Dave ran inside. "Time to go. Now. We got a plan yet?"

I jumped to my feet. "What happened?"

"Bunch of guys wearing hoodies coming up the drive in a Jeep. We're outmanned and about to be cornered." Dave flipped out a Swiss Army knife and swiped at Luke's ankle ties. He yanked Luke to his feet and yelled. "Let's go."

We ran outside, following Dave to the cars. He tossed me a set of keys and pointed at Amity's DeLorean. "Luke, Cloud, you're with me. We'll try to distract them from the girls."

"Why can't you just Sirenate them?" Danica asked as we slid into Amity's car.

"I don't fight humans with my power." A rule I'd instated after Chad's death.

"You're sure they're human?"

I stole a peek at the Jeep, packed full of guys in forest green hoodies. "No way," I breathed. "They're human. And I've met them before."

WHILE I TRIED TO FIGURE OUT WHAT THE MOTHER EARTH groupies were doing in such an un-eco-friendly car, I was also puzzling out what to do with the key Dave had thrown at me.

"You didn't happen to learn how to drive over the summer, did you?" I asked Danica.

Her heavy-lined eyes went Neri-wide. "You're the one who's been on the road nonstop for the past six months!"

"Okay then. Driving school, here we come!" I shoved the key in the ignition and turned it over.

It clicked.

The Jeep full of the groupies from Taco Bell, whom I no longer believed were groupies, was getting close enough for us to hear their chant over the roar of the engine. Dave fishtailed his car in front of their Jeep and they took off in pursuit, giving us a moment.

"Try turning it the other way," Danica suggested.

I rolled my eyes at her but did as she suggested. Nada.

"Umm…" She wiggled her lip ring.

"How have neither of us paid attention to how taxis do it in the city?"

Danica's eyes went feral. "How have *you* not learned how to drive when you've been doing nothing but driving for *half a year!*"

"Calm down, screechy-woman."

"We're about to die from a bunch of hoodie-wearing freaks because we can't turn on a car. I will not calm dow—"

I found the pedals at my feet, pushed both, and tried the key again. The car roared to life, and the scent of gasoline filled the interior.

"How'd you do that?" Her voice was all Danica-chill again.

"I don't know. Found pedals and pushed."

"Well, put this thing into drive and let's skedaddle 'cause the boys are back in town." Danica sang the last part of her sentence and pointed out the front window.

I grabbed the handle in between our seats, pushed it from the letter P to the letter D, pressed what I thought was the gas, and the car lurched forward.

We weren't going to win the Indy 500, unless it was a golf cart race, but we were moving. I pressed the gas pedal down, the engine rumbled and vibrated the floorboards, and Amity's DeLorean shot forward like it was jumping back to the future.

The Mother Earth gang stopped their Jeep. Let us pass.

They raised synchronized arms high into the sky, except for the blond with the green, spiked tips. He slammed his arms down to his sides and moved his mouth.

"Restore her." A whisper filled the DeLorean. "Restore her. Time is running out. The puppeteer comes to power. Restore her before you cannot."

"You sure they're human, boss?" Danica pressed her nose against her window as we sailed past the Jeep, left them in our dust.

I gritted my teeth. *Idiot.* I was an idiot.

"I'm positive. But *their* boss is an Underworld princess who has decided I don't have enough on my plate."

CHAPTER 18

We met up with the boys an hour down the road to Sedona, at a highway rest stop. It didn't look like we'd been followed, and it didn't look like the Siren Hunters had tracked us, but I still made everyone wait in their respective cars until I cleared the area.

The highway stretched into the distance, long and desolate, and the hum of bugs whirred through the warm air. A dragonfly flitted in front of my face, and my song leapt into my throat.

"Breathe, Korrina." I rolled back my shoulders, tried to relax. But something felt off.

I checked under the park benches, cleared the bathrooms, walked the perimeter, even tugged on my power to see if it recoiled against anything else supernatural in the area.

We were alone. No one, and no thing, else. Just three humans, one Luke, and one Siren.

Luke wasn't human. Not totally. I wasn't exactly sure of his lineage, but now that I understood what I was looking for, he felt *other*.

I circled my hand in the air. "All clear. Everyone out."

The DeLorean wingaling doors rose in the air, and Danica

climbed out carrying our Taco Bell takeout like the queen she was. The boys, more or less, fell out of Dave's truck with the grace of drugged cats.

Cloud walked over to Danica, his long legs eating up the distance between them, and he gathered her into his arms, checked her over, made sure she was okay.

I turned my head, not sure how to handle my two friends being with each other like this, not sure how to not run away screaming that I'd once had that…and lost him.

Dave left me in charge of Sully and Luke while he used the facilities.

I grabbed the Taco Bell sack and gestured for Luke to join me at a nearby picnic table. "I need you to tell me everything you know about Persephone and Demeter." I raised my hand, cut Luke off before he could begin his lecture. Luke, having grown up on the other side of the veil, was a mythical Wikipedia. "More specifically, the *groupies* of Persephone and Demeter."

Luke raised one eyebrow and leaned forward. His sleeves rose above his zip-tied wrists, skin reddened and raw around the plastic bindings.

A sludge of guilt gunked up my chest. He hadn't complained once. And I refused to be as heartless as my enemies.

I pulled out my hunting knife, cut off his ties, and passed him a taco.

He didn't say a word. I didn't say a word. He just rubbed at his wrists, licked his lips, and began.

"The Eleusinian Mysteries. It's one of the most famous cults in the world and the most secretive. The followers of Demeter and Persephone would be those initiated into the Lesser Mysteries, and those who were purified were selected for the Greater Mysteries."

I pulled out my sketch book and showed Luke the three-seed logo from green-haired groupie's hoodie. "Look familiar?"

Luke looked from the sketch to me and back again. "Where did you see that?"

"I met those guys from the Jeep before. And they were all wearing hoodies with this emblem."

His violet eyes went wide. "The priests are *here*? What did you do?"

"Since when do I have to *do* anything to have crazy people track me down?"

"Touché." He spun the paper around to get a better look. "Those who wear this emblem are either preparing for the rites of the Greater Mysteries ritual, which happens sometime in September, or they are guiding initiates through the purification rites."

"September is now."

"Thank you, Calendar Jane. I realize that."

I resisted the urge to slap him and shoved my hand inside the takeout bag instead. It was hard, but I'd grown.

"The Greater Mysteries are thought to happen in late Autumn, so more than likely we have a few weeks. But no one really knows. The initiates are very good at keeping secrets. The question I have is why are the priests here, tracking you?"

"Persephone sent them."

He dipped his chin, waited me out.

I huffed, unwrapped my burrito. I had to trust someone at some point, and even though Luke was the least trustworthy person here, even though I *had* trusted him before and got burned, I didn't have many options. He was the only one with answers.

"Persephone has been sending me visions. At least, I think it's Persephone. She gave me a message. The priests showed up shortly after the first vision and gave me a similar message as we left Amity's."

"And that message was?"

"Restore her before time runs out. And then something about a puppeteer."

"Oh that was totes creeps," Danica piped in from behind my shoulder. "'Time is running out. The puppeteer comes to power. Restore her before you cannot,'" she intoned, pulling chills all along my skin. It was an almost perfect mimic of the priest's whispers.

Luke straightened. "That's what the message said? Exactly? That the puppeteer comes to power?"

Danica and I exchanged glances.

"Word for word," I said.

Luke dropped his head into his hands and rubbed at his forehead. "It was foretold that Demeter's grief would become so great that she would cease to be goddess of the harvest and instead become Goddess of Retribution. I fear"—he looked up, the purple circles under his eyes even more pronounced—"I fear we are losing Demeter. If Persephone sent the priests to you to restore her mother, if that's indeed what the message means, then things are even more dire than anyone has guessed."

"Stop being cryptic, Lukester."

"At this year's Greater Mysteries ritual, Demeter will transform into the Goddess of Retribution and whoever is the puppeteer will have complete control over her and her powers. And because Demeter is the goddess of the harvest, the puppeteer essentially gets control over the food source of the human world."

I looked down at the burrito in my hand. "No more Taco Bell?"

"No more Taco Bell."

"For the love of all things holy and refried, we have to save Demeter." I pounded a fist on the picnic table, new resolve coursing through my blood.

"And this puppeteer has Amity?" Dave had snuck up at some

point, and I could kick myself for not paying better attention. What if he'd been a Siren Hunter? Or a Demeter groupie?

I had to stay on top of my game to keep everyone safe.

"Good point, Dave." Cloud sat next to me on the bench and rubbed his chin, his master plotter mind hard at work. "Our working theory is that the puppeteer is collecting Sirens and wants control of Demeter. What's the connection?"

I dug my fingernail into the soft, worn wood of the picnic table. "Besides the fact that Demeter hates Sirens with a passion that could heat the Underworld? I'm not sure."

Luke shrugged, at a loss as well. Not good when our resident all-things-mythological expert had not a clue.

"Figure out the motivation," Cloud muttered, drumming his fingers against his knee.

"What?" Dave growled. The guy was going to snap if we didn't get closer to saving Amity soon.

"We need to figure out the motivation of the puppeteer. Once we figure out their motivation, we can anticipate their next step, maybe even discover who is the puppeteer."

"We think this puppeteer will show his face in Sedona, right?" Dave was already on his feet, arms rigid at his sides.

Luke nodded, shooting careful glances at the rest of us. Dave was the outsider, as much as we'd like to think it was Luke. But right now, Dave was the unknown. And with Sully by his side, I was feeling less and less safe.

Dave headed toward his truck without another word.

"Everyone load up," I ordered.

Danica gave Cloud a smooch and bounced over to the DeLorean.

I pulled Cloud to the side. "Be careful. And watch him."

"Which one?"

I sucked in a deep breath. "Both."

～

Fifteen hours later, we rolled in to Sedona. Red rocks towered like skyscrapers against the midday sun, and their alien shapes looked like something out of a sci-fi movie.

We'd driven all night. On some of the back roads, we'd passed pitched tents, so my guess was we could camp pretty much anywhere. Or at least anywhere we wanted until we were kicked out. But I'd wanted to get here before we stopped. Needed to get here.

Amity was my responsibility.

And so was this next Siren chick.

I rubbed at my eyes and looked for a motel with a sign that said "Sirens Sleep Free." No such luck.

"Stupid Sedona," I muttered. I had never needed caffeine like I needed caffeine at this moment. "Yo, Dan. Wake up."

Danica's soft snores from the passenger seat sputtered. "Lemme sleep. I'll pay you." She snorted and turned her back to me, asleep once again.

"Whatever happened to you saying you had my back? That'd you keep me awake, no matter what? That you were the, and I quote, party animal who never quits?"

She snored louder in response.

"Some co-pilot you are…"

The sound of wind rustling through bare branches rushed through the car.

Danica sat up, wide awake. "What the—?"

Low voices chanted, a deep reverberating sound that pulsed, pulsed, pulsed against my bones.

Let me help, a dark voice whispered at the back of my mind.

"Danica, take the wheel—" I screeched, slammed on the brakes, and the world melted into darkness.

CHAPTER 19

Demeter wasn't here. My lungs could tell.

When Demeter was in a vision or dreamwalk, she hogged all available air. Right now, I was breathing easily.

I looked around an old amphitheater, lit by smoking torches. The air felt cold and wet and unused, and the scent of soot and incense wafted around the drafty space. I wiggled my bare toes against cold, uneven stone. A white gown fluttered around my ankles, and my wrists were tied with a thin, red thread. Not anything to keep me captive, but something symbolic.

No tattoo on my wrist. So I wasn't me. Or I was me, but in someone else's memory.

I walked forward. A line of people dressed the same followed my lead, our footsteps hitting the ancient stone as if there was a drumbeat directing our march. The path curved in front of my feet, spiraling further and further down until the torchlight disappeared and darkness took over.

"Welcome, Chosen Ones," a voice whispered through the flickering dark, speaking in Greek. Thankfully, the visions always came with a built-in translator. "You who were the purest, selected to become the essence of our dark queen, so that our goddess may live in the light. Continue forth, daughters, and know what it is to live in the shadow of death."

Creepy.

My feet stumbled forward, and we entered a giant cavern.

But it wasn't dark.

My eyes adjusted.

The cavern was set up as a massive glamping site. Elaborate tents awaited, the tent flaps pulled back. Plush rugs covered the floor. And by each tent, on either side of the door, kneeled a man and a woman.

Dressed in white tunics, they seemed to glow in the dim light.

I approached one of the tents, and the two waiting at my door bowed their heads.

"Welcome, my queen," the man said, his voice like a quiet forest, hushed and serene. "We are your guides through the shadows. We have walked your footsteps before and know what it is like to worship life under the light. But unlike you, we also know what it is to love death surrounded by darkness."

The woman stood. "Come and let us show you the way." She reached out, took my hand, and led me inside.

The tent was lit by tiny candles spread all around, so it looked like fairies dancing in the corners of the material. Pillows were strewn across the floor, and a low table occupied one corner. A bowl of fruit waited on the table.

"In the Lesser Mysteries, you learned what it is to hold both joy and sorrow under the bright light of the sun. In this, the Greater Mysteries, you will learn how to hold peace while surrounded by the darkness of death."

She led me to the table and the three of us sat down. "Like our dark queen before us, taste the fruit of death and acknowledge death's sacred place in life."

The man grabbed a pomegranate and cut it in half, scooped

the seeds out with his fingers, and held out the red pearl seeds. "Eat and begin to truly live."

Screaming filled my ears, distant, growing louder. The vision people didn't flinch. And the person I inhabited continued on…like there wasn't screaming, and the sound of metal crunching, and the scent of something burning.

The woman grabbed my arm, her long fingers digging into my skin, and she wasn't her anymore.

Persephone looked into my eyes. "Remember that the darkness isn't always to be feared, Korrina. Time is running out. Save my mother."

The vision faded.

I was suffocating.

My eyes strained open. The air was on fire. Smoke filled my lungs and burned the inside of my throat.

The DeLorean creaked, groaned.

"Danica?"

Her door was open, she wasn't there. I tried to move, but something was heavy, tied to my limbs. My fingers reached out, fumbled for the door.

The door wasn't there. Everything was topsy-turvy. Nothing was where it belonged. My Siren song exploded in the face of danger, but the flames, the smoke stifled my song. Stole my power.

"Cloud? Dave? Luke?" I gasped. Tried. My vision was going black, this time from loss of consciousness.

The air burned. Fire licked at my skin. Glass exploded.

"Jared?" I breathed. Hoped.

My breath left my body. The world went black.

STRONG HANDS GRIPPED MY SHOULDERS AND SILENCED MY struggling song. They moved under my arms, got a better grip, and lifted me out. My leg scraped against something sharp and hot, shocking me awake.

Fire crawled up my legs. I kicked, fought, pushed. Against him, against the fire, against the visions taking me against my will.

Against what had happened to Danica. Where was she? Why wasn't she here?

"Korrina. Babe. Calm down."

My stomach churned with something sick. Something bitter. I couldn't breathe.

Luke dragged me across the red clay ground, away from the burning DeLorean.

My eyes burned. Everything burned.

Nearby, someone moaned.

"Where's Danica?" My vision wasn't what it needed to be to see in the…broad daylight. #Crap

"Here," someone croaked. Did not sound like Danica.

"I'm over here," someone else said. Sounded like Cloud.

"Here," Dave called out. "We need an ambulance. Danica may have a concussion."

"Korrina, you have smoke inhalation and a bad burn on your leg." Luke poked at my knee. Pain exploded behind my eyes. "And there's no way in Tartarus we'll get reception out here to call an ambulance."

I blinked away some of the smoke and looked around. I could just make out the scene. The DeLorean lay on its side. One of the front tires was shredded. Smoke puffed out the door and flames curled around the hood.

We were in the middle of a field dotted with cacti and scrub trees. The sun looked no higher, no lower, than when Persephone had pulled me into the vision.

"What did we hit?" For all appearances, it looked as if Amity's car had hit an invisible wall.

Luke crouched a few feet from me, face crinkled in what the

uninitiated could take as concerned. He pointed behind us. "First a ditch. Then a fence. Then that cactus. Then you somehow hit a boulder and launched yourselves into the air. And here I thought you were mildly coordinated."

"Danica had the wheel." I rubbed at my face, throwing Dan under the bus without remorse.

"Why? You were driving," Cloud asked, his voice sounding like it'd been through a cheese grater.

"Vision." I sucked in a whistled breath as another wave of pain curled out from my leg...which I still hadn't been brave enough peek at.

Danica groaned just outside my periphery. My fault. Once again, her getting hurt was on me.

I needed to check on her. We needed to get help. I braced myself up on my elbows, tried to move. Lightning bolts of pain shot from my leg to my head.

My back hit the dirt, and I gripped on tight to consciousness. Danica groaned again.

"Luke?" I rasped and groped in front of me, my eyesight still blurry. "Didn't you say I could heal people?"

"Yeah, but we run the risk of blipping the Hunters' radar." He shifted on the sand and rustled closer.

"Not going anywhere." I gestured between myself and Danica, cringed at my voice. I sounded like one of those anti-smoking ads. "No choice. Teach me."

Luke let out a giant sigh. "Can you sing?" He moved closer, squatted on my level.

Use my scorched throat? "Do I have to?"

"The Sirens of old, before they were cursed, could heal with their song. Very advanced, but I supposed, given the circumstances, it's worth a shot."

Neri's words of warning flitted briefly through my head. I still hadn't mastered using my power without also using my life force.

Meh.

I took a deep breath, which felt like it was full of nails, and nodded.

Luke sat crisscross applesauce in front of me. "I don't know if this will work, but focus on the wound. Forget the pain."

A breeze kicked up and blew bits of sand against my leg. "Ha. You funny."

"Pain is temporary. Healing can last forever. Look at what you did to me." He shrugged and held out his hands, palms open to the sky. "Healing is stronger than pain."

I gritted my teeth. I couldn't see my wounds. From the way Luke was talking, I probably shouldn't look.

My lungs were the most distracting at the moment. I shifted my attention there.

I tested my voice, hummed softly, and if it wouldn't have hurt so bad, I would have screamed.

"My lungs are burning," I gasped.

Luke shifted closer. "Focus on how your lungs feel when they're not injured."

This boy was crazy.

But I tried again.

I pushed thoughts of *ow, ow, owee* out of my mind, concentrated instead on the function of my lungs. They breathe in. They breathe out. Breathe in. Out.

My aura turned purple.

Honey coated my throat, my tongue, the roof of my mouth, and it was cool and soft and relieving. The urge to cough disappeared. My breathing grew less ragged. The pain in my chest lessened.

The tone of my song changed. Rather than a hoarse whisper, it strengthened and harmonized with the deeper undertones.

"Good, Korrina. Very good." Luke's whisper held something I'd never heard from him. Approval, but also...awe. "Find the source of your other pain. Continue until you are completely healed."

Completely healed you are, my mind Yoda-translated his words.

Now that the air had stopped burning, other pain roared into existence. My leg being the biggest. Then my arm. Then everything. I was one big ouch.

I closed my eyes and focused. Took deep breaths, entered my meditative state. I pushed against the pain, shoved it from my mind. My teeth chattered. The sun disappeared behind the tip of the plateau. My power flared, and I hummed, sending a thread of the purple light along my body to my leg. I wrapped the thread tight, crisscrossed it around the wound, let it sink in deep. Warmth chased away the pain.

Coyotes yipped. Loud. Close. Ripped away my concentration. My power flickered, the thread loosened and rushed back into my chest. Pain coursed through my skin again. Searing, aching pain. In the sudden absence of my healing light, the pain roared, growled, gnawed on my leg. Screams ripped out of my throat.

"Korrina, shh." Luke got close, not touching me with his silencing skin, but too close.

My throat tightened around my screams. Hot tears trailed down my cheeks.

My Siren song reacted. Reacted to the pain, to the possibility of danger. To him.

My purple aura grew, brightened the darkening valley.

"No, Korrina, don't!" Luke jerked toward my hands, but it was too late.

The scepter bled out of my chest, a blueish-white ball of energy with the power of ten nuclear bombs. It floated in front of my face, spun around and sent out a horizontal beam of light.

The ball burst and the scepter formed. I grabbed hold. The jeweled scepter warmed under my hands, the crystal rod topped with a giant blue stone carved in the shape of a wave. It lifted me in the air. Blue light burst from the stone.

The only other time I'd used the scepter, it'd disintegrated mythological monsters, healed a torn, inter-dimensional veil, and thrown my soul into the void. But here, there were no monsters. The beam searched the valley, then ran across my friends, across Luke, Dave. It spread into an umbrella of light and covered us all. Energy coursed through my skin, my veins. The pain in my leg lessened.

The scepter collapsed in on itself, turned back into a ball of energy, and flew into my chest.

My aura dimmed, disappeared.

I sank to the ground. The pain was gone. The cuts and stale bruises on Luke's face had disappeared. Danica stood, taking her hand away from her head.

"You did it." Luke pulled away from me, releasing me from the familiar warmth of his arms. "You healed…everyone."

There was one quiet moment. One moment when I thought we'd be okay. That we'd reached the bottom of the hole and the only way was up.

And then I realized what I'd done.

Jared could sense the scepter…from anywhere. This wouldn't be a blip on his radar. This was the bat signal. My danger-meter flew from oh-crap to impending-disaster.

I lifted my head, all my strength gone. "We have to get out of here." I dragged myself to my elbows. Collapsed. The ground was warm. The air cool. Getting colder.

"You have to rest," Cloud said. "You look exhausted."

"No." I shook my head. "Jared…" His name was grit between my teeth. "He's…coming."

Realization dawned. Panic skittered across everyone's faces.

The scepter had healed us all.

The scepter had betrayed us all.

CHAPTER 20

My song, unfortunately, did not heal cars.

And Amity's poor DeLorean could use some magical healing.

Dave pulled out a fire extinguisher—I was starting to think his truck was related to Mary Poppins's purse—and put out the DeLorean.

At least we wouldn't be starting any forest fires.

Luke and Cloud carried me to the truck. Thanks to wonders of the scepter, my life force energy was running on low. Danica slid in next to me and wrapped an arm around my waist. I leaned into her. "We got you, boss," she whispered. "And when you're feeling better, we're going to talk about why you drove the car through that desert obstacle course and then blamed it on me." She pinched my arm.

"But...you had the wheel." I tried to turn my head to look at her. Too much effort.

She snorted. "As if you were letting that thing go. I don't know what happened back there, but you have from now until we find a place to sleep to figure out a good story."

Dave got in the truck before I could answer. Luke and Cloud hopped in the truck bed.

I crashed us?

I was still…functioning…while in the vision?

And here I thought my body would just shut down if I wasn't in it. Like a robot powering down.

Not the first time I'd been wrong.

Sedona appeared in a twinkle of lights. It wasn't a big town. But the ratio of crystal shops to people had to be one to one.

Despite Danica's threat, she held me tight and patted my hair.

When the scepter had drained me before, it'd taken weeks to recover. Even my song had disappeared. I didn't know what we'd do if Phorkys and his gang showed up while I was out of commission.

How could I keep everyone safe when I couldn't even lift my arm?

We grabbed Chinese takeout and found a Motel 4 on the edge of town that agreed to let us rent a room, since none of us were over twenty-one, and all stay in one room, against most hotels' policies.

Danica and I took one bed. Cloud and Dave took the other. Luke stretched out on the floor by the door, his limbs no longer stiff, even the rawness around his wrists gone. He hadn't filled out from his time in the block, but his coloring looked better, his eyes more like the dangerous Luke I'd once known.

I didn't like it.

I didn't trust him.

And I hated the way my stomach clenched every time he looked at me.

My meal's fried soy sauce goodness had given some strength back to my muscles, but my eyes were still heavy, my body requiring too much time to recover. I was going to get us all killed if I didn't find a way to reserve my energy.

Danica crashed before she could begin her interrogation. I cuddled against her back and ran through my mission—find Amity, save Demeter, find new Siren, keep everyone alive. Save Jared—until I fell asleep.

When I woke up the next morning, there was another flower on my pillow, white, fragile petals, and a yellowing bruise on one side. As if someone had crushed it.

DAVE MADE US TAKE ARMY SHOWERS. WHAT AMITY SAW IN THE guy was a mystery.

The lukewarm water hit my sore muscles, and I felt like I'd been given a free sample of a spa day—too short with Dave's annoying voice telling me my time was up. If I could've, I would've booked the shower for the rest of the day.

I told the group about my vision over powdered donuts from the vending machine. "Basically, Persephone is the one sending the priests and these visions and telling us our time is running out."

"Did she say anything about Amity?" Dave's powdered donut disintegrated in his fist, crumbled in his lap. Leave it to a lovesick guy to not flinch at a celebrity goddess sending visions to someone he knows and only care about the woman he's in love with.

I mean, not that I could blame him.

Been there. Done that.

Still kinda doing that.

I rubbed my finger against the silky smoothness of the petals in my pocket. I didn't want to ask who'd left these for me. I didn't want to kill my own delusions.

"No, Dave," I answered. "The Queen of the Underworld did not mention Amity. I don't think Persephone has any clue about what's going on up here."

"And you really weren't conscious while you were in the vision?" Danica asked. "Because the way you were driving seemed deliberate. It was like you were trying to kill us."

No wonder she'd pinched me so hard.

"I'm sorry, Dan. I really had no control. I wasn't there."

"Then who was?" Her fingers clenched around the blanket she'd pulled off the bed. "Because someone was inside you, and it wasn't someone I recognized."

Chills crawled up my spine, and my stomach did its clenching thing. "Maybe it was the person's body I was in? Maybe we did a Freaky Friday thing."

"That's not how visions typically work," Luke piped up. "That's how possessions work."

I rubbed at my arms. "Gross. Can we stop talking about this? It happened one time."

"You sure?" Dave bit his lip. "Because you've had other visions. What if you've done other things?"

A knot the size of a coconut formed in my gut. "I'm not dealing with this right now. We have a riddle to solve and two Sirens to find. Okay? Let's focus."

Everyone grumbled, but they followed the leader. Me.

Though Dave looked like he was thinking about staging a coup.

And Danica looked like she might let him.

"We've made it to the desert that sings," I said, "though I've heard no singing, and now we need to find the Siren who sees. Plenty of crystal shops and psychic reading places from what I've seen. Let's split up and search there first."

"What are we looking for?" Dave asked.

"Anyone who seems as if they're controlling their environment. Probably won't even know they're doing it. Guys will probably be plentiful around her, girls scarce. If you see someone who fits the bill, text us and we'll head over. My Siren song can sense other Sirens."

"Good plan," Cloud said. "I'm going with you and Danica. Dave, you've got Luke. Leave Sully behind."

I cocked my head at Cloud. He shrugged. "I'm *your* Second now. And I think you may need more support than Dave over here does."

Translation: Cloud doesn't trust me alone with Danica.

Honestly? Now, neither did I.

CHAPTER 21

There were mythological beings in Sedona.

We walked down the main street of the woo-woo town, following a pack of tourists. The mid-September sun beat down on my bare shoulders, promising a sunburn to match my hair.

I didn't know where the mythicals were, but I could feel them, like a forgotten plastic tag in the seam of my shirt. They were just there, just out of reach, just small enough to bug me without posing any real threat.

Not all creatures from the other side of the veil posed a threat. But mythicals weren't supposed to be here. And the fact that more of them were slipping through than I, or the Council, had known was concerning.

Luke had slipped through a back door between the dimensions. If there were more, there was no telling how many creatures were living in the human world.

Cloud, Danica, and I entered the last crystal shop on our list —Tanzy's Crystal Abode. A sign outside advertised tours to the vortices, as well as palm readings, tarot card readings, and free popcorn. Kids ran through the store like it was a snack shoppe at a theme park, and kernels of popcorn crunched under our feet.

It didn't exactly have the serene feel you'd expect from a crystal shop. And unless Sirens secretly thrived on chaos, I strongly doubted there was one here. I picked up a pink crystal in the shape of an elephant and searched for someone who looked like a manager.

I found her hiding toward the back behind a stack of brochures.

Her hair was either frizzy or she'd been pulling at her roots. Either way, she looked like Mrs. Frizzle, complete with a themed skirt featuring crystal balls and gypsy wagons.

"Hi, can we ask you a couple of questions?"

She looked up, her face full of regret. "Are we out of popcorn again?" She stood and started muttering. "What was I thinking? Popcorn day? I need kids running through here like I need another middle toe."

"No, no. I think you're fine on popcorn." I rattled my half-full bag and grabbed another salty piece.

She saw the pink elephant in my hand and her eyes brightened. "Oh, are you wanting to purchase that? Don't worry about keeping it safe in your luggage. We'll wrap it in bubble wrap and newspaper so it'll be safe. And you had some questions, didn't you?" She led the way to the counter without stopping for a breath.

"Uh, yes. But I'm not quite ready to buy this." With my non-money.

She dropped the roll of paper she'd been ready to wield.

"Are you Tanzy?" Maybe an owner would know a thing or two about some odd locals.

"Me? Lord no. That's the owner's niece. Who is a tourist attraction herself, you know."

Danica leaned in. "Oh, do tell." Danica had a penchant for

targeting gossipers. And for some reason, they loved to dish it all to her.

"Tanzy took a vow of silence when she was thirteen, so she could better commune with the spirits at the vortexes. She hasn't spoken in seven years, if you can believe that."

We all looked at each other. "That's commitment," I finally said.

"I know. Even better? She thinks she can see into the spirit world. Which if you ask me"—though no one did, she leaned in and lowered her voice to tell us anyway—"is about as much hogwash as this entire shop. But you didn't hear that from me."

She looked down at the pink elephant on the counter. "You sure you don't want to buy that?"

"We're sure. Where can we find Tanzy? We'd really like to meet her and see one of those vortexes."

"Vortices," Danica corrected under her breath.

I stomped her foot. I knew that, but I was trying to ingratiate myself with the locals.

Something familiar flashed in the manager's eyes. "I'd love to tell you, but I've really got to give my attention to *paying* customers."

Mischief. That was the familiar look in her eyes. I'd seen it in the mirror more often than not.

I nudged Cloud. He was loaded.

He slapped a twenty on the counter. "For the elephant. And your time."

She hmmed and rang us up. "Tanzy's probably at the vortex listed on the sign out front. But you're gonna need more than twenty bucks if you want her to see for you."

"See for us?" Danica pressed.

It was too close to the Council's riddle to be coincidence.

"Yes. See the spirits. Or whatever it is she thinks she sees. Not that she can tell you, with her vow of silence and all. But you'll get a chicken-scratch drawing in the sand of whatever she sees in the beyond." The manager did a woo-woo thing with her voice.

We refilled our popcorn and walked to the front of the store. In the window hung a massive poster of Cathedral Rock in the distance, with a robed woman standing in front, chin down, hands raised.

~

POPCORN WAS A BAD IDEA.

I slurped at one of the giant waters Cloud had bought us and stumbled over a dusty red rock. Thank whoever that his rich boy credit card was unmonitored and had a high credit limit.

The sun had reached max height and it was probably the worst time of day to begin a desert hike.

"Who thought putting a freaking vortex in the middle of the desert was a good idea?" I whined from my caboose position in our group. Luke shot me a look from the middle of the line. Cloud led the way—his agile gymnastic skills coming in handy when hiking *through the desert*—while my Siren power was best at protecting our butts.

Even if it wasn't back at full strength.

Pulling the scepter out of me had hurt. Not as bad as before, but my power had dimmed and I had no clue if I could take on *any* of Phorkys's minions. Maybe if they were small. Gecko small.

Something slithered just off the path, and a warning rattle came a second later.

"Rattlesnakes?" Danica squealed from behind Cloud. Not oh-my-god-it's-a-snake squeal. But Danica's-excited squeal.

She'd always wanted to dissect a snake's rattle.

"Not today, Dan." Cloud grabbed her hand and kissed her fingertips, as if she'd just said the most adorable thing in the world.

My friends were weird.

And in love.

It was sweet.

And heartbreaking.

Fire crawled through the lower chambers of my heart, and I blinked away tears my dehydrated body couldn't afford.

To the side of the path, a small pile of rocks guided our way to the vortex. Rock cairns, I'd overheard another group's tour guide say. Trail markers. Before he'd shooed me away, he'd also said that Cathedral Rock was a female vortex, and most people experienced a calm and comforting feeling once they arrived.

But groups coming down from the rock looked anything but calm. Definitely not comforted. Muscles tensed, checking over their shoulders, jumping at shadows.

The guides were even worse, with their everything-is-fine smiles.

Cloud led us from shadow to shadow as we crept closer and higher to Cathedral Rock. The trail markers appeared more frequently, guiding us to the center of the vortex.

Juniper trees—providing very little shade—typically grew tall and semi-straight. But here, on the rim of a vortex, the trees had grown twisted, as if they once had legs and were used to dancing. Their bark was worn smooth, and they arced gracefully toward the vortex, creating a semblance of movement across an otherwise still landscape.

It was otherworldly. Rocks twisted toward the sky in variating shades of red and I could easily imagine us trekking through an alien planet.

A bell rang.

I turned around, but no one else on the trail reacted. I'd bet they hadn't heard the note, soft, resonant, with an off-tune edge.

My group moved slower and slower. Cloud seemed to lose energy the closer we got. It wasn't a peaceful feeling, but more one of quiet suppression. Suffocation. The air grew harder to breathe, the pressure in the atmosphere intensified, the trees next to us groaned, limbs softly popping under an unnatural new weight.

On a flat outcropping of stone, the view opened up. Red rocks towered in the near distance, close enough to appreciate their magnitude but far enough away to see their outlines. In prehistoric days, Sedona had been under an ocean, and the way the rocks were formed looked more like untamed corals than mountains or plateaus.

And in the center of all this massive earth sat a woman in a stained white robe, legs straight in front of her, arms raised above her head, sweat pouring down her temples, a sweatier version of the poster we'd seen in the crystal shop.

"Looks like we found Tanzy," Dave said and gulped at his water.

"Who does she think she is? A monk?" Danica muttered.

"I don't know, but stay back," Cloud muttered back, putting his arm around Danica's waist, clearly seeing Tanzy—from the manager's description it could be no one else—as a threat.

My group stood on the edge of the stone, some instinct telling them to go no further.

But the woman was calling to me.

Siren to Siren, our silent songs met and pulled me toward her. Bells continued to clang, low and deep and chaotic, and I couldn't understand how she could sit there, so quiet, so still, among the cacophony.

I stepped onto the stone.

Luke yelled at me to come back, but his voice was distant. Unimportant.

The bells amplified, sounds attacking from all sides, as if I had taken shelter in a windchime garden in the middle of a hurricane.

Tanzy stood, reached her hands out to me, and pulled me into her world.

The sound of bells grew deafening. The scenery popped like it'd been put through an over-saturated filter. Tanzy's hands were dry and cold and strong, and her fingers dug into my wrists. Her bright green eyes stared into mine. Wisps of long brown hair that had escaped from her impossibly long braid stuck to the sweat at her temples.

"You're here." Her voice was a whisper. Raspy and tentative, her lips barely moved. "You feel her pain too."

I jerked back. "I'm sorry, but did you just *talk*? You are Tanzy, right?"

She nodded. "I've been waiting for you." She sounded as if she'd stuffed her throat full of mothballs. Her song puffed out with each word, sparkly and dusty.

But not unused.

She'd found a way to silently use her power.

"You must see what I see." She pulled me in close, pressed her head to mine, and the world around us flipped upside down.

CHAPTER 22

We were standing on the sky.

Impossibly blue, impossibly high, impossible.

This was nothing like skydiving with Amity.

This was like dancing with gods.

Tanzy held onto my arm, tight. Her robe whipped around my legs, and she reached up, toward the ground. Only the ground wasn't far away, as it should have been. It was at her fingertips. She touched it with one finger, and the ancient red rocks, here since before humans, rippled like impermanent reflections in a pond.

"What must I see?" My voice stretched and warbled, as if the watery reflection of the desert had filled my lungs.

"Many pieces. Do not fit together. The pattern unravels. The threads tighten. She becomes weak." Tanzy's grip tightened around my elbow, her voice grew desperate, not wholly sane. She placed a flat palm against the reflection of the world and swished it aside.

The water parted.

Darkness covered bare rock, our sun reflecting against the stone and giving it a ghostly glow. Demeter hunched in the darkness, crouched on a rock, bare toes hugging the stone. Her arms wrapped around her knees, and her long hair had become matted, tangled, bathed in dirt. She lifted her chin to the sky, to us, and wailed.

The bells clanged together harder, faster, so that there was no space between the goddess's cries and the clashing chimes.

Her knee lifted. Then an elbow.

Then Demeter, goddess of the harvest, scary Siren-curser, was yanked to her feet.

Gossamer strings glinted against the sunlight, a web of lines connected to her knees, her elbows, her ankles, her chin.

Her golden eyes shone through the darkness and froze on Tanzy and me.

"The Puppeteer has me," the bells whispered. "Has *her*."

Demeter fought against her strings, managed to lift one trembling leg.

Huddled on the ground at Demeter's feet was a small woman, dreadlocks cascading over her shoulders.

Wings attached to her back.

THE WORLD SPUN AWAY, ROTATED AROUND LIKE A GYROSCOPE. Wind whipped at our bodies, yanking me from Tanzy's grip.

She grabbed hold of my shirt, pulled me back to her, and wrapped her arms around my waist.

The rocks rushed up to us, and we fell to the hard, powdery stone, rolled onto our knees.

My stomach twisted, tightened, shrank into a hard ball.

"Demeter has Amity." My voice scratched out of my throat, and I dug my nails into the dirt to better anchor myself to this world.

The bells went silent.

Tanzy lay on her back on the stone next to me, chest heaving as if she'd swum through the world's reflection. Maybe she had. Her arms stretched to either side, like wings. Like Amity's wings.

"And the puppeteer has them both," she rasped.

Cloud, Danica, and Dave prowled at the edge of the vortex, instinct…human instinct…still warning them to stay away. Luke was a few steps closer, but no further—which made me question the safety of this vortex.

"What just happened?!" Danica shouted.

Leave it to Danica.

"Amity? You saw Amity?" Dave took one hesitant step onto the stone, the look on his face at once hungry and childlike.

I took a breath, turned my back to him. My legs trembled, or maybe that was the ground. I bit my lip and reached out a hand to Tanzy.

Despite my title as *Elpida*—hope—all I ever seemed to do was take hope away.

Tanzy took my hand, and I heard bells in the distance as I helped her stand, but no tilt-a-whirl water-desert this time.

Sheesh. If she heard those bells *all* the time, no wonder she'd taken a vow of silence. Anything to not add to the noise.

"We saw Amity," I said, my back still turned to Dave.

"Is she okay? How do we get to her? She's close, right?" Dave's footsteps crunched behind me as if he was pacing the plateau, as if Amity was hidden behind a rock, instead of trapped in another dimension.

"She's okay," I lied. Squeezed Tanzy's hand to make sure she went along with my tall tales. "But Demeter has her."

"And they're both prisoners," Tanzy finished.

Cloud stepped closer. "Prisoners of whom?"

"The puppeteer," I said. "Whoever he is. Demeter is fighting him, but she's growing weak. She won't be able to fight much longer."

"Harvest time is coming," Luke said. "Demeter is strongest at the peak of summer, but as it gets closer to the autumn equinox, she grows weaker. It's a turning point for her, a time when the earth begins to sleep. And so, her power wanes."

Danica stayed on the edge of the giant rock, her bare shoulders covered by a growing shadow. "So what now? Can we get to Amity from here? Save Demeter?"

Tanzy shook her head. "We must go. The patterns have changed and I do not trust the new threads I see."

Our group gave her identical what-the-what looks, looked to me to interpret. I lifted my shoulders. "I suck at riddles. We all know this."

Luke groaned and smacked his head. "Of course, why did I not pick up on this earlier?"

We waited. He groaned again.

"Lukester, would you like to share with the class?" I monotoned.

"Aglaope's line isn't the melody. It's the maestro." He dropped that on us and walked away, taking shelter in the shade.

Cloud took Danica's hand, and the rest of us followed, me last of all as my head was still spinning and ringing.

By the time I joined them, they had cracked open the water bottles and were bathing themselves in water supposedly bottled in Fiji.

I dabbed my neck with water from my own water bottle. "So maestro, not melody, huh?"

"You're going to hold this over my head forever, aren't you?"

I didn't respond. There was no need. He already knew my answer.

"Who's the melody then?" Danica asked from Cloud's side.

"Amity," Dave answered. "She's the Songwriter. Songwriters don't just write the lyrics. They write the melody."

"She's the Maestro?" I pointed at Tanzy, who was twirling slowly while staring directly into the sun.

"It's like sightreading a dozen pieces of music, all at once," Tanzy explained, in the clearest way we'd yet heard from her.

Luke nodded. "She sees the cues, the musical hints, and helps direct the song. But she can't see them until they are there in front of her. She sees the possibilities, not the future."

I cocked my head, propped my hands on my hips. "Let me get this straight. Whenever we ask you a question, you're not answering us with what you know to be true, but instead what you *think* to be true. Do I have that right?"

Luke shrugged.

"So we could be going off on an entirely wrong path and you would have no idea."

He shrugged again.

My song hummed in my throat. Angry wasps. "I need some air."

I turn back down the path leading away from the vortex, before my song started spitting stingers at Luke. A white petal floated by on the wind. Another caught on a juniper tree's twisted branch.

"The pattern changes again," Tanzy whispered.

CHAPTER 23

My friends gave me my space.

Which was probably not a good idea.

Flower petals identical to the ones in my pocket fluttered by on a breeze. Wilted and bruised, they danced down a small footpath away from the main trail. Siren bait, irresistible clues, a broken heart's hope.

I couldn't not know.

Because whoever had been leaving me flowers didn't hate me.

Hadn't hurt me.

Still had to have good in him, somewhere.

The footpath led into the rocks, away from the vortex, away from the beginning of the trail, deeper into the desert.

Red stones towered on either side of me, a hallway of ancient rock worn smooth by unrelenting winds. Petals littered the ground. Petals that had been beaten, torn, ripped, abused.

By the time I exited the open-air tunnel, the sun had dropped behind the rocks, the moon had brightened in the dusty orange sky, and the sweat had cooled on my skin. I wasn't on a path anymore, and I could no longer see trail markers or signs of other tourists.

A circle of stones surrounded a dead juniper tree. Stars peeked into the sky, one by one, low on the horizon, and super-clear.

I edged forward.

A flower rested at the entrance of the circle, and smoke curled lazily behind one of the rocks.

Someone waited for me.

Honey coated my throat, my body grew lighter, seemed to float across the barren desert.

I grazed the warm stone with my fingertips, held still for a breath, for two. The fire crackled orange and red, spitting sparks dangerously close to the dry, dead tree.

A figure unfolded himself from the other side of the fire. He pushed a strand of dark hair out of his face, shoved his hands in his pockets, and his eyes flickered from brown, to scarlet, back to brown.

"Hello, Korrina."

I took a step closer, and my breath trembled. "Jared."

His name was a song trapped in my throat.

"Stay there, please." He held up a hand. "Don't come any closer. I'm not sure…I'm not sure I'm safe."

His eyes flickered red-brown again, and he brought the point of a knife to his fingertip and dug it in. Black blood welled up around the knife and trickled lazily down his hand.

I swallowed, tried to, but my throat was knotted all up. My heart did some kind of crazy beat, totally off rhythm, and I leaned against a rock, tried to still my shaking legs.

"Why are you here? How…how are you here?" *And not trying to kill me.* I didn't need to say those words. He heard them.

"I dream of you. Even when I'm awake, you're there." Another fingertip met his blade, and the point dug under his nail. "No matter what I do, how hard I try, I fail to get you out of my head. You...torture me." He rolled his shoulders back, and his eyes flicked to red, stayed there a beat too long.

I stepped back.

He held his breath. His shoulders dropped, and he went back to Jared-brown. "I cannot be who my master needs. And I cannot be who I was. So I am here, lost, following the only light I have." He reached out his black-blooded hand. "You."

I walked closer to the fire. He shuddered, but his eyes stayed brown. He stayed Jared.

Flames sparked between us, soft pieces of ash floating into the air. Heat coursed along my skin, but I didn't care. I reached through the flames for him.

And he returned my touch.

A feather-light graze of our fingers, no more than a whisper, but it brought both of us to our toes. My song purred at the back of my throat.

"I miss you," I said, tears burning at the corners of my eyes.

He pulled away. "I shouldn't miss you. But I do." His expression fell, the turn of his lips curving downward.

I pulled my arm back, toasty warm from the flames. "Are you here of your own free will? Phorkys didn't send you?"

His fists clenched. "Do not speak his name with your cursed tongue."

Ooooo-kaaaaay.

"You must go. But I will find you again. I—I need you. Somehow, I need you."

I walked backwards out of the circle.

When we couldn't see each other anymore, he answered, "Phorkys sent me, but my will is not his. Nor is it mine."

~

THE NIGHT CHILLED. STARS SHONE CLEAR THROUGH THE cloudless sky, a spilled container of silver glitter. I walked back through the rock tunnel. My friends had to be worried. I hadn't meant to be gone so long. But...Jared.

He was in there. He was fighting.

I blinked away tears, not sure if they were happy or sad or some brand-new emotion entirely. Like...griefoy. Or sadpy.

The red rocks shone dully under the half-full moon, and something howled. Something else snuffled in the scrubby brush.

I walked faster. My commitment remained—harm nothing of this world with my song.

But were rattlesnakes *really* of this world?

I hummed, sent out my mythological creature radar, but nothing but a dull blip behind me popped up—and that dull blip had to be Jared.

That he registered on my radar was disturbing. He was no longer completely human.

The Cathedral Rock vortex was empty and silent. No bells rang, or maybe I couldn't hear them without Tanzy nearby. My friends had left, probably had contacted the National Guard or the desert patrol or whoever was the rescue team out here was.

Either that or they knew me and were waiting in the parking lot for me to return.

I checked my phone, but the signal flicked between weak and nonexistent.

They'd better have snacks.

I headed down the trail to where we'd parked Dave's truck. Thankfully, the path was clear, the trail free of stray rocks and debris, and the light of the moon bright enough to show me the way.

The only light I have...you.

Did he mean that? Could I trust him?

My fingers tingled from where we'd touched, and I knew I

would not wash this hand for days. Germs be damned, love was at stake.

The trail flattened, and I passed through the wooden fence that marked the end of the vortex journey, the beginning of civilization. Voices flitted around the night air like fireflies, and I recognized Danica's dry humor and Cloud's totally-in-love laugh. It didn't hurt as much this time.

Maybe because I had brushed the other half of my heart.

Danica and Cloud sat in the back of Dave's truck, heads resting on the sides of the truck bed, looking up at the stars. Luke and Tanzy lay in the middle of the parking lot, head-to-head and spread-eagle. Dave was asleep in the driver's seat.

"Nice to see you guys were worried about me." I propped my hands on my hips.

Danica and Cloud sat up. Luke didn't move, but his foot twitched. "When you get mad babe, you need a *lot* of space. You done with your fit? Because we're starving."

Was Luke truly of this world? Because my song itched to remind him who was boss. R-E-S-P-E-C-T.

"Ignore him," Danica said. "You get lost?"

"Nope, just needed some time to process."

Tanzy sat up, cocked her head at me, but didn't say anything. She knew. With her powers, she couldn't not know that I'd met with Jared.

But it seemed that Tanzy was no snitch.

"Took you long enough to *process*," a voice said from above. An annoying, thinks-she-knows-it-all-because-she-straddles-dimensions voice.

Neri floated to the ground.

I looked to Cloud, who shrugged. "She showed up about an hour ago."

"And you are now late, *Elpida*," Neri huffed.

"For the ball?" I quipped and looked down at my worn tennis shoes. Still no glass slippers.

"For your meeting with the Council."

Luke sat straight up, went still.

A rush of *something* rocked through my chest. Burned like fire, then went cold.

The Council didn't meet with pawns.

CHAPTER 24

Sometimes when things get too heavy, I pretend I'm a superhero. That I have an armband that deflects all the shots fired my way, that I have magical powers that knock my enemies to the ground, that I can solve everything with a wiggle of my nose.

Following Neri into a Chinese restaurant in a broken windowed strip mall, all my pretending didn't help.

I was not a superhero. I was a Siren, who didn't have a clear path forward, who had failed mission after mission, my own and the Council's. I had a magical song, but fat lot of good it had done. More harm than good. I had loved, and I had lost, and I hadn't found my way back again.

"This place had better have good egg drop soup," I said, shoving my hands into my pockets, clenching Jared's bruised petals in my fists.

"And orange chicken," Luke said from behind me.

The Council had wanted to see him too.

Which made me even more nervous.

The restaurant bell ding-a-linged above our heads, but what we walked into was no Chinese restaurant.

Lightning cracked on either side of a tall mountaintop. Greek-styled columns rose to either side of us, with pink check- ered curtains draped from column to column fluttering in the wind. A picture of the Great Wall of China banged against one of the columns, and in the midst of this weird scene, the Council of the Gods sat around a linen-covered table filled to the brim with steaming white rice, chicken in brown sauce, crispy crackers, fortune cookies, sauteed vegetables, and lo mein noodles.

My mouth watered, and I had to give my digestive system props. Even in the literal faces of the gods, it could still be ravenous.

Two empty seats were positioned on our side of the table, but we stood there as the gods ate, waiting for them to acknowledge us.

They didn't look like anyone special. If one of them had followed me into Taco Bell, I doubt I would have noticed them. But here, on the mountaintop that was at once sunny and stormy, their auras glowed.

One goddess, three gods, three Fates.

Demeter wasn't here, though she should be.

I'd seen Hades before, though we hadn't met. And he was just as hot as he was in Tartarus.

The other two gods had to be Zeus and Poseidon. Zeus, with his George Clooney beard and fitted golf shirt, and Poseidon, with his *The Dude* hair and surf shorts.

But the goddess…

"Hestia," Luke whispered. "Goddess of home and hearth. She'll be the closest thing we have to a friend here."

Leave it to Luke to know what I didn't.

Hestia's long brown hair fell over her shoulders in tousled waves, her pink dress accented her rosy cheeks.

The three Fates sat at a table to themselves, low to the ground in the traditional Japanese style. I peered closer at the three women, their figures dissolving with every brush of the wind, then reappearing with every crack of lightning. At times, they appeared beautiful, long cascading hair, white as the moon, spilling over their scantily dressed bodies. Long legs folded and tucked under their bums. Then a breeze would come, blow them away, and they'd reappear in a crack of lightning as three hags, with missing teeth and curled, yellowed nails. They slurped at soup with their loose lips, blew away again, and reappeared as some Frankenstein version of a Siren. Goose bodies, with old hag heads in place of beaks.

Ca-reepy.

"Takes the phrase, 'fate is a fickle bi-atch,' to a new level," I murmured to Luke.

"Where do you think the phrase originated?" he muttered back.

Touché.

Neri pushed off from the ground, gave two flaps of her wings, and landed on an outstretched tree branch that I swear wasn't there a moment before.

White bark and blue flowers peeked over Zeus's shoulder, with a branch that was the perfect size for Neri. Zeus picked up what looked like a soy-soaked dragonfly and tossed it into the air. Perfect throw, of course. Neri didn't have to move *at all* to catch it in her open beak.

Hestia stood, walked to our side of the table, and pulled out the two empty seats.

"Korrina, daughter of Molpe, granddaughter of Mnesynome, welcome. Luke, son of Phorkys, grandson of Gaea, you are granted sanctuary. Please. Sit." She held out open palms to the empty seats on her left and right.

My heart jumpstarted. Son of Phorkys? I glared at Luke. He avoided looking at me.

Like that would save him.

We slinked by Hestia and sat in our seats. She smelled of freshly baked cookies and rain.

Zeus nodded to the plates in front of us. "Eat. Join us."

I reached for the nearest platter, but Luke grabbed my hand under the table. Shook his head so slightly I would have missed it if I didn't know him, if I hadn't studied his looks so closely last year.

"Um, no thanks. We just ate." My stomach grumbled, and Zeus raised his eyebrows.

"Forget it, brother," Hades said. "This one has the scent of the Underworld on her. She understands that part of the game, at least."

I didn't, but it didn't hurt to let them all believe I knew more than I did.

I cleared my throat. "Why are we here?" Despite Neri looking all warm and cozy with the gods, despite Hestia's you're-home essence, we weren't safe.

They saw me as a weapon.

They saw Luke as the enemy.

And if they knew about Dad disobeying their orders, they'd see him as a thing to smite.

"You have found the one who sees, but you have lost the weapon who sings." Voices whispered from behind the gods, and the flickering images of the Fates rose to their feet, passed through the gods like ghosts, and stopped in the middle of the feast. "All four weapons are needed. The *Elpida* is damaged and cannot complete the mission on her own."

"Damaged? I'm not damaged!" I leapt to my feet.

Luke bowed his head, grabbed my knee, and gripped tight until I sat down again.

"Soul-damaged," the Fates whispered, a blue orb floating between the three of them. They lifted their hands to it, grazed its light. "A soul-damaged Siren cannot wield the scepter without losing her life. Such a thing would cause the scepter to fall into enemy hands once again."

Right. Not concern about my life, but the scepter. Always with the scepter.

"She is *Ania*. She is *Elpida*. A dyad. Two wholes make up only one-half. But together…" The Fates clasped their hands together, and the blue orb transformed into the shape of another being, completing their circle. Light shot up from the center of them, pouring out of the steamed rice. "Together, their power is enough."

Ania…

My heart beat faster, harder.

Ania. My darker half. The Sorrow of the world. Foretold to destroy everyone, everything.

Let me help…

Her voice. It'd been her voice I'd been hearing as I drifted into visions.

Hestia turned to us, oblivious to the revelations screwing with my mind. "This is why you were given the mission of finding the other weapons, Korrina. Not to save them, but to save everyone in both worlds. You must save Amity."

I gathered my thoughts, pressed my lips together. "I know. But how? She's trapped somewhere with Demeter. We can't get to them."

"Demeter?" Hestia looked to her brothers. "You said she was preparing for the equinox." And in her voice I heard a sister, fed up with the lies of her younger brothers.

The three gods shrank back.

Zeus cleared his throat. "She—uh—has not been heard from in seven days. We thought she was taking a vacation, you know. Getting ready for her big day."

"When has Demeter *ever* taken a vacation?" Hestia said something under her breath that sounded a lot like Ancient Greek for *idiots*. "Tell me more of what you know, Korrina."

"The puppeteer has taken both Demeter and Amity. But we don't know who he or she is, where to find them, or how to rescue them."

"The puppeteer has long threads," the Fates whispered. "And even the puppeteer does not know where they all connect."

"And you three." Hestia stood and pointed. "Can't you ever talk plainly? No one knows what in Tartarus you are saying."

"The first goddess is angry with us, but Tartarus does not have the answers. Only the Siren dyad who sits before us can answer her anger." The Fates bowed, flickered, and disappeared.

"Great," Poseidon murmured. "There goes our quorum. Meeting adjourned." He sat back, yawned, and fell away in a wave of water.

Hades faded in a cloud of smoke.

Zeus raised his hands, and a crack of lightning reached for him. He grabbed it like it was a rope, then turned into crackling electricity himself.

Hestia rolled her eyes. "Gods. Always with the drama. Come on, I'll walk you out." We followed her to the Chinese restaurant door, which had appeared at our backs. "You did well to not eat food from the table of a god, but I am not a god, and this was not served at a god's table, so please enjoy. From my hearth to yours." She held out a cloth bag of what smelled like chocolate chip cookies.

I reached out and accepted the cookies. "Thank you for your hospitality, goddess."

Luke and Neri edged out the door, but Hestia didn't let go of her offering. "You're like her, you know. Molpe. Before she let the curse take her mind, she was my friend. Please count me as one of yours."

I nodded. It wasn't wise to turn down a goddess's friendship. Even if I didn't trust her.

I followed Neri and Luke out of the restaurant, Hestia's and the Fates' words battering my ears. *The curse took her mind. Dyad. Both Ania and Elpida. Soul-damaged.*

Damaged.

I'm damaged.

And if the curse had taken Molpe's mind, what was going to happen to Amity?

CHAPTER 25

I tried to look on the sunny side.

The Council didn't mention Dad's disobedience.

The Council didn't know I'd had multiple chances to kill Jared.

No one knew we'd touched.

We'd touched and the world hadn't imploded. He hadn't gone crazy. I hadn't sprouted wings.

The sun was there. Hidden behind my damaged soul, apparently, but it was there.

Neri led Luke and me into the parking lot, where everyone waited for us in Dave's truck. Behind us, the Chinese restaurant looked just like the rest of the strip mall. Lights off. Windows boarded. Graffiti'd glass.

"What did Hestia mean by the curse taking Molpe's mind?" I asked.

Neri huffed. "The longer a Siren has her wings, the less human she becomes. She acts more on instinct rather than logic."

"And that's bad?"

"Not bad, just not always controlled. If Molpe decides she's lonely and wants male company, all she needs to do is sing and an entire ship of men will land on the island."

"Hence all the shipwreck Siren stories," Luke added.

I turned to him, my hands in fists, my song sparking purple. "You."

He held up his hands and took a few steps backwards. "I told you, my family has served—"

"Yes. Has *served* Phorkys. Not *son of* Phorkys. How could you not tell us? After you showed up, begged for our help. *My* protection?"

"You weren't exactly receptive. I doubted you would've taken that confession well at that moment."

"You lied. Again. And I was idiotic enough to trust you. *Again.*"

For once, he didn't say anything in his defense. "You're right. I did lie. I was desperate. I *am* desperate."

Neri landed on the cab of the truck, and Tanzy, Dave, Danica, and Cloud poured out.

I crossed my arms, widened my stance. "It's time for you to tell us everything, Luke. Start from the beginning."

Danica looked between us. "Come to Jesus confession time? Awesome." She pulled out a bag of popcorn and started snacking. "I'm ready. Squirm away." She looked Luke up and down and wore a sadistic smirk.

Cloud wrapped an arm around her waist, and they cozied up together against the truck. Dave hopped on his hood and crossed his arms. Tanzy sat cross-legged on the dirty pavement, spine straight, palms open to the sky on her knees.

I stayed ready, alert. My song still hadn't made a full comeback, but I could hold my own against Luke. Descendant of Phorkys. Liar extraordinaire.

"Yes, my family's bloodline started with Phorkys," he said. "He mated with a human woman, my great-great-something grandmother, and since then, we have served as his spies into the human world. Our family has mind control abilities, and for some reason, I specifically have the power to take away others' abilities."

My stomach sank. "Not just Siren songs?"

He nodded. "All powers. But I have to touch them."

He continued to talk, but it was all in the background. A new plan had started to percolate, and the noise of new ideas was loud.

Tanzy's eyes focused on me, as if she could see everything I was thinking. With her powers, maybe she could. Or at least see the possibilities of where my ideas could take us.

"How about god powers?" I interrupted him.

He narrowed his eyes and cocked his head, his long hair falling over his shoulder. "Yes."

"Goddess powers?"

His eyes narrowed to squinty slits. "Yes."

"Phorkys's powers?"

"What are you getting at?"

"Are you on our side? Truly on our side?"

"Since my escape from the Grotto and my reconditioning, my entire family has sworn to kill me and deliver my head to Phorkys for him to devour, so yes, I'm on your side. I have no choice but to be on your side."

"I need proof."

"What?"

"I need proof that your family is out to murder you. We need to be able to trust you."

"Beyond the obvious working-as-a-group reasons, why?"

He knew me too well.

"Yeah, Korrina." Danica stuffed her mouth full of white kernels. "What's going on in that head of yours?"

Apparently, they all knew me too well.

"I have a plan. And if Luke can prove he's to be trusted, we may have a shot."

"A very good shot," Tanzy added, her words a breathy, float-on-the-wind monotone.

"A shot at…" Cloud tried to lead us, but I wasn't ready to reveal my hand. Not yet.

"Winning everything." I grinned, turned to Luke. "But first, we need your family to kill you. Where should we start?"

~

Neri had the best solution.

We couldn't exactly trust Luke to lead the mission to get himself killed. But thanks to Neri's mythical connections, she was able to send a message to one of Luke's cousins about his "hideout" at a campsite in the middle of the Sedona desert before she left and headed back to help Dad on his illegal mission. Now that Dad knew Mom was in the Grotto, he was researching a way to break in.

Luke was watched at all times, to make sure he didn't contact his family to warn them of our plan. I didn't even allow him to close his eyes, just in case he hadn't told us all his powers, like mind-speaking. I was pretty sure your eyes had to be closed to mind-speak, though Dave thought my reasoning was stupid.

We walked for half an hour into the middle of the desert, not risking any private roads as we doubted the owners would like that.

Nice thing about the desert? Lots of open space with easy-to-hop-over fences.

We set up Luke's "hideout," with a ratty blanket draped over some mesquite branches for a tent, an overturned box for a sitting area, some canned food, bottled waters, and Dave's old sleeping bag for his bed. Looked pretty convincing…except for one thing.

"Luke, roll around in the dirt," I ordered.

"I am not—"

Dave cocked Sully. "You will. Amity's life is on the line, bud."

"Easy, Dave," I said. "I think we're done with Mister Sully for a while. Just unload him, put him back in his case." I shot Cloud a look.

Dave followed my instructions, walking back to where we'd left the truck with Cloud on his heels. If we didn't find Amity soon, not only would she lose her mind to the curse, but Dave was going to lose his mind as well.

"Now that Scary is gone, I need you to look like you've been roughing it, instead of being pampered by three lovely women."

Tanzy's and Danica's eyes brightened. The three of us were more than capable of forcing Luke to get down and dirty.

He looked between us and huffed.

"C'mon, Lukester. Time is a-tickin'." Danica snapped her fingers.

He sighed, got down on his knees, and laid on his back.

"Stop, drop, and roll, baby," I said.

Luke groaned.

When he was good and dirtied up, he sat on his box while we surveyed him.

"He needs wounds." Tanzy's dreamy voice made her sound like a drugged-up psychopath.

Danica picked up a stick. "I got this."

Luke jerked his gaze to mine, all panic-filled.

I shrugged. "Payback's a butthead. Besides, this has to be believable."

Danica went to work with the same glee that she'd dissected formaldehyde-soaked animals at school.

When she was done, Luke's clothes were ripped, he had a cut on his cheek, two on his neck, and his hair was tangled and knotted with leaves.

We circled him. "Good job, Dan." I yawned—still not recovered from the stupid scepter—and nodded at her, then turned to

Luke. "We'll be hiding nearby, which means you'll have to hold your own until we get here. And if I see anything that could even be perceived as a signal from you, I let Danica tear out your eyes, no questions, no regrets. Got it?"

Danica showed her teeth.

Luke gulped. Nodded.

I led Danica and Tanzy down the path so we could meet up with Dave and Cloud and find a good hiding spot. Luke looked scared. But the only thing he'd ever proven to me was his extensive acting skills. Time for him to level up.

Or get killed.

Truth was, I had no idea if we could get to him in time. This felt a little bit like a witch trial. If she sinks, she drowns and hey, good news, she's not a witch.

Only Luke had real powers.

And he'd shown himself to be a liar on more than one occasion.

We met up with Cloud and Dave and found a hiding spot on a nearby ridge. High enough to see Luke's campsite with enough brush to cover all five of us. Near enough to maybe get to him before he was murdered.

The early evening sun drooped in the sky, and the buzz of insects gettin' their bite on hummed around us. Sweat prickled at my neck, rolled down my spine, and below our hiding spot, Luke shaded his eyes from the lowering sun.

There was a sponge in my gut, soaking up all the stinky guilt it could hold, and it still didn't get it all. Guilt puddled in my stomach, spilled down to my toes. I couldn't stand this. Betrayer or not, Luke was a part of my life. I couldn't watch him be killed.

I jumped to my feet. "I'm getting closer. Can't see."

"Uh-huh," Danica muttered. "Softy. We're coming too."

Of all people, Danica should want to see Luke punished the most.

Seems like even she was starting to believe him.

Dangerous.

We crept forward, easing from clumps of mesquite trees to big rocks to thick cacti. Closer in, we belly-crawled, finding cover behind some thick scrub.

"I really hope there's no rattlesnakes around," Dave whispered.

Tanzy hummed her agreement.

"Korrina can just heal us if we get bitten, no prob bob." Danica slapped my shoulder.

"Exactly," I whispered, all cheery.

They didn't know that healing them was slowly killing me.

They didn't need to know.

My friends had been, were, and would be in danger because of who I was. I'd give my life force to them any day.

"Shh. Something's coming." Cloud pointed to the lengthening shadows on the other side of Luke's campsite and went still.

Luke noticed as well, but he kept drawing in the sand with a stick.

Which was impressive, because his so-called cousin was not-so-human.

CHAPTER 26

Luke's cousin was an ogre.

Granted, a very humanoid ogre, but an ogre. He—she?—had gotten more of the Phorkys genes than the grandma genes. Two beady eyes, hair hanging down in strings from a half-bald head, and pudgy fat in all the wrong places.

"Baby Luke!" Its voice was pitched high—female then—and she ran into Luke's campsite with open arms. "Good to see you. My, you've grown." She hugged him, picking him up to his toes, and he squeaked.

Not signal squeak, but all-the-air-crushed-out-of-his-body squeaked.

This was not the reunion we were expecting.

"Good to see you too, Olnar. I think."

"I think not, and you know it, little buddy. You know what has to happen, yes?" Her oversized mouth flipped upside-down, a car-wreck of a frown.

Luke took a few steps back. "I won't go easy on you."

She laughed, slapped her knee. "Nor should you, cuz. But do not worry. Even in death, you will serve Phorkys, feeding him and strengthening him with your power and knowledge."

Huh. Luke wasn't kidding about being fed to Phorkys.

"Now come to me and let me crush your skull." She said it as if she were asking Luke to come over and play.

Luke fell back into a defensive pose, something that looked a lot like Bruce Lee. Or Kung Fu Panda.

Olnar's smile returned. "You are sooo adorable!" She cracked her knuckles, bent her knees, and sprang into the air with a grace that defied her body.

My heart slingshotted into my throat.

He rolled out of the way as Olnar pounded into the ground, barely missed being crushed into Luke powder.

I held us back. Not until I saw Luke in real danger would I believe this wasn't an act.

He'd fooled me too many times before.

Olnar grunted, flung Luke's tent to the ground, snapped off the branch it'd been hanging from, and whipped the five-foot-long, three-inches-thick limb around her like a half-shelled Donatello.

Cloud and Danica tensed at my side.

"You are making this difficult, little Luke." Olnar's voice deepened, and something in her demeanor shifted. Turned sharp. Less playful. More monster.

The pudgy fat around her neck, wrists, knees, rippled. Moved. Her muscles bulged and hardened, and she doubled in muscle mass. Not pudgy. Not fat. Not friendly.

My heart lodged in my throat. This was the beast parents used to scare their children. This was the reason you didn't walk into dark forests.

She slashed at Luke with the branch, wielding it like a giant kebab spear.

"Korrina," Dave growled.

"Hold. Your. Position." I clenched my teeth, hated how much I wanted to jump up and fight for Luke.

Tanzy hummed. "We fail without Phorkys's blood, *Elpida-Ania*."

She knew I was a dyad? I shook that away. *Stay focused.*

This could still be an act.

Olnar's elbow popped backwards, and my blood slowed, thickened, congealed. I knew what was coming. Had seen the move too often in my training. Had done it myself.

Luke had fallen for it.

He was watching the big stick.

Instead of the big fist.

I jumped to my feet, roared out of the bushes, my song burning honey on the back of my tongue.

Her hard knuckles, each the size of Luke's ear, connected with the side of his head.

I screamed. Luke flew, blood spraying out like glitter, and then he was falling. Falling. Falling.

He crumpled to the ground. Didn't move.

The Mischievous sounded the battle cry, followed by an ear-splitting screech that could only be from Tanzy.

My song burst out of me, an electric firestorm that ripped toward Olnar as if she were encased in metal. I fell to my knees as my power hit her, wrapped around her, winked her out of existence with a blood-curdling scream.

It didn't matter.

We were too late.

I crawled to Luke. The world fell silent except for the soft rasp of my skin against the sand.

I reached for him. Tanzy pulled me back.

"You cannot. I have seen that path. You will drain yourself entirely by saving him."

"But you said we fail—"

"We do not win by you sacrificing yourself." She stared deep into my eyes, her palms warmed around my wrists, and her confidence in her visions seemed to give me a little bit of strength.

Dave stood. "We do this the old-fashioned way. Cloud, grab that blanket. Danica, give me that stick. We'll make a rescue sled, get him to a hospital."

Tanzy swayed. "He won't make it."

"We have to try." Dave's voice rose, cracked along the edges. "We can't just stand around and do nothing."

Cloud cleared his throat. "Dave's right. Tanzy, you yourself said that your powers are like sightreading a dozen pieces of music all at once. You see possibilities. Not truths."

Tanzy's spine went straight, and her bony, vegan arms went stiff. "They are more than possibilities. They are outcomes, places the present could lead."

I slipped behind her, let them argue it out, and placed my hands on either side of Luke's head.

He was angled all wrong, his color too sickly, his body too still.

I breathed in through my nose, focused on my breath, on the burning heart of the scepter in the center of my chest. "I'm sorry I didn't believe you, Lukester," I whispered. "But FYI, you did make it really hard to trust you."

And then, I sang.

Everyone fell back into slow-motion. Dave, Danica, and Cloud leapt away from the brilliant light, covering their eyes. Tanzy leapt for my arms, but already, the scepter was forming in front of my body. Already, Luke's gaping skull was knitting itself back together. Already, my world was going dark. My hands started to slip from Luke, but I forced my muscles to stiffen. I had to hang on long enough to make this right.

Tanzy stopped fighting me. Something passed over her eyes, and she folded her knees under her and placed her hands on top of mine. She hummed along, and my world stopped darkening.

My power focused. Rather than being this explosive, wild

energy, it became targeted, thin but strong. Not controlled, but given a more solid direction.

From the Maestro.

I fell into her lead, trusting where she was taking us. Only she seemed to be taking cues from me, from my song, my power, my passion. Together, we formed a dance of notes, where there wasn't one leading partner, but two people who knew their own steps.

And it wasn't killing me.

It hurt, I was getting tired, but it wasn't killing me.

And that right there was good enough for me.

I poured more of my power into the scepter, not taking hold of its cool body but letting its light cover Luke's body, heal his wounds. Tanzy narrowed her eyes at me, as if to say, "Don't push it," but she wasn't scary enough to make me stop.

Luke sighed under my hands. His violet eyes fluttered open, and he covered Tanzy's hands, which were covering mine, with his.

My song hummed against Tanzy's palms, but hers went silent. She gasped, yanked her hands away, and I knew what she'd felt. Empty relief. Foreign silence.

Luke placed his hands against mine and pulled them away from his head. My song went silent. The scepter winked out, flowed back into my chest.

"Thank you, Korrina. But you give too much. This hurts you."

He knew. Tanzy knew. I needed to stop the bleeding of my secrets.

"Both of you, swear to me that this stays between us," I said. "The others can't know. Especially Cloud. They think I can protect them. I can. I will. But if they know, they'll put themselves in danger trying to protect me." I bounced my gaze between Luke and Tanzy, now my closest confidants. "Swear."

Tanzy leaned away from Luke. "Of course. I do not foresee and tell. That can cause unpredictable change."

"Secrets have never served you, Korrina," Luke said. "Are you sure?"

"Positive. Do it."

Luke cursed below his breath. "I swear to keep your secret."

Dave, Cloud, and Danica peeked out from our old hiding spot. I couldn't help but notice how fragile they seemed…how human.

"That was brighter than before." Danica pushed her sunglasses on top of her head. "What changed?"

Luke groaned and rolled to his knees. He sat back on his heels and pushed his long hair out of his face. "Two are stronger than one. Tanzy combined her power with Korrina's, and together, they went supernova." He smoothly left out the piece where I'd almost died.

"I'm gonna need better sunglasses when all four Sirens get together." She wiggled her lip ring. "Glad you were telling the truth, Lukester. Now you can get us to Amity."

"We need to get out of here before any more of my family, or the Siren Hunters, show up." He started down the path back to Dave's truck. No one followed. Luke huffed. "Fine. Dinner first. Then, we cross the veil."

CHAPTER 27

Tanzy invited us over to her digs.

Dave followed her sing-song directions inside his cramped truck cab. We turned down an unlit road and drove into the heart of Red Rock State Park. Lights from random houses occasionally spotted the night, but they were few and far between.

"Are we there yet?" I whined. But really, I was starting to wonder what Tanzy's so-called digs were like. Did she live in a tent on the side of the road? A cave? Was there a coffee machine?

"Next right," Tanzy answered.

Dave slowed, made the turn. His headlights glanced off a deer and her Bambi crossing a gravel road that curved and climbed down into a shallow valley.

Under the bright light of the stars, I saw rooftops. That was promising.

The road ended, and Dave circled the truck around an empty cul-de-sac.

"You may park here," Tanzy murmured. "This is my uncle's

home, but he moved to Colorado a while back. Gave me this place."

We climbed out of Dave's truck and stopped in front of a giant wooden gate, carved with mandalas and birds and suns. Tanzy stood in front of the gate, her hand on the too-big-to-be-practical latch.

"This house is special. It has a magic of its own that must be recognized and respected. You will leave this house changed, but do not expect change to be easy." She pushed open the gate without further ado and revealed a small courtyard littered with glowing rocks and climbing vines.

We crossed the threshold, and the weight of the place settled on my shoulders. Not heavy and burdensome, but more like an anxiety blanket, calming and safe. Water trickled down moss-covered rocks into a koi pond and hanging from the roof were multiple hammock chairs that looked comfortable enough to sleep in.

She led us through a breezeway lit by Christmas lights, with a door on either side of the outdoor hallway. "This is the meditation and yoga room." She pointed to the right. "And this is my home." She placed her hand on a giant round doorknob in the center of a blue, wooden door that looked inspired by Tolkien and twisted.

Music poured out of the open door, soft and unearthly. It had the quality of the chiming bells of the Cathedral Rock vortex, only softer, more soothing. The others walked in, as if deaf to the notes, but Tanzy and I waited at the entrance, waited for the house to finish its welcome song.

"You weren't kidding," I breathed as the notes winded down.

"I rarely do. I'm not good at humor." She shrugged, let her lips tilt into a lopsided smile. "My home is yours for as long as you need. We are family, after all." She slipped her hand into mine, then pressed our palms against the wood grain of the carved front door. A light from inside the house warmed and glowed brightly at our touch, then faded. "The house now recognizes you. It will always open to you and those you love."

"Thank you, Tanzy." Warmth filled my throat, and something that felt a lot like coming home filled me up from the inside out.

She nodded, ever graceful, and stepped into the house. But paused. Kept her back to me. "Just be careful who you love, Korrina." Then kept walking.

LUKE LINED US UP IN THE MIDDLE OF THE MASSIVE LIVING AREA. We'd pushed giant-sized couches and loveseats out of the way, rearranged tables carved out of tree trunks, and circled around a window set into the floor that revealed a giant healing crystal. It was pink, or at least the light under it was, and it set the room in a warm glow.

"Crossing the Veil is more than passing through a piece of material," Luke said. "Within the Veil exists a void, a space of nothing designed to trap those crossing without permission."

"Lost souls void." I elbowed Tanzy. "Been there. Done that. Mom hangs out there sometimes."

Danica rolled her eyes.

"Yes, well, for whatever reason, Korrina is one of the very few who have crossed without a guide and survived." Luke stretched out his neck, like a jock would before entering a fight or a competition, and dove into his lecture.

Even with everything I'd found out about Luke, I still thought he'd look great in tweed.

"If you let one of those lost souls touch you, you will experience their same death and join them in the void, trapped forever."

I could feel our circle shudder. Luke petrifying them with his warnings was not helping.

"Neri is a guide," I said. "She's gotten me through the void tons of times and we've been just fine." Easy-peasy.

Luke shook his head. "She's a spirit guide. Not a corporeal guide. We need our bodies once we get there."

Dave, Danica, and Cloud shot each other looks.

Luke didn't notice. "Besides, she's been flagged. Everyone knows that she's compromised her unbiased status by remaining with you and your father in the human world. If she were to guide us through, we'd be immediately captured."

"Wait, so even the gods know that she's—"

"Probably lying to them about things to protect you and your dad. Yeah. They just don't have proof. Yet. But once they do, Neri will be demoted, and your dad…"

I didn't want to think about what would happen if the gods found out that Dad had disobeyed. "How do you know this? And why haven't you said anything before now?"

Luke shrugged. "Sorry, babe. You haven't been open to free speech from prisoners until recently. Plus, gossip abounds in the Grotto. The guards think inmates are too far gone to process anything they say."

Inmates. Luke. My mother.

Guards. Jared. My birth father.

My life was really screwed up.

"With the three of us connected"—he pointed at me, Tanzy, and himself—"we shouldn't need a guide. Tanzy has the ability to see if we're heading in a dangerous direction. Korrina, you have the power to push us through with your song. And I have the key to light our way."

"Great. So we're through the void and into the other world. I've only ever been to Anthemusa. Siren Island," I clarified, for those uninformed. "Where will we land once we get through?"

"The strength of our thoughts will guide us," Tanzy hummed.

Luke raised one eyebrow at her. "She's right. If we can focus our thoughts on Amity or Demeter, hopefully we'll land some-where close to where they are."

"This plan sounds really easy to screw up," Cloud inter-jected. "We're depending on our thoughts? Have you met Korrina? We're just as likely to end up in some supernatural coffee shop."

"Ouch, Cloud. I can focus."

Danica and Cloud looked at me, crossed their arms, gave me identical, *really* looks.

Luke shifted slightly in front of me. "Let's assume Korrina can stay focused for the thirty seconds it takes to cross the void, okay?" Luke jumped to my defense.

Sorta.

"She and Tanzy have seen where Demeter is being kept captive, so they'll be able to envision the space. Once there, the real danger sets in. The gods' realm acts as a power caste system. Those with more power are both safer and more endan-gered than those with less."

Dave narrowed his eyes. "Explain."

"In the Veil, power is like a light, drawing insects in like bait." Luke tapped the healing crystal's window with his foot. "Most of those can be swatted away or zapped. But get a big enough bug…"

"Kapow," Tanzy whispered.

"Yeah." Luke pressed his lips together. "Kapow. As soon as we land, Phorkys will sense us, the gods will sense us, basically anything that could eat us, thinks it could eat us, or wishes it could eat us will sense us. We have very limited time to get in, get out."

A thin string wrapped around my heart, squeezed tight. "Figure out how to save a goddess and a Siren while fighting off a bunch of baddies?" I confirmed.

Luke nodded.

I didn't say the other part of what we'd have to do. Keep the humans safe while saving Demeter and Amity and fighting. I didn't know how we could.

"One last thing," Luke continued. "There are all sorts of alarms fashioned to detect humans who have found their way to the gods' realm, barriers and obstacles to keep them out, and of course, the moment they so much as wiggle a toe on the other side of the veil, their life is forfeit."

"Sounds like a great vacay," Danica spouted and edged closer to Cloud.

"Sounds like we need better weapons," Dave said.

Cloud looked between the two of them, then at me, then Luke. "Sounds like we're being told to stay."

Luke nodded. "We need a conduit to guide us back. You three need to stay here, hold down the fort, and guide us home."

I could kiss him. He'd given them a mission while also keeping them safe.

Danica looked relieved. Dave looked pissed.

Cloud looked like he knew exactly what Luke was doing. "And if you three don't come back? What then?"

Tanzy swayed. "Run." Her voice, quiet and raspy, seemed to break the room in two. "Get as far from this place as you can. If we do not come back, the dethroned sea god will rip through our world…starting here."

CHAPTER 28

Luke wanted to leave at three in the morning. Veils between worlds were weakest then, and he wanted us to have as few obstacles to overcome as possible.

The rest of the group trickled off to sleep, finding their own space in the big house. Each room had a different personality, but they all radiated with the warm magic of the home.

I found myself on the back patio. Overlooking a dimly lit pool with a stone sun at the bottom of the water and beyond that, the other-worldly red rocks glinted dull and gray under the starlight. Like shadows of sleeping giants, they seemed real and impossible, scalable and enormous. Inviting. Terrifying.

A light flickered down below, and the scent of salt and sand floated up to the balcony.

He'd found me.

Like he said he would.

My heart flickered in response. A small flame of something I didn't want to name, but that had grown with Luke's passed test. Luke had said my song had healed him.

What if I didn't have to break a curse?

What if all I had to do to save Jared was sing?

My steps quickened down a set of winding, metal stairs. I passed the pool, found an unlit path. Pomegranates hung from trees that bordered a small, beaten trail, and if I reached up on my tiptoes, I could just barely graze the lowest fruit with the tip of my finger.

The path wound down into the valley, followed a dry creek bed littered with smooth, flat stones. Ahead, there was a rounded stone hut, with smoke escaping through an opening carved into the top. The entrance glowed with flames.

Jared seemed of the fire. As if the green Hunter flames had entered his veins, and wherever he went, he burned.

He stood at the entrance of the hut, his face shadowed by the night and the flickering flames.

"You're here," I breathed.

He held out his hand.

I reached out without thinking, but my training kicked in. I pulled back. "How can I trust you?"

"You can't. Don't ever let down your guard around me." Still, he moved forward.

"Are you…safe?" I used his words from our last meeting.

"I am…in control. Move slowly, but please join me by the fire." He kept his hand out, and stupid-in-love me took it.

He shuddered at my touch but held on tight, rubbed my knuckle with his thumb. His hand was warm against mine, callused where it had never been before. He'd grown. Gotten taller. More filled out. A dusting of stubble on his chin.

This person wasn't a killer. But he also wasn't Jared. He was someone in between. A someone I needed to know. To understand. To see if I could salvage.

I let him lead us into the hut and took a seat beside him next to the flames, keeping an eye on the shadows, on his hands, on any tricks that could drop in from above. I was vulnerable. This wasn't safe. This was bad bad bad decision-making.

But Luke had changed.

And I couldn't not try.

We sat in silence, him holding my hand, taking deep breaths as if he was struggling to maintain his control.

I studied him. His face half in the light, half in the dark, his eyes haunted, his lips troubled.

"Tell me what makes you happy," I said, wanting to get his mind off his thoughts.

His brown eyes flicked to mine. "You do," he responded, without hesitation. "Or rather, dreams of you. Your scent. Your" —he took a deep breath, one that shuddered all the way in— "touch."

My heart went tipsy-turvy. "Oh."

"Now ask what makes me sad." His gaze penetrated mine.

"Tell me." My fingers trembled in his grasp. I didn't want to hear what made him sad. Or happy. Or anything else.

Because my heart was already broken. My soul was already damaged.

And I was afraid of what else he could do to me.

"You do." He shifted, and his knees pressed against mine. "And mad." His hands left mine, trailed up my arm, traced the lines of my neck. "And maddened. At peace. At turmoil." He brushed the hair away from my neck, stroked my cheek. "You soothe me. And cause me pain."

My song hummed at his nearness. From being close to him, close to danger? "I don't want to cause you pain."

"Tell me to stop." His breath brushed my lips.

I leaned into him. "I won't."

"Be ready to run. Fight me. Kill me."

I reached up to him, mimicked his touches, felt his skin tremble under mine. "Never."

His lips curved up, pressing his cheek against my hand. "That's my girl."

He grazed his lips against mine, and my world went golden-green. His taste, salt and sweet. His fingers curled into my hair, and my song burst in my chest. A whirl of energy, a storm barely contained. As if my song had grown wings and forgotten how to fly.

Something deep inside me cracked, reshaped itself, super-glued back together into something I didn't recognize. The memory of our first kiss washed into me, swirled around this newness, this sharp edge of danger, this knife-point of a kiss. He wasn't my Jared. I wasn't his girl. We were something more. Something else. Tied together, linked heart to heart, insepara-ble. My heart forever tangled with his, for life.

For death.

He could kill me.

And I would let him.

But first, I had one thing left to try.

I focused my energy on the power tied to my fractured soul and called the scepter.

"Please don't, *Elpida*." He pulled away, but barely, just enough to whisper against my lips. He placed his hand over my chest. "It will not bring healing. It will bring death. And I will not be able to control myself around it. Or you."

My purple light dimmed. I rubbed my forehead against his. "I promised you I'd find a way to save you. I still hold that promise." My nose traced his, and he grabbed me back to him.

Not soft this time. Not gentle. Not hesitant.

My stomach twisted. My heart fell into a hole.

"I remember loving you." His voice followed me down that hole, deep, dark, ragged on all the edges. His lips crushed into mine, and then, I was in his arms, straddling his lap, letting him kiss my neck, everything moving so fast I could feel the world spinning beneath our feet.

Fire burst between us, an electric pulse so strong it pushed us apart, flung me against the side of the stone hut.

"Begone from here, Hunter. She is not for you."

Over my shoulder, the three priests of Persephone stood in a dyed-green-hair bunch, holding a weapon that looked a lot like something out of LOTR.

Jared stood, ignored them, focused on me. "I remember you. I will not forget again." He dumped a bucket of water into the fire and disappeared into the steam.

ON THE ONE HAND, I WAS BUMMED.

The scepter could not heal a Hunter. I should have known it wouldn't be that easy.

On the other hand, I'd kissed Jared, I'd kissed Jared, I'd kissed Jared.

On the other, *other* hand—because apparently I needed three hands to make this thought process work—I was freaked out. Felt like I'd been caught making out with my boyfriend on the couch in the dark. By priests.

By groupie priests.

I stood, brushed off my knees and my derriere, raised my hands in the air, and faced Persephone's messenger boys.

"I'm not armed." I held up my hands.

"A Siren is always armed. And you are mating with the enemy." Main Groupie kept his weapon raised.

My ears burned. "We were not mating." *Gah!*

"It looked like the beginning of the mating ritual to me." He shoved his weapon in my direction.

The rest of them yes-man nodded. The three original Taco Bell band members.

I *gahed* out loud. "Since you're not blasting me, I assume you're here to deliver Persephone's message and not kill me or my friends."

They furrowed their pierced eyebrows. One of them had even dyed his brows green. "We do our queen's bidding. She has not bid us to kill you."

He didn't need to say the *yet*. As Queen of the Underworld, I was fairly certain Persephone's hands weren't exactly clean.

Even if she'd never wanted to be there in the first place.

"We are here to guide you to our queen. Now that you have received Hestia's boon, you may converse with her directly."

I patted my pocket. "You mean the cookies?"

They nodded, more serious than I'd ever seen anyone respond to cookies. Even me.

"They are a token through the veil. Safe passage."

I took out the cookies, counted them. "There are six here."

"For yourself, your Siren sister, and your disesteemed companion. One token for the way there. One token for the way back. Now come. We are wasting time."

They left the hut, clearly expecting me to follow. Their lime-green hoodies glowed in the midnight air, like fireflies leading me home.

I stopped the priests by the back door.

"Your ultimate goal is to save Demeter from the puppeteer and becoming the Goddess of Retribution, yes?"

"We must save the mother so that we may save the daughter," they intoned.

Not quite an answer, but good enough. "So let's keep the whole mating ritual out of the conversation, okay? Because if *they*"—I pointed indoors—"know about *that*"—I pointed down the path—"there will be no saving the mother or the daughter. Got it?"

They bowed the tips of their noses to the tips of their fingers.

Guess that's a yes.

Between Tanzy and the priests, we could lead a woo-woo convention. And also, cool band name: Tanzy and the Priests.

I took a deep breath, turned the handle, and let them into the house.

CHAPTER 29

Tanzy was curled up in a big reading nook by the fireplace like a cat warming its fur. I wanted to trade places with her. Have a place to curl up and feel safe. To sleep without dreams and visions. To have a home.

Luke sat up from the couch, his long hair pulled into a knot at the back of his head.

"Hey guys," I called out. "We've got company. And a change of plans."

The priests fanned out behind me, and Luke jumped to his feet. He reached for the back of his pants, as if he were used to hiding a weapon back there. He fumbled for a moment, and I knew what that was like. To have muscle memory stronger than logic, stronger than reality.

Luke jumped off the couch. "Have you lost your mind? What are *they* doing here?"

"Helping, I think," I responded. Luke's reaction was over the top. These priests were creepy, yes, but this…

"Interesting company you choose to keep, *Elpida*," the head priest said. "Should I care beyond the demands of my queen, I would warn you to be careful of your companions."

"Bite me, Crannik," Luke retorted, and it was a totally un-Luke thing to say.

But— "Wait. You two know each other?"

Crannik crossed his arms. "In another life, Mr. Carter pretended to be one of our initiates. He should be commended on his ability to infiltrate impenetrable forces. Though from what I have observed here, it looks like his skills of manipulation are not needed."

"I told you, I had orders," Luke said. "I didn't want to be one of your stupid initiates, but Dad thought hanging out with my big brother would be good for me. Us. I didn't know he was using me to get to you."

"Brother?" I sputtered, storing the rest away to process later. "He's your brother? Is there anything else you need to tell me? Are you actually married with two kids on the other side of the country?"

He flashed me a *not now* grimace. "I didn't think it was important."

"You knew the priests were after us. You knew *your brother* was chasing us in Ohio. I think that's relevant information."

"He's not my brother. Not anymore."

Right. "I thought you said your family had sworn to kill you on sight?"

"Yes. Loyal family. Like I said, he's not my brother. Crannik left the family years ago. Found a new master to follow. One that allowed his penchant for tacky hair."

I will not comment on Luke's disheveled bun.

I will not comment on Luke's disheveled bun.

I will not comment on Luke's disheveled bun.

"We are blood, brother. No amount of words changes that truth." Crannik tightened his grip on his weapon, his biceps bulging beneath his robe.

I'd never had siblings, but I didn't think this was normal.

They really did look like they were holding themselves back from killing each other.

I needed to increase the number of witnesses. "Tanzy, can you hunt down the others? We need to get everyone on the same page."

She'd sat up from her warm perch a while ago, her hair in a crazy halo. Her gaze flitted between Luke and the priests and I couldn't tell if the possibilities she was seeing were good or bad, but it certainly looked like they were giving her a headache.

She nodded, clutched her robe around her waist, and hurried into the depths of the dark house.

The priests went silent. Silent enough to hear the pop of the wood in the fireplace, the soft growl at the base of Luke's throat.

And I thought my family had problems.

I moved up a few steps, quietly putting myself between Luke and the three beings that could guide us to Persephone, who could maybe give us a clue of how to save her mother and Taco Bell without getting ourselves killed.

Because there was still that chance. That we could save Demeter and she'd still kill us.

Or one of Luke's other family members could kill us.

Or one of Phorkys's other monsters could kill us.

Or just about anything beyond the veil could kill us.

Tanzy led a sleepy Dave into the room, followed by a cuddly Cloud and Danica. They had a blanket wrapped around their shoulders and collapsed together on the couch. Half-asleep, they didn't notice the green-hair band standing at my back.

I wanted to tell them I'd seen Jared. I'd kissed him. He wasn't as lost as we thought.

But I didn't trust him.

I didn't trust myself.

And I didn't trust them to trust me.

Besides, the less they knew, the safer they were. I rubbed at the little twinge in my gut.

"Dan, Cloud"—*snap, snap*—"say hello to my little friends." I donned an Italian accent and Scarfaced my voice.

They blinked, waking fully up.

"Hey," Danica said. "Those are the creeps that projected their voice into our car. They tried to kill us!"

"Nope. I believe they were trying to kill Luke. Us, they just wanted to talk to."

"Luke?" Cloud narrowed his eyes, looked between Luke and Crannik. He settled his mischief master gaze on Crannik, thumbed at Luke. "What'd he do? And can I help punish him?"

"Cloud, Dan, Dave," I said, "meet Luke's big brother, Crannik. Crannik and the priests, Cloud, Dan, and Dave."

"You have got to be kidding me." Danica leapt to her feet, walked over to Luke, and punched him in the arm. "You lied to us. *Again?*"

Crannik chuckled. "I see all your companions are not so stupid, *Elpida.*"

"It's Korrina." It had taken forever to get Neri to stop calling me by my title. A title I never wanted. FYI.

I relayed the new plan to the others and showed them the cookies.

"You have six." Dave stepped forward. "There are six of us."

"We need two apiece. One to get us there, one to get back."

"But we had a plan. Without the cookies. We could spare one. I could go. I can help."

I let out a sigh. I knew all too well what it felt like to watch someone you love be trapped. To be helpless to do anything. I touched his arm. "You'll help Amity the most by being here. No matter what, Amity needs an anchor to get back. You're hers."

"Dave's right." Luke crossed his arms. "Why do we need to meet with Persephone? We have a plan. She's not in it. You and your dead queen are not needed, Crannik."

"Our queen has a key you must have in order to find the

goddess. The mother has sequestered herself deep inside, and it is impossible to get to her without the daughter's help."

I looked to Tanzy to see what her song thought about all that.

She swayed a little on her feet, hummed. "We are more likely to succeed with the daughter's help, but not all will come home." Her eyes met mine and drilled deep.

I swallowed. Hard. Turned to my human friends. "See. It's dangeroso. I need you three to stay here. Please." Dave didn't know me well enough to hear what I wasn't saying. But Cloud did. Danica did. I needed them to stay here. To stay safe. So I could focus on my mission without also feeling like had to watch them every second.

They nodded, held hands.

Dave huffed when he realized they weren't standing with him, looked to Luke for help.

Luke shook his head. "Sorry, man. Boss says no."

That's right. I do.

Crannik stepped forward. "*Elpida*, three tokens please."

He held out his hand, and I passed over three of Hestia's cookies. One of the other priests pulled a pomegranate out from his robe, broke it apart, and let the juice of the blood red seeds run over the cookies, staining them red, before Crannik handed them back. "Your tokens have been seasoned to take you to our queen. Place your token on your tongue but do not ingest until we arrive. Humans, please keep your friends in your meditations and you will bring them home."

With that, the three priests grabbed hold of Crannik's weapon, and Luke, Tanzy, and I placed Hestia's tokens on our tongues.

～

CHOCOLATE AND POMEGRANATE AND SOME AMAZING SPICE I HAD no words for cascaded over my tongue. I groaned my way into the dark void. Spirits were floating lanterns of blurry light, obstacles to be avoided at all costs. Mom's spirit was stuck somewhere in here, and I should look for her—she'd visited me, saved me before from this place—but all my efforts were focused on *not* swallowing the utter awesomeness on my salivating tongue.

If I'd gotten my love of sweets from her, she'd understand.

The Void blurred past like we were at warp nine, streams of light painted over a nothingness so black it hurt to look at for too long.

In times past, I'd been a spirit without a body floating through here. This was my first time experiencing the Void with skin and bones, and it was cold and hot, windy and still. It was a cacophony of opposites, devoid of sound, and my brain, with its almost purely human experiences, felt like it'd been twisted into a poorly shaped pretzel.

Which brought me back to food. And not swallowing Hestia's homemade goodness.

It took too long, and no time at all, for the edge of the veil to appear. A wall of shimmering light waved lazily at an indescribable distance, but its warmth curled out, singed my toes and fingertips, as if it was pointing out my body's deep freeze state.

My hands began to tingle, awakening. Golden light wrapped around me in a solar blanket, warmed me up from my marrow to the tips of my hair, and with an audible *pop*, I landed on gravel.

I blinked away the sun spots, pushed myself to a wobbly stand.

Manicured bushes, perfect and without a twig out of place, surrounded the most beautiful garden I'd ever seen.

And there, beneath a huge pomegranate tree, sitting on a throne of vines and flowers, was Persephone.

I choked on Hestia's cookie.

"Korrina. At last, we meet."

CHAPTER 30

A golden orange light shone from Persephone, the hue of sunlight when it hits dew-covered gardens for the first time. She was the first light of the day, and if I was still painting, I'd have spent a year trying to get that color just right.

All flowers turned their heads to face her. Even the trees bowed toward her, as if they were her court and she their queen. Or perhaps a vortex herself. Green vines twirled from her throne like veins, leading away into the depths of the garden, feeding it life.

Her lips and fingertips were stained with pomegranate juice, and the tree at her shoulder dripped seeds into a silver bowl at her side. It reminded me of the IV set up in Tula and Danica's hospital rooms last year, during their recovery time after Luke. A slow drip of medicine to keep them alive.

Other than that, she looked good. Much better than the deathly pale, gray-eyed, bone-crowned girl I'd seen in the Underworld.

Here, Persephone glowed.

"Wow, Seph. Life looks good on you." I felt like rushing her for a hug, but awkward for wanting that. She was an internet friend, and meeting in person was too weird, too strange, too close.

"Seph?" She looked confused for a moment, then a smirk crooked her seed-stained lips. "Molpe had the same name for me, but only after we'd known each other for some time. Though I suppose you and I have known each other for a while now." She picked up one of her seeds from the bowl and balanced it on the tip of her finger.

"How are you here?" I asked. "Without Hades? From what I saw in Tartarus, he doesn't like for you to be out of sight."

"Even prisons can be beautiful," Persephone sighed, lifting her chin. She stood and took a step forward, but no further. Thick green vines, a darker shade than the rest of the garden, wrapped around her wrists, her ankles, her waist. Flowers draped from the restraints, delicate pink and pure white, like precious jewels. "Hades's leash is long and comfortable and breathtaking, but it is still a leash."

She sat back on her throne, not elegant and graceful, but with the enthusiasm of a girl having to do what she's told.

I wanted nothing more than to snap those vines in two and let her have the biggest tantrum on the planet if that's what she chose to do. Because then she'd have a choice. But even me, with all my can-do attitude, knew there was no way Hades would allow her topside if those vines were easy to break.

"I will find a way to free you from him, Seph. I don't know how yet, but I will make him let you go."

A light breeze danced through the garden, chilled and wintery, and it sounded like a laugh. Self-deprecating and out-of-place. "Will you now? I think you'll find that more difficult than breaking a few chains. Even a garden requires sorrow."

Riiiiiight. Moving on. "Where are Tanzy and Luke?"

"Your friends? They are at the gates. I have not given my protectors permission to let them in."

"Gates?" I looked around, but the garden stretched as far as I could see.

"Gates guarded by creatures with swords of fire. Some have called this garden Eden." Her lips thinned.

Her tone made me hesitate, but the question had to be asked. "What have others called it?"

"A crime scene." Her gaze blazed into mine. "For this is where I was betrayed by your family, captured by Hades, and forgotten in the Underworld by all but my mother, who has lost herself in her grief. And now, the world suffers. Yours. Mine. Ours. For the sins of your family, we *all* suffer."

"But...Molpe...she grieved for you. Searched the world for you."

"And is the only one I count innocent. Therefore, *you* are the only Siren safe from my wrath. Do not trust the others, for betrayal is in their blood." Her eyes flashed, and the garden burst into red and orange flowers. The scents went at once from floral to cloying, and it became hard to breathe.

I'd once visited a museum exhibit about all the ways nature could kill you. Flowers are rarely innocent and seldom *just* beautiful. They had defenses, and Persephone was calling them to take up arms.

My knees hit the dirt, my lungs clenched in my chest, unable to get breath.

"You...like...me...remember?" I gasped, my fingers clawed in the ground, fingernails gathering garden.

A vine of purple flowers climbed up her throne, and she stroked them. "I'm afraid you'll find that I am a perfect match for Hades. Beautiful. Deadly. Silent in my approach."

I'd bet all of Cloud's money that those flowers were nightshades, and with the money I won, I'd bet all *that* on them being Persephone's favorites.

I heard, *felt* Persephone take a breath, and the flowers calmed, the air cleared. I sucked down air, looked down. The same vines growing on her throne were leaving my feet and hands, slithering away from my waist. My gut cramped for a second, made me nauseous. Hestia's cookie? Or Persephone's vine?

A shudder swept down my spine before I could suppress it.

Time to get this train wreck back on track. "We were told you knew how to find your mother. That's why we came." I stood, took a shallow breath, not trusting *at all* the air I was breathing.

Persephone didn't seem to notice how much she'd rattled me. Or if she did, she didn't care.

I'd been thinking of her this whole time as a girl, more human than goddess. Relating to her and putting myself in her shoes.

I'd forgotten that goddesses had no need for shoes.

She stopped petting her flowers, giving me her attention once again, and the purple nightshades draped themselves across her lap. "My mother's prison is wrapped in gilded power, but it is a prison just the same. Invisible to all but those who are imprisoned by the same ties. The same wounds. The same grief."

I didn't like the way her words made me feel. Sick and seen, all at once.

She twisted her hand at her wrist and held her palm open. A small, compact mirror appeared in her hand, glinting in the light. "Crafted from dew touched by first light, this will be your guide. And your key. But I warn you, Korrina, do not look too deeply lest your own leash become too tight." One of her vines grew a flower the size of a plate. She placed the mirror on top, and the vine brought it over and bowed low so that I could take Persephone's gift.

"Now go," she said. "Her restraints tighten, and soon, she'll be unable to resist."

Vines and flowers grew under my legs, fashioning themselves into a garden-sculpted Pegasus. Alive, but not, much like its mistress.

"When the time comes," Persephone called out, "remember me. Remember who I am and, through that, know how best to free me." Her gaze met mine once again, direct and focused, changing from shades of gold and green to shadows of blue and purple.

The enchanted shrub pushed off from the ground with its ivy wings and carried me into the empty blue sky.

I pushed the mirror deep into my pocket and tried to do the same with my unease.

Persephone made it sound as if she didn't want to be saved.

And that maybe Demeter's jailer wasn't someone I could fight.

Tanzy's words floated back to me, and I knew what I had to do.

Not all of us would make it back to the human world.

I just had to make sure that who she was talking about was me.

The sound of arguing reached me long before I saw the flaming swords.

My enchanted Pegasus landed just inside the gates, dug its hooves into the dirt, and turned back into a tangle of vines and flowers under my feet before disappearing into the ground.

Well then.

So much for us becoming magical friends and sliding down rainbows together.

There was a flash of light and a scream, followed by a growl and the sound of fist hitting flesh.

I plowed through the garden gates, barely noticing the two creatures and their imposing sabers. Because Luke and Crannik were rolling around in the dirt, fighting for reals. Crannik's fist wrapped around Luke's ear. Luke reared back, punched Crannik in the side. Crannik let loose, and the two fell apart for mere seconds, before falling back together like magnets.

"Have you two lost your minds?" I yelled. "Or does stupid just run in your blood?"

They stopped. Looked up. Luke held Crannik's hoodie strings, choking him with his own green tackiness. Crannik had Luke's ponytail wrapped in his fist, and looked ready to perform a Sweeney Todd.

"We. Are. In. Enemy. Territory," I continued. "And you are fighting like two boarding school boys with too much testosterone and no outlet!"

Luke loosened his grip. Didn't let go.

Crannik relaxed his hand. Didn't let go.

"Need I remind you that Luke's entire family has sworn an oath to kill him on sight? Phorkys just happens to live here and *really* wants to get his hands on me and my scepter. We have two Siren Hunters who can turn Tanzy and me into feathered monsters with a simple swipe of a blade. And that's not even counting all the other things that can kill us by looking at us." I wasn't yelling anymore. I was rabid. Livid. Mad.

Not in the angry sense of the word. The *Alice in Wonderland* Mad Hatter's Tea Party sense of the word.

Crazy-mad.

Crazy-angry.

Crazy-going-to-kill-two-idiots-if-they-screwed-up-this-mission.

Now that I had their full attention, I took in our surroundings. The stone-like creatures with the big wings, big claws, big talons, and even bigger fire swords. The wide-open meadows that rolled away from the gates like a royal carpet. The ancient forest that bordered the garden. The twinkling azure water in the far distance.

And Tanzy…

My stomach tightened, and a sharp pain shot through my gut.

"Where's Tanzy?"

Luke pushed Crannik away. Stood. Walked a step or two in either direction. "She was just here."

Crannik stood as well. Darted to the other side of the garden's entrance.

"Where. Is. Tanzy?" My song puffed out with each word, turned the world purple.

"I don't—" Luke's violet gaze went wild. "Korrina, I don't know." His voice hushed. His skin paled. "I heard her scream, but I thought she was screaming at me and Crannik. Not. Oh gods." He rubbed the back of his neck.

A dark urge shivered through my veins. "I will kill you. If one hair on her head is out of place, I will absolutely—"

Tanzy danced out of the forest with a halo of flowers on her dark hair. Following her was a creature.

A bird with a woman's head.

"Look who I found," Tanzy singsonged as this new Siren— not Molpe—snapped her half-crazed gaze in my direction.

CHAPTER 31

Luke and Crannik fell into a bow. Tanzy danced around like a hippie at Woodstock. I readied my song.

I'd only met Molpe in person. And *she* was intimidating.

The other three Sirens I'd seen from a far, safe distance as they'd tortured a creature they believed to be a spy. They were enough to give my nightmares nightmares.

This one pecked her way forward, more bird than woman. Persephone's words and my own suspicions rolled through my mind. Betrayal. They set her up.

They helped Hades.

She dragged her talons down a black rock.

"Who's your friend, Tanzy?" I tried to steady my voice, tried not to let the fear seep through. But fear's one of those emotions you can't always control. It creeps through your pores, rearranges the beats of your heart, shakes the structure of your bones.

And I was positive she could sense all of the above. Her lips tugged up on one side. Her eyes narrowed.

She had dark hair, like Tanzy's. Bright green eyes. Mottled brown and orange feathers.

"I am Aglaope. And you are the unnatural granddaughter of my sister Molpe." She cocked her head and sniffed the air. "You have met with Demeter's daughter. I smell on you the cold scent of death."

Tanzy beamed. "She's my great-great-whatever-grandmother."

The Maestro.

Aglaope let the rest of her mouth curve upwards in what was supposed to be a smile. She stretched out her wings, dipped her head. "I am the daughter of the Muse Melpomene, grand-daughter of the Titaness Mnemosyne, blood of Gaia, and hand-maiden to goddess Persephone." That last bit she said with a sneer.

Bitter much?

I nodded. Gestured for Tanzy to join me at a safe distance from her ancestor. "Korrina. The *Elpida*. Nice to meet you." Tanzy danced to my side. "What can we do for you, Aggie?"

She took a step back, snapped her wings closed. But hey, if she was looking for someone to bow down in awe, she'd come to the wrong great-niece.

"My sisters and I have come to offer you safe passage through the realm. You are the last of our blood, and we will not have it needlessly spilled."

Two more Sirens pushed their way through the trees. One with feathers as black as the dark moon. The other a jeweled, peacock green and blue.

"Careful, *Elpida*," a voice said quietly at my shoulder.

I jumped. Screamed.

Molpe had crept up behind me at some point, and her wing brushed against my shoulder.

It wasn't lost on me that Aggie and Company had come from a different direction than Molpe.

"Sister," Aggie hissed. "Nice of you to join us."

"Next time, I'll be on the lookout for your invitation."

Molpe's tone was a calm, steady don't-mess-with-me. "Thankfully, Neri was able to pass along the message."

Aggie's nostrils flared.

Molpe cocked her head. "Now I believe you are in violation of your contract to stay far from this garden. Since our granddaughters and their friends have limited time, I suggest we be off."

The three Sirens ruffled their feathers, seeming irritated that Molpe had taken charge.

"Wait, how do you know what we're doing?" I looked between the three of them.

"Neri keeps us informed," Molpe said. "Now, Korrina, do you know the way?" She edged closer, as if preparing to protect me. Her body hummed, and her white feathers vibrated against my skin.

"I do." I restrained myself from pulling out the mirror. If Molpe was being this cautious around her sisters, I'd do the same.

"Good. Aglaope and I will carry Tanzy and yourself. Your friends—"

Crannik stepped forward. "Forgive me, daughter of air, but we will not be going. Our duty here is complete."

Luke turned his face to the sky. "The gods do answer prayers."

I ignored him. "We could use the backup, Crannik. We are saving *your* goddess, you know."

Crannik, to his credit, looked like he wanted to say yes. "We have been given new orders. The equinox approaches, and we must be ready should you fail."

"Thanks for the vote of confidence," I muttered.

Crannik bowed his head, and his two priest pals placed their hands on his staff. The air glowed green around them. Moss grew at their feet. And then they were swallowed by the ground.

"We must go," Molpe said.

Tanzy pulled herself onto Aggie's back and got comfortable between her massive wings.

"I will carry the young man," the peacock Siren said, a hushed eagerness to her voice.

"Thank you, Thelxiepeia," Molpe said. "Make sure he arrives in one piece."

Thelxiepeia—Amity's ancestor and the original Songwriter—flashed Luke a not-so-trustworthy grin.

That meant the last Siren was Peisinoe. The one who had most enjoyed torture. The mistress of the beat. Out of all of them, I trusted her the least.

I pushed off my toes and scrambled onto Molpe's back. A sharp pain tore through my belly, and I doubled over.

"Korrina, are you all right?" Molpe checked over her shoulder.

I breathed through my nose, taking one shallow swallow of air at a time until the pain lessened. "Yeah. Must be something I ate." Like goddess cookies.

Molpe crinkled her brow, but nodded and turned her focus back to her sisters.

Once Luke had secured himself on Amity's grandmother, Molpe lifted her wings, thrust them down, and with a puff of dust and dirt, we rose into the air.

MOLPE FORCED THE OTHER THREE SIRENS TO GO AHEAD OF US. We led from behind, with Molpe chirping out directions every once in a while.

I hadn't pulled out the mirror, and wouldn't until I had to. For the moment, I drank in the mythical world. Impossible colors, hues and palettes I could never replicate, taunted me from below. The air rushed around my arms and neck, cold and frigid, but Molpe's thick down feathers kept me warm.

We were quiet for a while, let the sunlight beat down upon our heads, let the wind make our conversation.

Molpe broke the silence. "I wouldn't have hurt you."

It took me a few seconds to connect what she was talking about. The first time I'd seen her had been one of my first dreamwalking experiences. With Luke. We'd witnessed Molpe's transformation, the first to be hit with Demeter's curse, and then she'd seen us. Me.

"I know." Now, I knew. But back then? I'd thought I was going to be bird food.

Her muscles relaxed the tiniest bit underneath my legs, then went tight again. Tighter than before. "Neri asked me to deliver a message."

"That sounds ominous." I tried to lighten the mood, but I forgot that mythical beings rarely have a sense of humor.

"Yes, it is. Your father has failed to find your mother. The Council knows of his betrayal, and he is to be tried at the equinox, in two days' time." She said it like she was reading the daily headlines. Like she had no skin in the game. No imagination or empathy in her air-filled bird bones.

I went still. My elbows locked. "What do you mean *tried*? As in trial? Judge? Jury?"

"And conviction. A Council trial is an honor given to Guardians, but it is simply a chance for him to beg the Council's forgiveness. His verdict has already been declared—guilty."

Guilty. The word resonated through my bones, filled them with lead. My song tuned to a low pitch. *Ania* pounded at my mind's door.

Go away. He's not dead, yet.

"What does that mean? If the Council forgives him, will they let him go?"

"No," she said, so quietly I almost missed it. "If he is forgiven, he will be granted entrance to the Elysian Fields after life, as would any other Guardian who performed his duties to the best of his ability."

My mouth went dry, my song swirled around my stomach, honey burned my throat. "And if he isn't forgiven?"

We hit some turbulent air, and Molpe went silent as she navigated the stormy atmosphere. I held tight. Waited.

"You've heard of the River Lethe?" Molpe finally said.

"The River of Forgetting," I whispered.

Molpe nodded, her long red curls tangling in the air.

"He will be forced into the River Lethe, his memories will be wiped, and his soul will be restrained in the caves of Oblivion."

Plans swirled in my mind, escape routes designed to fit my dad's exact shape, a reflex reaction to bad news. "Where is the trial?" It wasn't a question. My song sparked around the words, solidifying them into a command.

But of course, Molpe was immune. "You cannot reach it, *Elpida*. It happens on another plane of existence, determined by the Fates."

"So what? You're saying we have no chance of saving him?" My hands clenched her feathers.

"I'm saying that it's complicated. And that you have other priorities."

Like hell I had other priorities.

I hadn't told him I loved him. I hadn't told him goodbye.

My song went dark, *Ania* slipped in, and I felt her dark voice directing my thoughts, stretching her fingers toward the center of my power.

Our power.

The world went void-black. There was screaming. There was nothing.

CHAPTER 32

I floated in white nothingness. Soft and warm and safe. Time scurried away like a little mouse, and I was the well-fed, lazy cat who had no need to give chase. Here, I could stay. Not deal with any of that…

My mind went blank.

The other place had too many colors. Too much to hurt my eyes. My heart hurt there.

Here, I didn't feel. I couldn't remember what it was like to feel pain. Didn't want to feel pain. I'd carried its heavy burden, had grown calluses on the shoulders of my heart from its friction. None of that was here.

Elpida

A distant voice yelled, but that was the other place. I didn't have to listen.

A soft song entered my hazy nothing, drowning out the Other, and I fell into its soothing rhythm, its hypnotic beat.

The nothing shook.

Korrina, you have to fight her.

A new voice. I liked this voice. It was warm and safe too, but not soft.

I liked that it wasn't soft.

Korrina, fight your shadow self. Fight Ania.

Ania. Sorrow. The darker side of my split and damaged soul.

The nothing grew jagged edges. Razor-sharp corners that turned into bars. Bars with a roof. A floor.

A cage.

I was in a cage.

I tested the bars. They zapped me.

On the other side of the bars, dark colors swirled. In them, pain flowed and twisted with sorrow. Grief tied them all together, and it was a beautiful kind of dance that flowed around my safe spot like a river.

My cage.

It wasn't so bad. I mean, sure, a couch and Netflix would be nice, but this. This was easier. I could stay here.

Warmth pressed into my distant body, strong arms wrapped around my ribs, soft breath tickled the lobe of my ear.

Fight her. You're stronger than her. You deserve more than a caged life.

How did that voice know?

I *really* liked that voice.

I tested the bars again. They zapped me again.

But this time, it pissed me off.

No one puts Korrina in a pretend-nothing-that's-really-a-cage and then zaps her.

This was my body. My life.

Those were my ribs and my ears that wanted more of the squeezing and touching from the voice.

That was *my* Other. *My* pain.

I stood. Grabbed hold of the bars. Held on through the pain.

And ripped it all apart.

∼

THE WORLD EXPLODED INTO COLOR. NOT NORMAL COLOR. NOT the extreme hues of the mythical world. But reddish-brown. And dark, almost black, purple.

"You're back." His voice was rough, as if he'd been screaming, and he held me tight, brushed the hair away from my forehead with one hand.

With the other, he held a knife to my throat.

"So are you," I managed, each word scraping my skin against Jared's blade. "Mind removing the sharp cursed object from my neck?"

Because if that blade drew blood, I'd become Molpe's twin.

Where was Molpe?

"I cannot. You've let *Ania* out, and she has caused destruction." Jared broke eye contact and looked around us.

I looked with him.

Beyond the purple shadow of my power, ancient trees laid out from us in a sunburst pattern, ripped from the earth by the roots. It looked like an explosion had happened. And Jared and I sat in the middle of the blast site.

"I did this?" My ears drummed, everything went echo-y.

"*Ania* did this. Look at me, Korrina." His voice lowered, commanded, demanded, and it had this nice vibrato that settled into my bones. But he kept that knife pressed tight against my skin. "You can control her, and you must. You remember what the Fates foretold, yes?"

That *Ania* would destroy the world. Yeah, kinda hard to forget.

I nodded.

"*Ania* is a Siren of old. Acting purely out of her own desires and pain with no regard for anyone else. There is no humanity inside of her. She belongs totally and completely to this world. Do you understand what I am saying?"

"Yeah. *Ania* bad. Korrina good. Got it." But they were both me. And no one seemed to grasp that.

Jared nodded. "Same here. Siren Hunter bad. Jared good. When I let the Siren Hunter out, it is next to impossible to drag him back inside." The blade wiggled at my throat, Jared's eyes flashed red. "And *Ania* brings him out in full force." His voice deepened to a growl, and the hands gripping me stopped holding. Started restraining. Morphed into a predatory grasp.

I went still. Tried not to breathe. My song hummed in my throat, the air around us brightened as my song gave it new power.

"I don't want to hurt you." My power sparked on my breath, and Jared dodged the sparks.

"I don't think I can stop." His eyes narrowed. The blade pressed tighter against my skin.

Fight, flight, or freeze. Couldn't fly. Freeze wasn't working.

I tensed my stomach and another slice of pain ripped through my belly. *Not now...* I pushed the pain to a back corner of my mind, thrust my head into Jared's chin, and knocked his blade off-balance. I grabbed Jared around the neck, rocked back, used his momentum to launch us forward.

He landed on his back, gasped for air.

I scrambled to my feet. Kicked the blade away from his hands.

He recovered quickly. Launched himself up and into a crouch. "There'll be a time, *Elpida*, when I cannot, nay, will not, restrain myself. You let me get too close." Green fire sparked to life in his palm. "You will look lovely with wings." He blew on the flames, and they leapt out of his hands and cometed at me.

I took a page out of my mother's book and threw my song up like a shield. The fire blazed around me, held back by nothing other than the force of my song, a purple light that fought against the fire, fought to live. I pressed my hands in front of me, pushing my power forward, but Jared's fire ate away at my light, slowly, steadily, acid burning through metal.

Let me help.

Ania's dark voice whispered in my ear.

The pain makes you strong. Makes us strong.

I shut her down, splicing my power between pushing against Jared, pushing against *Ania*, two tectonic plates sliding against me, crushing. Winning.

Something barreled out of my periphery into Jared. A blur of long hair whirled around Jared, and two manly grunts popped into the air. Jared's fire disappeared.

Thanks to Luke.

They rolled around on the ground, punching wherever there was an opening. Jared wrapped Luke's long hair in his fist and pulled his neck back, exposing his throat. The blade lifted. The point pressed into Luke's skin.

My song stammered. I rushed forward. "Let him go, Jared." Words of power enforced my command.

Jared's mouth strained into a grimace, and he dropped Luke, backed away. "Thank not your Siren witch, but instead the courtesy you've granted to me in the past. My debt to you is repaid." He slashed the air, opening a dark wound in the world, stepped into it, and disappeared.

My song's power faded. I brushed the dirt off my backside. "What debt did he owe you?"

"Covered for him in the Grotto. Made sure Colin didn't know where he'd gone."

I narrowed my eyes. "I thought you were in a prison cell."

Luke shrugged. "They let me out from time to time. Some of the guards were old friends."

Again, Luke hadn't told the entire story. The horror he'd described of the Grotto sounded like someone else's story. Not his.

I pushed it aside. Right now, we had other issues. "What happened here? Where are Tanzy and the Sirens?"

Luke crinkled his brow. "*You* happened here, Korrina. You let your power explode out of you and destroy part of an ancient forest. You did this."

My stomach twisted. Not me. But *Ania*.

"Tanzy and Aggie flew off," he said. "My Siren dumped me and flew after them. Molpe crashed into the forest. What happened? Did Molpe get fresh with you?" His tone teased, but he was serious. Searching. Prying me apart for the truth.

I shook my head. My mouth went dry. "*Ania. Ania* took over." And the truth hit me. Finally. Why Danica said I'd wrecked the car, why things seemed out of place, why it seemed as if I hadn't been catatonic during my visions...but active. "She's been taking over."

CHAPTER 33

We found Molpe plucking broken branches out of her wings. She glared at us, growled, and went back to fluffing her feathers.

She looked ruffled. But not hurt. My chest relaxed a smidge, and for the first time since *Ania* had taken control, I realized how tense I was holding myself. I took a few deep breaths, unwrapping tension from around my ribs with each exhale.

"Hey, Molps. What's up?"

She growled again—didn't know birds could growl—and muttered something under her breath. Power sparked around her, little firecrackers of violet and lilac.

"It wasn't her, Molpe." Luke stuck his arm out, soccer-mom protecting me from my grandmother.

"I know that, Betrayer. She does not need you to rise to her defense. What I want to know is how, Korrina, you have not yet learned to control your shadow self?" She rose to her full height, shivered, and fluffed out her feathers to twice her normal size.

"I didn't know she was a she until now," I retorted, folding my arms across my chest, defending myself against what I should've known, should've recognized. Should've been able to stop. I huffed. "And if you'd known, maybe you could've shared that knowledge before my shadow self took over."

I glared. She glared. Luke looked worried.

Finally, Molpe let go a breath, was the first to break eye contact.

Ha. I win.

"Shadow selves do not typically manifest as yours has done," Molpe said. "They have a voice, yes, but it is usually only a voice that has influence. Not power. Your shadow self seems more sentient, somehow…" She studied me like I was her next meal.

"Perhaps because she is a dyad," Luke said in his professor voice. Dude even rubbed his chin.

Molpe hummed her agreement.

I hated being analyzed. "Good. Glad you guys have a working theory. When you know more let me know. For now, I know what to look for with *Ania*. I can stop her from taking over again." My chin jutted into the air, and I dared anyone to doubt me.

Molpe and Luke exchanged a look. They doubted me. And were probably going to keep a close watch on me.

Pretty much my plan as well.

Molpe let out a shrill call and a few minutes later, her sisters swooped into view. Thelxiepeia landed so that Luke could climb aboard. Tanzy, Aggie, and Peisinoe stayed aloft.

"Are you okay?" Tanzy called down to me.

"Yup. Just a minor split-personality issue. Let's fly, chicks."

"So irreverent," Molpe reprimanded. "You have much to learn about your ancestry, *Elpida*." But she knelt so I could climb on her back easier.

"And you have much to learn about me." Like how my so-called irreverence was sometimes the only thing keeping me from buckling under. I tightened my knees around her body, tucked my feet up under her wings, and we leapt into the air with a giant swoosh.

The air was quiet. Molpe's body hummed beneath mine. Distantly, the voices of Tanzy and Aggie floated to us, like voices crossing calm waters.

But these waters, this space, was anything but calm. The quiet was a lie. It was weighted, heavy. Like an invisible storm cloud about to break loose.

Worry wormed around my brain. Dad was on trial. And it sounded like he was getting the death penalty.

Plus, Jared.

I didn't tell Molpe about Jared. Wasn't going to.

But neither had Luke.

I wasn't quite sure why, but I knew this moment of getting-away-with-it wasn't going to last long.

I glared after the tail feathers of Molpe's sisters, searching for anything to stop more worry wormholes from burrowing into my brain matter. "Why did Hestia say the curse has taken your mind? You seem okay. More okay than those psychos."

She didn't show surprise at my mention of Hestia. "Demeter's curse changes us. Not just our bodies, but also our minds. Our needs. Our desires. And I am not—I have not been—always pure in my motives and actions. Sometimes, nature takes over nurture, no matter how hard I try to resist."

"Hey, I get like that about once a month too. No biggie."

"It is a—biggie. Never trust a Siren, *Elpida*. We are unpredictable on our best days." She banked steeply to the right, as if needing to emphasize her point, and I grabbed on tight to avoid plummeting to my death.

When I got done screaming, I leaned in. "How about a warning next time?"

"You want a warning, after what you allowed *Ania* to pull back there?" Molpe fired off over her shoulder.

I grunted. "Touché."

She huffed, and a little of the tightness flowed out of her body. "If you want to survive the task ahead of you, you must be prepared." The harshness had left her voice. "Life does not give warnings. Only death does that, and only if you know what you are looking for."

Man, she was a cheery travel companion.

She chirruped and swooped downward in slow, lazy circles. "We'll camp here for tonight. Too many creatures awaken at sundown, and you are too tempting a treat."

She didn't say it, but she was also tired. Her breath had grown more labored the further we'd flown, and I was positive whatever *Ania* had done back there had made her more than a little sore.

The trees below grew larger as we got closer to the ground. We followed the other Sirens through a small gap in the cypress trees.

Molpe coasted along the top of a large ruin and landed with a soft bump. Crumbles of stone littered the ground. Weeds poked through what had once been a floor, inlaid with intricate tiles that were now chipped and filled with dirt. The surrounding forest was quiet. No birds, no insects, no frogs. Just the quiet secrets the trees whispered.

"What is this place?" I asked, funeral-quiet. Something about it was tragic, and familiar, and painful.

Molpe took in a deep breath, looked all around, pausing on Tanzy, who was in a deep conversation with Aggie, and then on Luke, who looked as if he were about to be sick.

He leaned against a thick, wooden door that had been wedged between two large boulders and was half-rotted. "Mankind belongs on the ground."

"Molpe?" I reached out and touched her wing.

She shuddered under my fingertips. "Home. Or it was a very long time ago." She pressed her lips together, tossed her red curls over one feathered shoulder. "We'll be safe here. Even in ruins, our fellow mythicals leave the house of the Muse of Tragedy alone."

I nodded.

"My sisters and I will take first watch. Get some rest." And with that, the four Sirens took off and hid themselves deep in the trees.

An hour later, Tanzy, Luke, and I sat around a small campfire, roasting kebabs of mushrooms and some sort of root vegetable Luke swore was safe to eat. Since Tanzy didn't see us dying anytime soon, I trusted his swear.

I caught them up on my meeting with Persephone and my suspicions of the other Sirens.

"So Persephone claims the Sirens betrayed her?" Luke drummed his fingers against his chin. "Interesting."

"If they did so," Tanzy said. "Aglaope must have seen that it was the best path forward." Her normally calm and lucid voice contained steel.

"The best path for who?" I met her gaze until she looked away.

My heart sank. I wish she hadn't looked away. I wish she'd stood her ground. I wish I could forget Persephone and Molpe's words.

Never trust a Siren.

But I couldn't forget their words.

I shouldn't.

Not when I didn't really know Tanzy...or her intentions.

The stakes were too high and too many lives I loved were at risk.

Speaking of high stakes...

I picked at my food. Not my typical fare, but it was probably healthy to have a break from refried every once in a while. "Wanna tell me what you and Crannik were fighting about?"

Luke sighed. I was not going to like whatever came next. "You."

I let my kebab stick go limp in my hands. "Me? Why?"

"Said I shouldn't trust you. Said you were fornicating with

the enemy. I told him that was crazy, that you'd never—" He stopped, violet eyes going dark as he studied my face. "Korrina. What did you do?"

"I-I saw Jared. We...kissed." My stomach churned with nowhere to go.

Tanzy and Luke shrank from me, as if I were a disease. As if bad decisions were contagious.

"Here? Before I found you?" Shock rewrote his features, rearranged them into something just short of familiar.

I cleared my throat, held myself still. "No. Back at Tanzy's."

Tanzy shuddered, and some emotion passed over her eyes. "I told you to be careful of who you love. Your broken heart is no small matter, *Elpida*."

"Luke said something went wrong with his transformation to Phorkys's Siren Hunter. I've seen it too, and he's changing." I looked between the two of them, hoping they couldn't hear my desperation. Knowing they could. "He can be saved. I can save him."

Luke scoffed.

"You've let him in," Tanzy whispered. "You've made us all vulnerable. Cloud, Danica, Dave. They won't know he's coming."

"He's not going to hurt them." I jumped to my feet. "Somewhere inside him is the Jared we all know. The one who would sacrifice himself to save his friends at any given moment. *That* Jared is the one we trust. He'll hold his Siren Hunter self in check."

Luke looked down at his hands, at his split-knuckles, at his fresh wounds. "I know what I said about Jared's transformation, but I also know Siren Hunters. It could be a trick."

My heart went still. "I'd know if Jared was tricking me. I. Know. Him." My hands were fists. My song was a boulder lodged in my throat.

"No, Korrina." Luke looked up at me. "You *knew* him. You don't know him. Not anymore."

I shook my head, squeezed my eyes shut. My throat hurt from where Jared had held me too tight, pressed a cursed blade against my skin. "I need some air." I tossed my kebab into the fire and walked away. The angry glow of my song led me into the forest, but it was the echo of Luke's words that nipped at my heels.

CHAPTER 34

I kicked my feet against the edge of the cliff I'd almost walked off, shaking loose rocks and dirt down in little avalanches.

Luke was wrong. Tanzy was wrong. And when Cloud and Danica found out, they'd be wrong, too.

It wasn't a trick.

Jared's touch flooded my memories, his kiss fogged up my world, made it hard to see.

My song scratched up and down my spine. I sat straight. Went still. Listened.

My song was my sixth, seventh, and eighth sense. I'd learned to trust its warnings.

Something was here with me.

The forest was quiet. Even the frogs had stopped their late-night song.

I couldn't turn around, not without alerting whatever was here with me. And until I could get eyes or ears on it, I didn't want to scare it away.

I wanted to fight.

I slowly pulled Persephone's compact mirror out of my pocket, stretched my arm out, and pretended to fluff my hair.

Dark veins covered my reflection. Silver eyes stared through mine.

Persephone had said this mirror would be my guide to Demeter but that her prison was invisible. Invisible to everyone except those who also grieved.

Sadness curled at my reflection's lips, and in the mirror, my reflected image jerked her chin over her shoulder.

I followed her direction through the mirror, and there, almost out of sight, was the creature.

Instinct took over before training could kick in, and I froze.

Long teeth curved out of the creature's mouth and glinted under the starlight. The little beastie scurried from shadow to shadow, not a monster but an overgrown rat, able to blend almost entirely into the darkness.

I took a breath, pushed past my fear, and snapped the mirror closed. Readied for a fight.

My song tingled at the back of my throat, a bitterness hidden among the honey. A bitterness I was beginning to crave. I took a deep breath, tightened my abs, pushed off my hands into a back handspring. My feet hit the ground, my ankles wobbled. I kept my balance, and…

There was nothing here. No creature. Nothing.

I went still. Looked for those teeth, hidden among the shadows. I could feel it, in the danger-alert nerve in the center of my spine. A presence that did not belong. A nasty in the darkness.

If it liked darkness, I'd give it light.

I pulled my song in, compacted it tight inside my chest, tensed all my muscles, and let it fly free.

The cliff side exploded into a theme-park-worthy light show. Shadows tightened behind the trees, went rigid, straight, skinny. Insects took flight. Birds startled into the sky. Bats dipped and rolled away from my blinding power.

And still, noth—

Pain slid into my stomach. My voice broke on a high-pitched scream.

My belly was on fire. Brilliant, bright, bonfire pain. Pain that was white and hot and purple and cold and blue and unforgettable and beyond understanding. I looked down, and black blood seeped out of my skin, wetted my shirt, soaked my jeans. I grabbed a fistful of my shirt, yanked it up, away from my belly, but there was no wound, just seeping, inky blood that burned and gnawed, and with each new gnaw, a new gush of pain.

I hadn't stopped screaming. My throat was hoarse, my song was weak. This was the shadow creature's attack.

It became impossible to breathe.

A creature I couldn't see was killing me.

I fumbled for the mirror as I fell to the ground, thumbed it open, and there, hanging onto my gut by his long teeth, was a rat.

It met my gaze, its eyes full of intelligence, and it slashed at my skin again with its razor teeth and ripped away something long and squirmy.

A vine. Or a vein. A long cord that spewed black gunk. The same gunk that covered my clothes.

The shadow rat fell to the ground, wrestling the…*thing*…that had been attached to me, subdued it, and dragged it toward the forest. And with it went the pain that had been nagging my insides since I'd met Persephone in the garden.

Since her vines had wrapped around my waist.

My free arm covered my stomach, but I watched in the mirror as the rat scurried back into the shadows, trailing the long, snake-like cord behind its three-toed paws.

Peisinoe stepped out of the trees, hummed a deep, low tone, and my attacker scurried to her, hid behind her talons.

I dropped the mirror back into my pocket.

"You." My voice was raw, a few octaves lower than normal.

"Very few gifts come without a price, *Elpida*." Her dark eyes glinted in the moonlight, and she turned away and melted back into the forest.

"What gift?" I yelled after her, but no response came.

What was that? Some sort of Siren hazing? And gift? Was she talking about Persephone's mirror, Hestia's cookies, or her rat?

"Korrina?" Luke and Tanzy called out, came crashing through the forest.

"We heard you scream." Tanzy doubled over, resting her hands on her knees.

Luke matched her gasp for gasp. His wounds may have been healed, but his body would be recovering from the Grotto for a long time. And it was things like this that made me want to take him at his word.

"I'm fine, just—" I moved my arm away from my shirt, and it was clean. My heart skipped.

It'd been soaked. Black. I hadn't imagined it all. But…

It was clean.

"I'm fine," I finished.

They were already pissed at me because of the Jared thing. Already didn't trust me because of the *Ania* thing.

Pile on an invisible vein that was pumping black blood into my body and got ripped away by an invisible rat, and I'm pretty sure they'd throw me in the asylum-thing.

"Then why were you screaming?" Luke pried.

The man was a human crowbar.

"Bat. Bats. Big bats. C'mon, it's probably time for us to take second watch." Without waiting for them to respond or to see their reaction out of the corner of my eye, I headed back toward the birthplace of the Sirens, the ruins of my ancestral home, and the remains of a dying campfire that no longer gave enough warmth.

CHAPTER 35

The sun rose the next morning, pink and too bright. The Sirens gathered around our little campfire, pointing out their old rooms in the rubble and reminiscing about better days.

It made them seem almost human.

A dangerous thought.

I stretched out my legs, felt the compact mirror in my pocket. I wasn't quite sure how it was going to lead us to Demeter, but it was time. The autumn equinox was approaching in less than forty-eight hours, and with it, Demeter as we knew her would cease to exist. She was already a handful. I didn't want to see her in full-blown retribution goddess style.

And in forty-eight hours, Dad would be sentenced to death, a done deal, as Molpe had emphasized, with only his afterlife at stake.

No.

Just.

No.

"Let's hit the skies, people," I said, loudly, drowning out the squeak of my mental anxiety wheel. Somehow, I'd save Demeter, save Amity, and save Dad. Didn't know how, but I was a proven badass. I could do this. One step at a time. I drew in an uncertain breath, exhaled faux confidence, and beamed a sunny smile. "Molpe and I are leading today."

First step, figure out how to use this magic mirror.

But— "Where's Luke?" I looked around. Two semi-humans. Four birdy-Sirens. No Luke.

I should have known he'd wandered off. My side had felt particularly comfortable without the thorn named Luke shoved in it this morning.

Tanzy and the Sirens exchanged wary looks.

"Where's Luke?" I asked again, letting my voice drop, letting my anxiety squeak.

Tanzy took a couple of steps forward. "We talked. Decided it was best for him to go back through the veil and protect your friends."

I clenched my hands, dug my nails into my palms. "I told you that there was nothing to worry about. Jared would not—"

"There was an attack," Molpe said. "The humans are fine. Safe. But Phorkys reached them and broke through the barrier guarding the house last night."

"Reached them? How? They're in the middle of the desert." I denied, denied, denied. Because Jared wouldn't. He couldn't.

"*Elpida,* surely you know there is no escape from water." Peisinoe laughed, a cruel and dark sound. "It is the blood that runs through Gaia's domain, and like the innumerable veins residing under your fragile skin, it takes but a simple cut to make it bleed."

Leave it to Peisinoe to compare blood to water.

I had no comeback. No defense.

Cloud, Danica, Dave. They'd been attacked. A few hours after Jared and I—

Siren Hunter. He was a Siren Hunter. He'd warned me.

Ania wiggled at the back of my mind. I gritted my teeth, tensed my body. I'd make it up to them. If they let me.

"They're okay?" I pushed out the words out despite the desert-dryness of my mouth.

Molpe nodded. "Someone named Sully helped hold off the attack. They're a little shaken but glad that Luke is on his way."

Glad that Luke was on his way? They were more than a little shaken.

Stupidity was a force rising at the back of my throat. I pressed my lips together to hold it in, to remain somewhat composed.

They all saw through me. I lifted my chin, straightened my shoulders. "We have a goddess to rescue. Let's get moving."

We broke camp, climbed aboard our feathered and finicky transportation, and took off.

Molpe climbed above the clouds. Above us, the sky was a blue-black. Ahead, the way was clear. Behind us, three feathered beasts I didn't trust to watch my back. Especially after last night.

"How much do you trust Peisinoe?" I was treading on the bonds of sisterhood, but Molpe seemed to have her eyes open where her sisters were concerned.

"Not the slightest. Why do you ask?" she said, all nonchalant.

Her answer surprised me. Not the words themselves—I pretty. Much figured that—but the way she'd said them. No hint of regret, no tint of sadness. Removed. Distant.

But when you had tens of thousands of years invested in a relationship, maybe you could afford to be pragmatic.

"She followed me into the woods last night," I said. "Sent some sort of shadow rat after me."

Molpe twitched. "And did the rat find anything to sharpen its teeth on?"

Not the response I was expecting, but okaaaay. "Uh, yeah. My tummy."

Molpe's head sagged. "I was afraid of that. Pull out your mirror, Korrina."

"You're not in the least bit concerned that Peisinoe sent her pet after me?"

"Pull out your mirror."

I pulled out my mirror.

The silver casing flashed under the unbroken sunlight. I flipped open the cover, and the reflected world went dark, just like last night.

"Look closely, but not too deeply."

I looked closer. Focused. Waited. And then, suddenly, my eyes seemed to adjust, and I saw it.

What I'd thought was a solid shading of darkness was a thick web of cords. Cords like the one that had been gnawed off my stomach. I moved the mirror around, gazing into the reflected sky, the reflected air, our reflected bodies. The cords covered everything, went through everything, everyone.

Some were clear, but most were variated shades of gray. And black. Lots of black.

"The threads of fate tie us all together," Molpe said, "but if a being has chosen a dark path, those threads reflect that choice."

My heart dum, dum, dummed. "Threads. Like strings. Like puppeteer strings?"

"Exactly like puppeteer strings."

"So the Fates are the puppeteer?" I couldn't hide the excitement from my voice. All along, it was stupid fate. I should have know—

"No. The Fates simply spin the possibilities. They do not pull on the strings."

"Who does?"

Molpe was quiet for a while. "At some point in our lives, we all allow someone else to control our strings. The permission we give can either rise us up or destroy us, but it is not until we take the threads of fate in our own hands that we are truly free. For Demeter, her puppeteer has nothing but intentions of destruction."

I chewed on my lip, tightened my grip on her feathers. "And mine?"

Again, Molpe went quiet. "I do not yet know."

"Thanks for the vote of confidence," I muttered. "How do we use this to find Demeter?"

Before she could answer, the reflection shifted. I looked closer, deeper, and the darkest threads shone silver around their edges, an almost hypnotic gleam. They parted like waves around fallen rock and revealed one thread, so black it glistened as if it were wet. Thicker than the rest, pulled taut.

"That way," I whispered and directed Molpe with my knees, somehow knowing we'd find Demeter on the other end.

DEMETER'S THREAD GREW THICKER THE FURTHER WE SOARED. More joined the one we'd been following, and soon they braided together into a thick, not-even-a-shadow-rat-could-chomp-it rope. I'd taken to sitting backwards on Molpe, using the mirror to look forward and find our path. My hair was an impossible tangle in front of my face, and the back of my neck had gone cold. I wanted a scarf. And a scrunchie.

Without warning, the threads plunged beneath the clouds. I turned around on her back. Faced forward and gripped on.

"Molpe, here." I tightened my knees and she spiraled down, the rest of our posse following us.

We plummeted through the pink and gray clouds and came face to face with a mirrored lake. Red rocks towered all around the water, and it looked exactly like the world Tanzy had shown me.

I looked backwards, caught her gaze. Her mouth thinned into a serious line, and she nodded.

This was the place.

Demeter was near.

I searched the mirror again, and what should have been a too bright world darkened, became thick and sticky. Gray wind swirled around an impossible number of fate's threads, all tangled up and pouring into the lake. And all around were jagged red spires of rock that looked like they could cut the sky. No good spot to land.

I unhooked my feet from Molpe's wings, crouched on her back.

Tanzy looked at me like I was crazy, then she slouched. Defeated. On board. Or rather…off board.

"Thanks for the ride, Molp." Before I could think about how bad an idea this was, I leapt off her tail feathers. Her scream followed me down.

When I was skydiving with Amity, the fall had seemed to take forever. So long that my brain was tricked for a moment into thinking I was flying.

This was not that.

The water rushed up to meet my face, faster, sooner than it should have. I turned over at the last second and watched, helpless, as Tanzy and Aglaope slammed into Molpe's side. I screamed. Molpe crashed. Plowed into the rocks, rolled, and lay still.

The water opened, just like it had in Tanzy's vision, and swallowed me up. The world snapped into a gray, underwater light. My fall slowed, slowed, until I was floating like a leaf, spiraling down.

Down, down deep into the goddess's lair.

CHAPTER 36

Molpe.

Her scream, the echo of her silence, surrounded the writhing darkness. She was immortal. She'd be okay.

But a sharp pain in my gut said otherwise. The ability to live forever did not mean nothing could kill you. Tanzy had attacked her. She wasn't trying to stop Aglaope. She'd leaned in, clutched tight, and smiled.

Had she been against us from the start? Or had Aglaope triggered something in her? Something that explained that *off*ness I always felt around Tanzy.

I gripped the ground, cold, clammy, hard, gravel at my fingertips, an impossible place to climb out of. There was no escape down here. Not without someone tossing down a Rapunzel-length rope.

The air pushed against me, and no matter how hard I pushed back, the pressure grew until my ribs cracked, until I could barely breathe. I stood, but my spine curled over, my shoulders drooped.

Tanzy and the Sirens were off on their own agenda. Molpe was down for the count. Luke had left. Because I'd chosen Jared.

A Siren Hunter. Over all of them.

And then he'd left me too.

Or maybe he'd never been. Just another of my illusions, like that I knew what I was doing. That I was in control.

I felt my way forward. The ground rocky, sharp, unforgiving. The darkness thick, tangible.

But not silent.

I stopped moving, slowed my breathing. Listened.

Somewhere in this vast darkness, someone quietly cried. The sound was brokenhearted, lost. The sound of someone who had succumbed. Who saw no way forward. Who thought this would never end.

I pulled out Persephone's mirror. If Demeter's threads of fate led into here maybe they'd keep leading me forward. Better than stumbling around in the dark.

And when I found her? If I found Demeter? What then?

And Amity? Would she be friend or foe?

Use me. Let me help. Ania pulled at the dark corners in my head, shadows growing longer and more tangible without any light to fend them off.

"No." My refusal echoed through the darkness, and *Ania's* smile stretched against my skull.

Fight her, Korrina. Jared's words.

Keep going, you gorgeous badass you. My words.

I took a deep breath and gazed into the mirror.

It took a few seconds for my eyes to adjust, but then I saw them. A forest of fate's threads, lined in dark silver, pouring through this place as if they were water. My fingers trembled, but I reached up anyway and touched one.

In the mirror's reflection, the thread flashed a shade of purple I recognized. The color of *my* power.

I yanked my hand back. But smaller threads came away with my hand, as if I was now somehow tied to this cord of fate. Sticky, invisible, and no way for me to get them off. But maybe that was to be expected. You couldn't pass through someone's life without being tied to them somehow, even if that connection was a thin regret.

I bit at my lip, forced myself to grab hold, and pulled. The thread flashed purple again.

It was cold and felt alive. Deep within the membrane, something pulsed, and I followed. One hand on fate's thread, one hand holding Persephone's mirror.

Never thought I'd be double-fisting the impossible.

The pulsing led me through the darkness. The mirror let me see. The thread was my tether. And soon, I arrived at a misty lake that glowed a faint silver in the middle of the darkness.

It was empty. Quiet, except for the broken sobbing that had grown no louder, yet seemed to be everywhere. I crept to the edge of the water, where all the threads plunged deeper.

The water was like glass, still and dark, and I was reminded of all the horror stories of the Underworld's waters.

The River Styx, the river of hatred.

Acheron, the river of woe.

Phlegethon, the river of fire.

Cocytun, the wailing river.

And finally, the River Lethe, the river of forgetting. Where Dad's soul would soon be washed then imprisoned in the caves of Oblivion, lost.

Ania grew stronger.

A faint cry echoed from beneath the pool at my feet.

This water was dark. Darker than it should be. Dark enough to have bubbled up from Tartarus. If I touched it, it could be the last thing I knew.

If I didn't…

I put Persephone's mirror away, leaned forward.

Fate's threads disappeared from under my touch, but in the water's reflection, I *saw*.

My heart seemed to split in two, sinking to my toes and

lodging in my throat. My bones reverberated with a kind of electricity, a buzzing that went from toenail to hair tip.

It hadn't been the mirror Persephone had warned me against looking too deeply into.

I crept closer.

It had been this. This mirror. This water. This reflection.

A half-healed wound oozed at my lower stomach. A rope cut by a shadow rat.

But the creature hadn't gotten them all.

Fates threads pulsed from my shoulders, my elbows, my neck, my heart. More attached to my knees, my ankles. Still more rose above my back, like wings. Some gray, some silver, some indigo.

Some black. Very, very black.

I watched as they all flared green and tightened.

The tension lifted me to my toes, stole my breath, wrenched at my spine.

Like hell.

No one controlled my strings.

My song didn't tickle at the back of my throat. It roared. The scepter burned to life in the dark cave, turned the pool into a misty blue, ate away at my life source. My knees shook, my teeth trembled, I couldn't hold on.

Not like this, you can't, Ania said at the back of my mind. *At the rate you're going, you're going to kill us. You need me.*

"You are sorrow," I gritted out. "I will not...let you ruin... everything." It was getting harder to breathe.

Sorrow doesn't ruin anything, she coaxed. *It is needed, necessary, and only those who fight it lose.*

"Like when you took over during my visions?"

She was silent, but I felt her yes.

"And those who don't fight?" I was so tired. Tired of fighting her, fighting myself, fighting to use my power and fighting my power for my life.

They win. Sorrow makes you strong. It refines you. Prepares you for the darkness ahead.

"Way to look on the bright side," I gasped out, sarcastic to the last breath. I dropped to my knees.

The darkness isn't always to be feared, Elpida. She echoed Persephone's earlier words.

The scepter flickered.

Huh. It'd never done that before.

The cave was growing darker. Or, no…that was me. My vision. I dropped to my hands. My palms scraped against the rough gravel at the water's edge, and I looked deep, deeper. Close, closer.

Could I save Jared, stop Demeter, and defeat Phorkys like this? With dark threads of fate pouring out of me? Dark threads I had no control over?

Even with the scepter, I wasn't enough.

I hadn't brought our Siren family together. Tanzy was lost. Amity was broken. And we had yet to find the fourth Siren. The Council had warned that was the only way to stop Phorkys… because I'd damaged my soul in loving Jared too much, too hard, too fully.

Could I save the world?

"You were never supposed to," *Ania* whispered. No longer in my head, but standing in front of me.

I fell backwards. My heart stopped.

She was a mirror of myself but with silver eyes, dark auburn hair, and a raised arch to her brows. "No one person can save everyone."

"I could have," I answered her—my duality, my shadow-self, my other half.

"No," *Ania* smiled, no cruelty this time, but only sorrow. "No, you couldn't have. And that has been your biggest failing. Trusting no one, not even yourself, because everyone has either failed or betrayed you. But, *Elpida*, perfection is the only true myth. You cannot be everyone to everybody. And they cannot be that for you."

"Maybe not, but right now, I'm all they've got."

"You're wrong. They've got me as well. But it's up to you. Keep going down this path…or try something new." She held out her hand to me. *My* hand to me? Yup. Not thinking about that too hard.

"You want me to try becoming sorrow?" The air was getting thin, harder to breathe.

"No. Just take sorrow's hand and walk beside me for a little while. It's time to face your heartbreak, *Elpida*. It's time to take fate back into your own hands. Our hands."

I met her gaze. Even dying, she was confident. Not weak. Not grim. But something else. Something…burnished.

Ania lived in the fire of grief. But it didn't own her. It strengthened her.

"I can't," I gasped. "I can't trust you."

She pressed her lips together. "Then lean on me, just for a little while. But, Korrina, if you do not accept me, if you do not begin to trust yourself, I will be the cause of your death."

I nodded. My neck felt limp. My energy was zapped. I had no choice but to lean into sorrow.

Ania wrapped her arm around my waist. The air grew breathable, my muscles stopped trembling, and the scepter blasted blue brilliance everywhere. With *Ania's* help, I yanked and pulled at cords and bled from fresh wounds, but I didn't care. I'd free my ties from whoever was holding them.

Oh who was I kidding? I knew exactly who was holding them.

I stilled, placed my palm against the last one, the one coming from my heart, and breathed in, breathed out. The ache nestled there had settled so permanently that it'd found a comfortable space to curl up and slowly eat away at my life.

I miss you, Jared. I sent that message through the cord in a pulse of purple energy. *I'm sorry I didn't choose you. I'm sorry I couldn't save you. And I'm sorry for your pain.*

"I'm not ready to let this one go yet." I blinked back tears, and *Ania* smiled.

"Whenever you're ready, I'll be here," she whispered, fading into the dimness of the cave. "But now it's a conscious choice, *Elpida*. Look. See how you have changed fate's trajectory already."

I looked.

The cave was no longer dark. The few remaining strings pouring from me had lightened to a dark silver. The water had become crystal clear.

At the bottom, in a cage made of gold and surrounded by misty water, was Demeter. With Amity at her side.

I walked forward, took out Persephone's mirror, and tossed it into the middle of the pool.

CHAPTER 37

The mirror spun in the air, opened on its own, and landed in the middle of the water with a click. Not a splash. A click. With a burst of light, the water evaporated, and the lake became a crater with gently sloping sides.

"That's convenient," I muttered and heaved a sigh of relief. The mirror had unlocked the lake.

Demeter's crying grew louder.

I made my way down, grasping the cold earth to keep my balance, setting off miniature landslides. Pebbles rolled under my shoes like makeshift roller skates. At the base of the incline was the golden cage, its bars thick and polished to a gleam. Rocks from my slide pinged against the metal, but the cage's inhabitants didn't seem to notice. Or if they noticed, they didn't care.

When *Ania* had trapped me in the cage inside my mind, I hadn't realized I was imprisoned. I hadn't realized my own mind was keeping me captive, and only I had the key to set myself free.

Persephone had said that only those imprisoned by the same wounds could even see the cage.

And now I knew that only those who'd been through the same grief, the same heartbreak, the same trauma could shake you back awake.

Like Jared had done for me. Because he'd also broken free of his cage. For a little while at least.

I knew the edge of Demeter's grief. I'd shared in that pain. Even if the source of my grief was different than hers, it had the same scent, the same taste, the same slippery skin.

And Amity? Her wings pressed against the bars of Demeter's cage, trembling slightly as if she was silently sobbing. I knew her pain as well. Knew what it was to have caused destruction and death. I knew her guilt, her shame.

So yeah, these two prisoners? I knew their hurt intimately. It was fresh and raw and so sharp the point was invisible. But not the cage.

Not anymore.

I walked up to the locked door, grabbed hold of the bars, and sang. Not my song, but Amity's.

"*We are but mountains, and we crumble, we crumble.*" My power wove through each note, laced each beat with Siren compulsion. "*We are but mountains, be gentle, be gentle.*" Amity began to stir. "*We all break, we all break, we all break. You think I'm strong, but I'll crumble, I'll crumble, for you.*" The cage rattled, cracked, the bars began to crumble, and the door popped open.

Neither Amity nor Demeter moved. I propped open the door with a rock, making sure it couldn't slam closed behind me, and walked inside, skirting the edge.

Demeter let out another broken cry, this one muffled as her face was buried in her knees. Her long toes dug into the dirt. Her hair dragged along the ground.

I dodged her, because *hello, scary goddess,* and went straight for Amity.

Her shoulders were hunched over like her arms had given

out. She shivered. Her shirt had torn open at the back, where wings had sprouted.

Her wings looked heavy.

I hummed her song again, sang a few phrases out loud, and silent, dirty tears tracked down her cheekbones.

"Amity, can you hear me?"

She flinched, but didn't respond.

No matter. I grabbed Amity's hand, pushed my power into her, and sang a little ditty I'd learned from Elmo. "Wake up. Wake up. WAKE UP!"

It was super simple. Super annoying. Super effective.

Amity blinked. "Korrina?"

She didn't have threads tying her down. Not like mine. Not like Demeter's.

She just had wings.

Dirt smudged her cheeks. Her dreads hung lank around her wings. Up close, I could see little patterns running through her peacock-inspired feathers. Aqua-blue speckles spattered her brown and cream feathers, more subdued than her ancestor's brilliant colors. More like a peahen, rather than the garish colors of the peacock.

"Yeah, hun. I'm here. Sorry it took so long, but Demeter is really good at hiding." I thumbed over my shoulder.

Amity's eyes widened, and she scrambled backwards, digging the golden bars into her wings. "Demeter? As in goddess of the harvest Demeter?"

"Guess you paid attention in English class." I grabbed her elbow and hauled her up. The girl's petite frame was deceptive. This chick was heavy with tight muscles. Guess from all that jumping out of planes.

I wrapped an arm around her waist as her knees went wobbly, her feathers thick and warm against the chill of the cavern.

"Something's wrong," she whispered and reached up behind

her. "Korrina…what…what is this?" Her hand grasped the base of her left wing, her eyes went wide, and the glow of her Siren aura began to show. Sky blue. Like she was meant to soar.

"Demeter's curse." I urged her forward, but she didn't budge.

I had to get her out of here before she freaked out and woke Demeter up or alerted the Puppeteer that we were here. No telling what either one of them would do with two Sirens in their grasp.

"Demeter's curse?" Her hand hadn't left her wing. "Are you saying…"

"When Demeter's fire touched you, the curse of our ancestors did as well. Our…winged ancestors."

In the cold light of the cave, she went pale.

"Bright side? You get to fly without a parachute." I gently socked her shoulder. "Pretty neat, huh?"

She sank to the floor. "I can never go back to the human world, can I?"

"I—I don't know." My tone lost its playfulness. "I hadn't thought that far."

"You don't often, do you?" She dropped her hand from her back, straightened her shoulders.

Ouch. I bit my tongue to keep words from spilling out. The last thing she needed right now was a sarcastic retort. And as much as I wanted to throw some shade her way, she was right. My plans rarely took into account all possible paths. So far, I'd gotten lucky.

Or I at least had really good friends watching my back.

The cage door slammed shut.

Amity's blue eyes grew sky-wide.

I slowly turned, not needing Tanzy's foresight to know I wasn't going to like what, or who, was waiting.

CHAPTER 38

The sound of feet being dragged across the cage floor was the theme song to this horror movie. The scent of freshly tilled dirt and manure flooded the cage.

I positioned myself in front of Amity and readied my song.

Demeter was suspended mid-air by her elbows, the black threads that controlled her movements now visible, and glistening.

"Demeter?" I tried.

Her eyes fluttered open, and golden light and dark fear poured out of them.

"I cannot fight this," she gasped, even as she wriggled to get away, a moth caught in a web.

I took a step closer. "You have to try."

She met my gaze with her full-on goddess power. "You, of all creatures, help me. Why?"

Centuries of suffering rolled around my tongue like a hard piece of candy, sticky and stale. Suffering caused by this goddess, by her grief, by her loss.

Did my Siren ancestors have a hand in Persephone's kidnapping? I didn't know, but I wouldn't put it past them.

Did it matter anymore?

"No one should be made a prisoner of their own grief." I reached out a hand to her.

She reached back. And for one, very small moment, I thought we'd won.

A low whistling filled the air.

Amity screamed.

Black cords shot from all directions, dodging the bars of the cage. I hit the floor. The cords slammed into Demeter, threw her against the cage. The golden prison shuddered. The goddess screamed.

The binds that tied her down pinned me to the floor. Amity yelped, and the sound of another body hitting the bars reverberated through the cage.

"I won't let go that easily, *Elpida.*" The Puppeteer's toneless voice had returned.

I craned my head back, peered through the web of Demeter's strings, and through a small peep hole, I saw Demeter.

Demeter, with eyes now black instead of gold.

Demeter, with strings wrapped around her hands.

Not restraining.

Controlling.

Demeter tilted her head, her chin falling forward like a doll with a broken neck. Her eyebrow raised. "Surprised, daughter of Molpe?" The Puppeteer's voice drawled out of Demeter's lips.

I flexed my feet, getting a little leverage with my toes, millimeters from the web. "Yup. You got me. Didn't know you were a fantastic ventriloquist."

Demeter's head fell back, her mouth gaping wide to let a loud laugh boom out of her throat.

I took the opportunity to belly crawl forward.

"Tricks upon tricks I have up my sleeves," the Puppeteer half-sang, half-growled.

"Well, you definitely have creepy down," I retorted, drawing another laugh that let me get closer. The threads concentrated on Demeter's torso the closer I got, leaving me more room to maneuver along the floor.

"Careful, Korrina," Amity whispered from somewhere close. "She's not sane when she's like this."

Seemed Amity and Demeter had gotten to know each other a bit in their time together. If we survived, I had questions.

"When are the gods ever sane?" I muttered back and carefully stepped over and ducked under more of the web. The small thread I'd grabbed and followed was still attached to my wrist, and I didn't want to be more tied to her than I had to be. The string led to Demeter, and it was still purple. Not black. Which I assumed meant I still had some influence over Demeter's strings. She wasn't totally lost to us, yet. "I have to wake her."

I twisted my body around another knot of threads and popped up next to the bars between Amity and Demeter.

Amity leaned forward, threads pulsing from her wrists, the shadows under her eyes growing darker. "You sure that's a good idea?" Her quiet voice held no more faith in me than I deserved.

"It's the only way to stop something worse from coming." I moved away from Amity, closer to the trapped goddess.

"What if you're wrong?"

I sighed. "Wouldn't surprise me a bit."

The threads jerked, as if just now sensing how close I was.

Demeter's head swung in my direction, boneless and fluid. "Little Molpe on a string. Little Molpe sneaks to me."

Before I could second-guess myself, I took a breath, let my song fill my throat, and grabbed Demeter's hands.

The cage faded. Demeter's nightmare took over.

CHAPTER 39

It was dark, and sharp rocks towered on either side.

Demeter kneeled in a small pool of light, just enough for her to see where she was, and no more.

A prison, buried deep in the earth, with no room to lie down, no room to sleep, no room to stand without scratching her spine. A hole. Demeter had nightmared herself into a hole.

I turned Demeter's hands over in mine. Blood caked her fingernails, dried and black. Her nails were broken, bleeding. Dark tears stained her face.

I pulsed my power into her, through the thin thread that connected her wrist to mine.

"Goddess?" I could do reverent when I chose.

She lifted her head, her chin tipping toward the light. "Persephone," she sighed then let her chin fall back down, and the Puppeteer's threads tightened, pulled.

Demeter's elbows lifted before the rest of her, and there was a sound of rock grating against rib. Her strings yanked tight, and fresh black liquid flooded into them. But who held her strings? Who was her puppeteer?

I held onto her hands, somehow existing in the rock itself.

But I knew this wasn't reality, so maybe I wasn't bound by the same controls she was.

"Demeter, this isn't your life. This is your grief. I need you to wake up." And hopefully, not curse and kill me. I echoed the same concepts Jared had spoken to me, but threaded mine with puffs of Siren power, of the *Elpida's* hope.

Because hope could heal.

Demeter didn't respond, but the cords controlling her movements did. They thickened, as if fighting against my urgings.

"Hades took her from me. He keeps her from me. He's changing her. My sweet girl. No longer my girl. No longer sweet." Fresh tears bloomed in her eyes, fell down her cheeks like crimson roses being shredded.

My heart softened and tore a little around the edges. The blinders came off my eyes.

Demeter was past grieving about Persephone's kidnapping. Maybe in the beginning she'd been controlled by that grief, but not anymore. Or at least, not totally.

Demeter's grief, born out of the horror of losing her child, had morphed into grief over the death of the child she'd birthed and never knowing the woman she'd become. Her grief was about not seeing Persephone grow up. "Goddess…Persephone is alive."

Demeter's gaze jerked forward, meeting mine, and her focus was so intent, so full of power, I couldn't breathe.

"I saw her. In the garden," I gasped. "She sent me here to find you. She wants to meet you. Talk with you. Maybe even come home."

"She sent you here?" Demeter's voice was breathless, but there was something else about it. A duality I couldn't place. "My daughter wants to come home?" A light glinted in Demeter's eyes. She looked around. "Where am I?"

The nightmare shuddered.

"Yes, come home. But you can't help her if you're trapped in here. I need you to wake up. Persephone needs you to wake up."

"Persephone...needs me..." Her voice deepened. She stood. Looked at one of the threads holding her tight, her gaze dropping from mine, releasing me from her breathless hold. "This. No more." She reached back, wrapped the threads from her elbows around her wrists, and used the cords to pull herself up.

The nightmare faded, the cage reappeared. Demeter looked around like she hadn't seen it before. A smile played against her lips. "I see I took precautions." She palmed one of the bars. "Now, let's get out of here." Demeter's voice seemed to occupy two registers at once, and it didn't sound grateful. She nodded to Amity and gave a small flick of her wrist.

Amity stepped forward, released from the cage's bars. The shadows under her eyes were now black. She kneeled and began to scratch Greek symbols into the cage floor with a small knife.

"Amity, what are you doing?" I asked.

The cage began to shake.

She didn't answer.

"Amity, whatever you're doing, I'm not sure it's a good idea."

She ignored me. Slashed her knife against the floor, ran her fingers over the etchings, and stood. Blue Siren power poured out of her, and she began to sing in Greek.

I lurched forward. I had to stop her. Because whatever she was doing, she wasn't in control.

My wrist, the one still tied to Demeter, yanked back.

"We're done with our game, little Molpe," the Puppeteer said.

Something cracked. Loud. Amity raised her hands in the air, and belted out her song. The cage screeched, splintered, burst apart into millions of gold flecks.

The threads flew from around the cave and wrapped themselves around Demeter like some sort of weird runway fashion.

They snapped away from me and away from Amity. Amity shook herself, sat back on her heels, dazed.

But Demeter...she took a deep breath and sighed. The glint in her eyes grew stronger, but not brighter. The rotting scent of a farm field grew stronger.

"Thank you, *Elpida*. For giving me your hope. For helping me to fully wake." Her voice dropped, and it was no longer Demeter's broken voice, no longer the Puppeteer's monotone. This was someone deeper, darker. Someone who had given themselves over to pain.

"Now all shall pay for the death of my beloved Persephone."

My heart stopped. My stomach knotted. My insides froze. "She's not dead," I whispered, terrified to contradict her, not willing to risk the world if I didn't.

"The Persephone I knew and loved, fed and nurtured, bathed and sang to sleep...she has died. And I do not know who has taken her place."

So alive wasn't enough. Hades had taken Persephone and molded her into something Demeter would not have chosen for her daughter.

Gray light poured from Demeter's eyes. "The world will know my pain." She clasped her hands over her head and disappeared in an explosion of darkness.

"Korrina?" Amity's voice whispered through the empty lake, echoed around the empty cave.

"Yeah, I'm here." My voice was calm, my mind a storm.

It had been Demeter. She'd held her own strings. She'd been yanking on her own hurt, letting it grow and fester and manifest. And now...

Now I'd awakened her. The Goddess of Retribution.

CHAPTER 40

Amity gripped my hand and hauled me up the last few steps of the dry and empty lake. Dirt smudged the side of her nose, and her dreads had gone frizzy, but she had a look in her eyes that I knew all too well.

"A pissed off Siren is an out-of-control Siren," I said, mimicking words from Neri I'd heard way too many times.

"That witch took over my body." She was shaking, as if her anger was about to explode.

"Yeah. I saw."

"No. You didn't. She took me to some tree. Tried to get me to sing it out of existence. I brought us here instead. Then she went crazy, switched personalities, muttered something about stopping herself, then threw up a cage around us, switched personalities again, and shot a bunch of black liquid hoses into me."

Amity shuddered again. Her sky-blue power glowed around her feet.

I didn't blame her. There were no good words for situations like these. Times when someone had been violated, had power exerted over them.

But Demeter's shadow self's plans, the Goddess of Retribution, began to fall into place.

"I'm sorry that happened to you." I gripped her hand, gave it a squeeze. "Nothing about it is okay or right."

She nodded. Blinked too quickly.

"This tree. Was it in a meadow? By itself?"

Amity nodded, her power dimming as I got her mind redirected. "With red fruit hanging from it. Not apples, but…"

"Pomegranates," I breathed, something akin to terror budding deep inside my gut.

If Demeter destroyed the tree. Persephone's tree…

"We have to get to Molpe, my Siren ancestor." Who may or may not be incapacitated. But we didn't need to worry about that now.

"You've got a plan to get back at this goddess-hole?" Her lip snarled. Even her wings had a snarky tilt to them.

I snorted. "Goddess-hole. I'm so stealing that. Yes. I think. But we're going to need help. We came to wake Demeter. We came. We got woke. Now flap those flappers and let's get outta here."

"You know that's not what 'got woke' means, right?" She raised a pierced eyebrow.

A few dozen false starts later, Amity lifted off—me attached to her like a spider monkey baby—and flew toward the distant surface.

"By the way," I said. "Tanzy's another Siren like us and she's gone over to the dark side and may be waiting up there with our Siren ancestors who have all gone more than a little insane, and also, I kinda wrecked your DeLorean," I spoke into Amity's boobs, kinda hoping she didn't hear me, but also feeling responsible to provide a disclaimer of what we may be flying into.

"You wrecked my car?" she half-screamed, half-sang.

Well, at least her mind was off her trauma at the hands of a psycho goddess.

~

WE POPPED THROUGH THE SURFACE TO THE RED ROCKS TOWERING all around and the sight of our Siren ancestors hovering over a crumpled Molpe.

Amity landed us next to the rest of our so-called family, though I wasn't sure that was the best idea.

Molpe was alive, groaning and complaining about fate's interference with reality.

"What the hell, Tanzy?" I stomped forward to confront my Siren sister. Cousin. Crazy relative.

She held her hands out to me, palms up, universal sign of hippie peace. "If Molpe had gone with you, you would have failed. Every path forward both I and Aggie saw foretold so. What we did was the only way."

I huffed, not quite trusting her, but also seeing the merit of her words. And the fact that she'd called Aglaope Aggie. Maybe she wasn't lost after all.

"She failed anyway." Amity thumbed over her wings at me. Traitor.

Tanzy brightened and took Amity's hand in hers. "The Song-writer. I am so pleased to meet you."

"And I as well." Thelxiepeia sashayed forward, her peacock feathers prim and indignant. "Though no one has thought to introduce *me*."

I sighed, the long hours spent in Demeter's nightmare catching up to me. "Amity, your ancestor Thelxiepeia. Thelx-iepeia, Amity. Amity, it's up to you to come up with a nickname for this one—I got nothing."

Amity grinned. "That's easy. Nice to meet you, Thelma."

Amity was my people.

Peisinoe nodded as she was introduced. No one was brave enough to give her a nickname yet.

I knelt next to Molpe and surreptitiously checked her for

injuries. On the surface, she seemed okay, her ego bruised more than anything. But when she stood, she balanced on one talon and one toe, not putting her full weight on her other foot.

"Korrina, you were unable to awake Demeter?" Molpe asked, dependable in any situation to get us back on task.

"No…I woke her."

They all leaned forward.

"Annnnd…" Amity pushed.

"Annnnd kinda woke Demeter and set the Puppeteer—who was really dark-side-of-the-force Demeter—free."

Mouths dropped open. Human and Siren alike.

"Annnnd…" Amity pressed again.

"And Puppeteer Demeter is also the Goddess of Retribution," I said as quickly as I could. I turned to Amity. "Happy?"

She just raised an eyebrow.

Oh man, she and Danica were going to become best buds. I wasn't so sure that was a good thing for society."Good news is," I said, "she isn't collecting Sirens like I thought she was."

They all waited for the bad news bomb.

I sighed. "Bad news is, she tried to use Amity to write Persephone's tree out of existence. And she wants to share her pain with *everyone*."

"This is bad, *Elpida*," Molpe stated.

Great. She'd gone back to formal titles.

"Super bad," Tanzy agreed.

Not so good that our seer saw a super bad future.

"I have a plan." I swear, they'd rehearsed a group eye roll at some point.

"Your plans haven't gone well so far," Aggie pointed out.

"This one might. But we have to go back to our side of the veil and get our friends on board. If we fail on this end, they're our last defense system."

Molpe nodded. "Protect your side of the veil. Send Neri to us when you are ready. The Goddess of Retribution has risen, and there are no safe havens left."

~

OUR FOUR SIREN ANCESTORS STOOD IN A CIRCLE AROUND US, wings raised and wingtips touching, so that we were completely surrounded. Tanzy, Amity, and I huddled in the center, hands held tight.

Aggie lifted her chin, and all four Siren sisters took a deep breath. She dropped the first note and let it ring, stronger and stronger. Molpe joined in next, a half-step higher, giving the tone a haunting sound. Peisinoe came in super low, her voice pulsing against Molpe's and Aggie's. Thelma joined last, her voice a cymbal crash of Greek words against the minor keys of Molpe and Aggie. With her words, a portal began to open, one that would jump us over the void and dump us right where we started, in Tanzy's living room.

The Sirens' voices rose, became louder, stronger, and the portal became clearer and clearer until finally, it was time to step through.

I pushed Tanzy through first. After what she'd put me and Molpe through, she deserved to be the guinea pig. She stumbled through the portal and gracefully landed in a runner's stance next to the healing crystal set into her living room floor.

Startled screams came from the other room as Dave, Cloud, and Danica reacted to Tanzy's sudden appearance.

Tanzy shot me a you're-gonna-pay-for-that look, then turned her attention to somewhere behind the portal.

Cloud, Danica, and Dave couldn't see the portal or the veil— it wasn't a gift given to humans. But Sirens could.

Only the *Elpida* could hear voices from one side to the other.

"Amity, you're next." I didn't shove her. She didn't need it.

Dave was on the other side, and wings or not, she couldn't wait to see him.

She reached out with one hand, touched the portal. It shivered under her touch. She flattened her palm against the opening, pressed hard. It remained sealed. A little squeak escaped her throat, and she pushed with her other hand, her shoulder, her full weight, until her spine slumped. She rested her forehead against the portal home—a home where she was no longer allowed.

The curse had only half-touched Amity, so she looked more angel than Siren. We hadn't known if she'd stay that way, go back to being human, or eventually turn into a full-fledged Siren. But for now, the transformation was enough to keep her from making the journey back with us.

Because I'd failed.

"Amity…" I reached out, but she jerked away before I could touch her.

"Don't." Pain seemed to tear through her eyes. "Get back, save them, use your head before you put people in danger."

"Korrina!" Tanzy screeched through the portal. "Hurry!"

Tanzy's living room lit up like something was on fire, then Dave was hurled across the room.

Adrenaline buzzed my bones. They were being attacked. Again.

I pressed my lips together, gave Amity one last look, and dove through the portal.

Tanzy's foresight had come true—one of us had been left behind.

The living room quickly took shape. The thick glass windows had been busted in by what looked like an explosion. Fire licked up the curtains and tasted the silk pillows.

My stomach clenched.

Tanzy was curled up in her reading corner, her leg bent in an unnatural position. Dave must have landed on one of the couches and flipped it over on impact. He stood, wobbled, leaned against one of the wooden posts to hold himself upright. Cloud held Danica, like he'd just caught her.

I rushed to Tanzy and sang my healing song over her broken leg, then attended to Dave. My aura was a darker purple than usual. *Ania* was still lending me some of her power but, for the first time since Jared was turned, not draining my life force.

Dave wrapped his hand around my arm as I healed him, his grip bruiser-strong. "Where's Amity? Did you find her?"

I smiled, reassuringly I hoped, and nodded. "I did, and she is safe. She stayed over there to help, but she really wants to see you."

Dave's body relaxed, and a smile peeked out from under his beard for the first time since Amity was kidnapped.

Once I was sure he was okay, I stood and looked around. "Anyone want to tell me what happened?"

Cloud turned to face me, finally, his expression an encyclopedia of hurt and betrayal.

"Guys?" I tried again.

Cloud dusted himself off. "What happened?" He scoffed, something I'd never heard him do before. "You did, Korrina."

Danica gripped his arm, as if to hold him back, but he shook her off.

"Your Siren Hunters came here, to this place that was magically warded to all but those *we* allowed in. You let Jared in."

I knew where this was going, but it was a car crash, a bad one, one I couldn't stop, but just had to sit behind the driver's wheel and watch, split-second by split-second, powerless to stop it, powerless to change course.

"They waited for you, Korrina. They held us here, waiting for you."

It was only then that Cloud's black eye, the dried blood on his knuckles, the swelling around his cheek, registered. All too old to have been from the explosion.

He took a step closer. "Luke told us what you did. How Jared wormed his way back into your life. Our lives. How you let him."

"Jared did this?" I couldn't believe it. I could, but…I couldn't.

"He and Colin. Nice guy, your dad, by the way," Cloud sneered and rubbed at his bruised cheek. "Said you'd awakened the Goddess of Retribution. That you were the only one who could have awoken her. They were *happy*, Korrina. Giddy. Because you did their dirty work."

"Give her a break, Skylar." Danica pushed in, calling Cloud by his given name—a name he detested.

He snapped his head around to look at her, and she gave him a cool-it look. "She's been through enough. It's not like she held us hostage and tried to kill us."

"She might as well have," Cloud yelled. "How many more times do we have to get hurt, and almost killed, because she chooses Jared over us?" He turned back to me. "How many?"

My throat swelled. I couldn't answer.

"It's always him over us, Korrina. Again. How"—Cloud's voice broke and a single tear darkened his lashes before making its escape—"how could you do this to us?"

And I saw, finally I saw, just how badly my friends had been hurting. We'd all lost Jared. We'd all been through hell.

But I'd gotten to leave. Push the bad memories to the background and fight. I'd grown stronger, physically and in my power. But Cloud? Danica?

They'd had to stay behind. Confront the memories. Go back to normal life with big Jared-shaped holes following them around their day. They hadn't gotten to punch their feelings away. They'd had to figure out a way to begin to heal.

They didn't have my power. But they had more strength than I'd ever noticed.

"There's no way for me to make this better," I said, low and filled with regret. "But please know, from the depths of my heart, that I have never and will never make the choice between Jared and you. I have no choice."

Danica reached for Cloud's hand.

"I would go to the ends of the earth and beyond for any of you. I *have* to." It was my voice breaking this time. "You and Danica? You're strong. Stronger than you probably know. Way stronger than me." I sniffed. "And yeah, being my friend means getting hit with shrapnel. I tried to stay away, to protect you. But you guys chose to come here. To help. Just like I would have done for you. Just like I am doing for Jared."

Cloud went rigid.

"He needs our help," I continued, stronger, pleading. "I had to make a sacrifice, and that sacrifice was him. He didn't get to choose that. He doesn't deserve this fate. And until he is saved and restored, I will not stop trying. I love you two, more than anything, but you don't get to ask me to sacrifice him again. You just don't."

Danica let go of Cloud's hand and rushed me. I braced for small-packaged violence.

She threw her arms around my neck and squeezed tight. "Of course we don't get to ask that. And of course we want to help save Jared. It's just hard to keep that in mind when he's trying to kill us."

I laughed. "Yeah, I know. I get that."

Danica walked us around one-hundred-eighty degrees without letting go of my neck. "Cloud? Do you have something you'd like to say?"

I heard him huff. "I see your side of the issue, Korrina. I don't necessarily like it because I really hate getting punched in the face, but I see it."

I wanted him to come over and join our hug fest—a friend sandwich with me in the middle—but it was too soon, too much for him. He'd get there, but not yet. The wounds were still too fresh.

I knew the feeling.

"Where's Luke?" I asked.

Danica let me go and glared at Cloud. Cloud shook his head, ever so slightly. Danica gave him a get-some-balls snarl.

Cloud sighed. "Jared and Colin took him back to Phorkys. Said he had to answer for his betrayals."

A knife of pain twisted in my stomach.

Dad, Luke, Jared, Mom. Who needed enemies when you could have me.

CHAPTER 41

We sat around the healing crystal, took stock, and I updated the team on what had happened on the other side of the veil.

"Now what?" Leave it to Danica to get right to the point.

We turned to Tanzy, as if a knee-jerk reaction. She shrugged her shoulders. "Until a direction is chosen, there are too many futures to sort through."

I huffed. My main direction was to fix my mistakes. Save them all. I had a plan.

Not that my plans had the best track record, but this one was good. Solid. Solid-ish. A plan that could save them all. Though if my crew knew my plan, they wouldn't like it.

Tanzy's eyes flashed, and I quickly backtracked my thoughts. If she foresaw my plan, I'd have no chance.

"Crannik," I said.

Tanzy narrowed her gaze, as if she could see my double-thinking. I refocused all my energy back on the present. Stop Demeter. Because if I couldn't stop her, there would be no additional plans, no saving anybody.

Dave, Danica, and Cloud tilted their heads.

"Crannik. Luke's brother. He works for Demeter. Not the Goddess of Retribution, but good ole Demeter. He'll know where she is." Despite my gut feelings—which were usually spot on—I'd promised Amity to use my head more. Justify the danger. And Crannik would be able to provide clarity on his goddess.

Danica jutted out her chin. "So you gonna text him? Snapchat? What? Get on it, woman." She waved her hand at me in a go-on gesture.

I went to the back room, found my bag, and pulled out the old, battered coin inscribed with something Greek—which at some point I should really learn.

Rejoining the others, I flipped the coin into the air. It glinted once, twice, and I called out the magic words. "Yo, Neri."

Purple, shimmery light filled the room, and Neri appeared with a flap of her wings and a roll of her eyes. "You rang?"

"Whoa. Did you just drop an *Addams Family* reference?" Color me shocked. And a little in awe of myself.

If she could've smirked, she would've.

"How's Dad?"

Her color dimmed, and my heart quieted, waiting.

"He is…resigned." That pause in her words, it told me more than she wanted me to know.

Ania stretched against my bones, and something sharp pinched my heart. I blinked back tears. "The equinox is still a few hours away, right? We still have time to get to him. Tell him that, okay. Tell him we're not giving up. Not yet."

"Korrina…" Danica reached out her hand, but I shoved her away.

I met her gaze. Held it. "No pity. Not yet."

She firmed up her lips and nodded. She understood the need to put on a brave face, to stay strong, to turn yourself to stone, until you couldn't anymore.

Tanzy held out her hands. "I'm sorry, Korrina, but no future that I see shows—"

"Can it, psychic." Danica held up her hand, stopping Tanzy mid-unwanted-prophecy. "You don't know everything."

I turned back to the more-helpful-than-Hedwig owl. "Neri, we need to speak with Crannik. Can you help us get in touch with him?"

"What is it with you and these Carter boys? Give me a minute." She flashed out of existence and, less than ten seconds later, returned with her talons hanging onto Crannik by the ear.

"Letgoletgoletgoletgo." Not once did Crannik raise his voice or change his tone. It was a monotone beg, like a monk's chant.

I snorted. Danica flat out cackled. Even Dave and Cloud broke a grin.

Neri let Crannik go, and he fell to the floor, then gave us all the best stink face I'd ever seen. He stopped once he reached me. "You were supposed to stop her. Not help her."

"It's not like she came with an instruction manual." I grabbed his arm and helped him stand.

"What's the plan?" He crossed his arms and waited.

I liked that. He didn't waste time on the past, on things we couldn't change.

"I need you to confirm something first. You know where she is?"

"I know where she is headed. The Goddess of Retribution seeks justice, to correct perceived wrongs." He paused for dramatic effect. "She is going back to where this all started. What she'll do once she gets there, I'm not sure."

"Persephone's tree," I deciphered for the rest of the group and looked to Crannik for confirmation.

He nodded.

"She's going to destroy it at the peak of the equinox. She's already tried to do so once." I sounded a little too giddy. But I did so enjoy being right.

Crannik crinkled his brows. "How do you know this?"

"It's why she kidnapped Amity. Tried to use Amity to write the tree out of existence. When that didn't work, she shifted gears."

Neri nodded, so I kept going.

"That tree is Persephone's link between Demeter and the Underworld. It's where she reappears each spring and disappears at the end of each summer. If she destroys it at the equinox, just before Persephone is supposed to rejoin Hades…"

"It'll stop summer from turning to fall." Crannik hopped on my logic train. "Persephone will be trapped above ground. Hades will rage."

"A civil war between the gods?" Cloud asked.

"It will be anything but civil," Neri responded.

"Hold up," I said. "Before we go to war, two questions." I waited until I had their attention. "First, won't making it always summer plunge us all into an even worse global warming?"

"Crap," Danica said.

Cloud rubbed his brow. "Civil war *and* eco-disaster."

"Second," I continued, "how does any of this help Phorkys?" Lest we forgot who the real baddie was in this scenario.

Everyone went silent.

Except for Dave. He sat straighter. "War creates a power vacuum. Leaves weak points in the system. If Phorkys is orchestrating the whole thing…"

"Phorkys uses the mayhem to grab all the power," I finished.

"Crap," Danica said again.

"Yeah-uh."

Things were about to get a whole lot worse.

CRANNIK CALLED IN THE REST OF HIS CULT BUDDIES. THEY appeared in a flash of dark green light, staffs raised, faces hidden by their Mother Earth hoodies. Once they'd settled, we went over the plan.

I turned to Crannik. "Do you think Demeter will come through one of the vortices here to seek her *justice?*" I put the last word in air quotes.

He mashed his lips together in thought. "Since the goddess in her Demeter form used the female vortex here, it's likely she'll return to this area. And the vortices here are some of the most powerful. The Goddess of Retribution will need a male-energy-powered vortex to emphasize her strength and control."

Tanzy hummed dreamily. "In that case, it'll probably happen at the Airport Mesa vortex."

"In that case," I said to Crannik and his yes-men, "you guys will go with Danica, Dave, and Cloud to the Airport Mesa vortex."

"Yes, we will go with the humans," Crannik confirmed.

Danica rolled her eyes.

"Danica," I continued, "use Betty and your tech prowess to hack the news channels. We'll need a live feed of Demeter invading if anyone, besides flat-earth people, is going to believe our story."

She nodded and cracked her fingers. "Fun."

"Dave, take Sully. Probably won't do much good, but who knows."

He grabbed his trusty, well-oiled friend.

"Cloud…"

"Don't worry about us, Korrina," he answered. "I've got this."

I grabbed his hand and gave it a squeeze. "I know. I'm depending on that scary smart brain of yours."

He just grinned in response. Not a happy grin. An evil genius grin.

Cloud was back.

And it made me think we might stand a chance.

I took a deep breath. "Okay, we've got our side of the veil

covered. It's up to you guys to keep everyone safe, or at least, prepare the world for Demeter-On-A-Rampage. And you know, tell everyone the gods are real. And stuff."

Neri scoffed. "'And stuff,' the *Elpida* says," she muttered.

"Neri, we need you to gather the Sirens on the other side. We'll need all of our combined power."

"Molpe is already working on a plan for her and her sisters to support you. Rendezvous at the garden's entrance." She bowed out and disappeared.

I should've known my great-whatever-grandmother had my back.

"Crannik, can you and the boys get us near the gates? Preferably without anyone knowing we are there?"

Demeter's groupies exchanged glances, but Crannik was the one to answer. "Persephone will know. Nothing happens in or near the garden without her knowledge."

One of Crannik's boys spoke up. "Spring is fickle. It will either be a beautiful day to be near the goddess, or it will be a day you fear for your life."

The cloying memory of Persephone's poison made me twitch my nose. "Awesome. So she'll either be in the mood to help us or make things very difficult as we try to stop her mother."

"And since the turn of the season is so close, as is her reunification with the dead god, her powers weaken, and her resolve darkens."

I looked to Crannik for translation.

"Expect trouble," he said.

He and the two other priests of Demeter slammed their staffs into Tanzy's living room floor. The healing crystal flashed, and Tanzy and I were sucked into a portal through the veil.

CHAPTER 42

Crannik's portal dumped us into a shadowy grove outside Persephone's garden gates. From our position, we could see the gates, see the flaming swords of the statue-like beasts, see that we appeared to be the first there.

The air felt heavy, weighted, dense with unseen spirits. It felt like being watched. I met Tanzy's gaze in the gray light, and her expression mirrored what I was feeling. We weren't alone. And nothing about this felt welcome.

I helped Tanzy stand, and we brushed leaves off our knees. Around us, vines curled and seemed to sniff the air, seemed to hunt.

I gestured toward the sunlight. Molpe and the rest of the Sirens were supposed to be here. Tanzy and I crept forward.

A black wing shot out, blocking our progress. More wings wrapped around our mouths, stifling our screams.

"Glad you could join us," Peisinoe growled and let us go.

"Where are Molpe and Amity?" I shot back, pretending that I hadn't just peed my pants a little.

"This way." Peisinoe walked away without another word,

somehow trespassing through the trees without making a sound. She was a feathered shadow, slipping away from the sun.

She led us away from the gates to a pavilion barely supported by crumbling columns. On its floors, a tiled mosaic peeked through a layer of dirt and dust. I swept aside the dirt with my foot as we trailed after Peisinoe, revealing a chipped and cracked picture of the day Persephone was stolen from her mother.

"This is one of Demeter's temples," I said. "How is being here a good idea?"

Amity stepped out from behind the altar. "Because Demeter has left the premises, thanks to you. No one will look for us here."

Molpe, Thelma, and Aggie joined her, but it wasn't enough to deter me.

I rushed toward Amity, but stopped short when I saw the expression on her face.

Something had changed. Gone was the bright-eyed, bridge-jumping, drop zone owner.

In her place was someone slightly more savage, something slightly untamed.

Hestia's words echoed through my brain. *Before she let the curse take her mind...let...let...*

Amity had a choice. And she was making the wrong one.

"Dave says he misses you," I said. "He wants to see you again, Amity."

"Yeah, well, thanks to you, there's little chance of that happening." Her hands fisted at her sides. Her wingtips trembled.

Her words were a knife to my back. "Amity, I didn't do this to you. But you can control this curse. It's a mind game. Mind over matter. You can fight it."

"How do you know?" Her gaze softened, sharpened.

I grabbed her hand, pushed my power into her. *Hope.* "You're the Songwriter. You write your own fate."

She didn't react. Not outwardly. She didn't cure her own curse, write away her wings. I didn't even know if she could. But the sharpness in her gaze faded, her hands relaxed.

Amity stepped aside, and Molpe took charge.

"Only Korrina and I are allowed through the gates. We will provide a distraction there, allowing the rest of you to sneak in through cracks in the garden's walls."

Peisinoe drew an outline of the garden in the dirt. "My shadows have identified weak spots in the walls here, here, and here." She pointed out locations around the backside of the garden. "We will have very little time to get to the tree once we sneak inside, before Persephone's guards detect us." She pointed at the gates, and I remembered those stone beasts, those fiery swords.

I shot a look at Molpe. "Please tell me our distraction does not involve those stone dudes."

She just looked at me.

"Awesome."

Peisinoe cleared her throat and continued. "Once we get within sight of the tree, Persephone's powers diminish. She is a prisoner of the tree and loses control of her power at the underground spread of the tree's roots." She drew in the dirt an approximate perimeter. "Our fight against Demeter must take place within this area. Otherwise, Persephone will decimate us before we even begin."

"This looks like an elaborate game of capture the flag," I muttered. "Are we sure Demeter is there?"

Peisinoe gave Molpe a hard look. "Show her."

Molpe kneeled so I could climb on her back. She lifted us into the air, staying close to the tops of the trees. "I'm going higher, just for a second, so you can see what we've spied. Any longer and Demeter may see us. She knows we're coming, but she doesn't know how. We'd prefer to keep it that way. Look quickly, my daughter."

At least Molpe liked me.

"Cast your gaze to the center of the garden, on three, two…"

"One," I whispered, and Molpe flung us higher into the air.

The garden dropped as Molpe spun us higher and higher. I scanned the ground, searching, and finally, there. Dead center. A tree in a field by itself.

Surrounded by green flame impossibly high, impossibly wide.

Molpe dive-bombed the ground, leaving my stomach back in the clouds. She flared her wings just before we hit dirt, and I tumbled off her.

"How are we supposed to get through that?" I yelped. Because that was Demeter's fire. The fire that carried the original curse.

Thelma and Aggie stepped forward, forming a line with Molpe and Peisinoe.

"We will provide the way," Aggie answered.

"The curse can do no more damage to us," Thelma said, "so we will block the fire's power."

Molpe stepped forward. "It is up to you three to stop Demeter. We will join you if we can, but if we cannot, we need you prepared to fight. Combined, the three of you have more power than Demeter. And hopefully, more power than the Goddess of Retribution."

I looked to Tanzy. I looked to Amity. I closed my eyes.

Three Sirens who had just discovered each other and our power.

Ania tickled the back of my mind, a small reminder that she was there too.

Three-point-five Sirens. Who barely knew the first thing about our powers.

Fighting a super-pissed goddess on our own.

I opened my eyes. "Let's go teach Mother some manners."

CHAPTER 43

The gates loomed large in front of Molpe and me. They weren't pearly, but made out of carved stone and covered in honeysuckle and thorns. Designed to make you want to lean in, probably so the thorns could shank you.

At either side stood the two stone creatures. Not quite identical. Not quite alive. But not dead. Not sleeping. Their wings towered high above the gates. Stone talons gripped the rocks at their feet. Sharp claws glinted against the base of their swords. Their eyes were half-closed, and underneath, blue orbs flickered.

We stepped closer, something hissed, and flames shot from the hilts of their swords to the tips.

"They don't look very friendly," I whispered.

Molpe ignored me and bowed, her wings spreading out in an elegant curtsy.

I followed suit, only my leggings and tank top didn't have the same effect. I looked to Molpe, so I could tell when we'd dipped our heads long enough. I still didn't know what our distraction plan was, but Molpe had taken command of this part of the plan. From my years serving as Second in Mischief and

Mayhem, I knew—you don't question your commander. If they want you to know the plan, they'll let you know the plan.

But Molpe still hadn't moved.

Korrina...

She connected to my power, talking to me through a silent song.

These are the judges of intention. Please step forward and allow your intent to be judged.

"What?" I hissed, not having learned the power of speaking in silence.

Remember. You have to get to the tree. You have to fight.

Don't question your commander. Rule number one.

I stepped forward, and the stone guardians' eyes flicked wide open and drowned me in a blue stare so penetrating I wouldn't be surprised at all to find a hole burned through my chest clear to my spine.

"I just want to get into the garden, man," I said, all cool, every bit of it true.

The blue in their eyes dimmed, and their eyelids slid back to halfway closed.

"Guess I passed," I muttered and stepped through the gates.

I turned back, waiting for Molpe, really curious to see what her big distraction plan was, but she hadn't budged. Except to suck in a deep breath.

Little dirt tornadoes swirled at her feet, twisted and grew along the dirt and clover foot path. Her plan hit me like a lightning bolt to the face.

"No," I gasped.

The tornadoes, powered by her song, had grown and converged into two dirt devils, one for each guardian.

The guardians stretched impossibly tall, stone cracking from their claws, their faces, their wings, the flames in the swords growing, beams of white light shooting from all the cracks in the stone, blinding.

Molpe screamed. The tornadoes grew to match the guardians, and I saw what she'd done.

To get all of us into the garden, she'd sacrificed herself at the gates.

She couldn't tell me her plan or I never would have made it past the guards.

Go.

I dug the balls of my feet into the ground and launched through the garden paths, leaving Molpe at the gates to the fate she'd chosen, hoping it wasn't in vain.

Hoping we were strong enough without her.

Ania whispered at the back of my mind, *Trust us, Elpida. Everything we've been through. We are enough. You are enough.*

I am enough.

I believed her. And even though my feet were pounding soft dirt and grass and flowers, making my way to the center of Persephone's garden, I felt as if I was being carried by wings, carried on a soft breeze, and a silent song.

At my side, something flew, keeping up with me step for step. I flicked my gaze over, not wanting to stop, knowing we were on a deadline that had probably already passed, and tripped.

The Pegasus I'd ridden before, woven from ivy and garden debris, flew low to the ground at my side.

With Persephone riding his back.

CHAPTER 44

I stumbled, caught myself before I fell. Persephone was a wild card. I really wasn't sure whose side she was on.

"Hey, Seph," I said, all normal. "Just going for a run."

She raised her eyebrows. Her eyes had darkened, and her long, Lady Godiva hair had lost its golden shine. She looked more like the Underworld Queen I'd met last year, more dead than alive. "Let's not play games, Korrina. You are trying to stop my mother. Your Siren sisters are all trapped outside the so-called weak areas of my garden."

My stomach dropped to my knees. Our plan had failed before we'd even started. I propped my hands on my hips, readied my song. "Fine. No more games. Are you here to help me or stop me?"

A smile curled at Persephone's full lips. It was beautiful. And terrifying.

"Never can tell with a fair-weather friend, can you? Spring is life-giving, destructive. It can rain and help the flowers bloom, or it can flood." She gestured in front of us.

Through the trees, Demeter's green fire blazed.

I was close. Close to where Persephone was powerless. Close to stopping Demeter.

Vines wormed out of the soil, thick and thorny. Flowers bloomed at their edges, bigger than nature intended. Though Persephone was essentially nature, so maybe it was exactly what nature intended.

An impassable wall formed, protecting Demeter's fire, sealing our fates.

Persephone turned to me, dark tears at the corners of her eyes. Gone was the goddess of spring. "Let's see if you've learned."

"Learned what?"

She stopped smiling. "Who to trust."

She stepped into a hollow tree and let it swallow her up.

"Really?" I shouted. We did not have time for this.

I stepped closer to Persephone's wall. On the surface, it was beautiful. Sculpted by a master gardener, every leaf, flower, and vine perfect.

But get just past the flowers, and sharp thorns blocked every opening. No way through, and I had a feeling my Siren power was powerless against those thorns.

Worth a shot anyway.

My voice rumbled against my throat, my purple aura glowed, and I pushed against the wall.

It thickened.

"That's just great," I muttered and paced in front of the wall. There was no giving up. No one coming to my rescue. Persephone knew exactly why we were all here and had stopped me with little more than a thought.

Something niggled at the back of my mind. Why had she let me come all this way, only to stop me at the edge of her power?

Like any god, Persephone liked her riddles.

Before, the only way I'd been able to use the key Persephone had given me, the key that unlocked Demeter's cage, had been to confront my own grief. To acknowledge it, to see how many ties it had on me.

And now? What had I'd learned?

Who did I trust?

My heartbeat slowed, my chest grew lighter, my power swirled around me, lifted me to my toes.

"Me. I trust me," I whispered.

I was a dyad. Two halves that made up more than one whole. *Elpida* and *Ania*, hope and sorrow.

Losing Jared, Dad, Mom, everything I'd gone through…it hadn't made me weaker.

It'd made me stronger.

I reached deep, connected with all that I'd lost, the pain that colored my memories, my decisions, my dreams. *Ania* reached out, and this time, I grabbed her hand without reservation, held her tight, and let her power weave with mine in a knot that couldn't be undone, a quiet mending of a broken heart.

Music poured out of me. Not just a melody, but a resonant symphony. My power filled the air, no longer a thin purple light, but rich and velvet and tangible. It didn't drain me but refilled me, as if I was a fountain pouring into itself again and again in a never-ending cascade.

I stretched out my hand and let a tiny drop of my power roll off the tip of my finger and drip onto one of the garden wall's leaves.

The vines rolled back and formed a pathway, not just through the thorns, but through Demeter's cursed fire.

I couldn't see Persephone, but I felt her approval through the gentle scent of the flowers and the distant smell of a spring rain.

I took a breath and walked through a tunnel of thorns and fire.

No longer was I broken. No longer two halves, but whole, and somehow…more.

I stepped out of the tunnel. Demeter's fire raged in a giant circle around a barren field. In the center, a pomegranate tree braced against the flames that licked its trunk.

Demeter—aka the Goddess of Retribution aka the Puppeteer aka Persephone's grieving, broken-hearted mother—knelt in front of the tree, her hands buried in the dry soil.

CHAPTER 45

Once upon a time, Neri dragged my spirit from my body and brought me through the veil to this meadow, cloaked us in the shadows of this tree, and thrust us deep into the earth, to Hades's dead domain.

We hadn't been there to rescue Persephone, though Hades had thought so at the time. We'd been there to steal an oath-breaker.

Back then, the meadow had been green. Full of flowers and soft grass that gently sloped upward to Persephone's tree.

Now, the meadow was a desert. The tree had lost most of its leaves. The pomegranates, once full and red, clung desperately to the branches, the fruit withered and leeched of color.

Demeter's hands were plunged wrist deep into the earth, and around her, the soil had cracked, exposing thick roots. Roots that were turning black.

She was killing the tree by killing its roots. It'd never grow back.

There was no reasoning with the Goddess of Retribution, so I didn't even try.

I held my power in my hand, whipped it out at the kneeling goddess, and lashed open her cheek.

She ripped her hands out of the dirt, spun around, and landed in a feral crouch. Golden blood leaked down her face. "I should have known you'd show up again. Sirens are a fungus with only one cure." She slapped her hands against the ground. Flames shot out like a bullet, targeted on me.

I jumped, rolled out of the way. The fire followed, swirling closer. I darted left. The flames met me there, cutting off any escape.

Great. The Goddess of Retribution had a missile targeting system.

Demeter had turned her back to me and refocused on destroying the tree, which looked sicklier with every passing second.

My song vibrated in my throat, but it would do no good unless I got past these flames.

Again, I balled my power in my hand, but this time, I let 'er rip. It baseballed at the fire, and the flames *darted away*.

Say what?

Demeter hadn't noticed. Her fire changed direction and came at me again.

"Okay, *Ania*, time for a new look," I whispered, rubbed my hands down my body, and coated myself in Siren dyad power.

Flames surrounded me, but didn't touch me, as if my new *Ania-Elpida* powers were a fire suppressant. I concentrated, kept my power pulled in close, and launched myself at Demeter.

My Siren power might not be enough to stop her, but I'd also been trained by a Guardian to fight.

I smacked into Demeter with my shoulder, shoving an *oomph* out of her and wrenching her away from the tree's roots.

She landed on her feet.

So did I.

"You have to stop," I gasped. "You're going to destroy the human world and start a war between the gods."

She shrugged. "Let them all burn. For all have had a hand in my daughter's demise."

Time for some fact checks.

"Uh, not true. Humans had nothing to do with Hades kidnapping your daughter."

She cocked her head. "The Sirens did."

"You punished the Sirens with the curse, remember? So check them off your list."

"And yet, you seem to have found a way around that." She nodded at my purple power suit.

I looked down, heard a whiff of wind, braced for impact.

Her dirty goddess foot kicked into my chest. Air rushed by my cheeks as I flew across the meadow. I uselessly gasped for air. My back hit the ground. Something crunched. Something sharp pinched against my lungs. Someone screamed.

Me. It was me.

Green flames towered over me. I flung my power out, barricading my body from hitting the curse. I'd lost my power suit somewhere along the way, and Demeter's curse missile was headed straight for me.

You've been through worse, Ania reminded me.

Yeah, I had.

I forced air into my lungs, forced my legs to stand, forced my power to cover my body, to seep into my bones, to heal whatever Demeter had just broken. The world stopped tilt-a-whirling, and I took a deep breath.

She'd already gone back to the tree roots, ignoring me, trusting that she'd knocked me down for good.

Not yet, goddess-hole.

A more subtle approach this time.

"We are but mountains, and we crumble, we crumble. We are but mountains, be gentle, be gentle." My voice poured out, soft and

whispered, singing Amity's song. A song filled with hushed sorrow.

Demeter froze, her back going straight.

I took a step forward, kept singing. *"We all break, we all break, we all break. You think I'm strong, but I'll crumble, I'll crumble, for you."*

Demeter's fire disappeared.

A new voice joined mine, a new power circled the meadow.

"But from the ruins of my grief I'll rise, I'll build a kingdom that's sky-high." Amity appeared by my side, gripped my hand. *"I'll not stop there. You'll not stop there. We'll not stop there."*

Tanzy joined my other side, humming the melody before we sang it, leading the way.

"From the ruins of you, we'll start anew, and we'll grow stronger, together, forever. Refined by the fire, by the past, by the memories that flood, that burn, that heal, that lead us back to where we are strong again."

These were fresh lyrics, new verses. More words to let live, hope to set free. A song that was written as we sang it.

"We are mountains again, we can do this again, come back to us again..."

The meadow flooded with a swirl of Siren power. New, strong, tested, and refined.

Demeter stood.

She stepped toward us. Darkness fell from her, and hints of the Demeter I'd encountered in Persephone's visions, hints of a Demeter whole and healed began to shine through.

"My daughter..." she sang, her voice breathless.

"She'll come back to you again," the three of us sang.

"She's broken..." Demeter stretched her hands out to us.

"Not forever," I promised, and we formed a healing circle around her, an ancient chain of all the women before us. Women who had grieved, who had lost more than one could bear, and together we lifted her up, lent her our strength, our hope, our words, let her see past her darkness, and into the hope of tomorrow.

A strong wind rushed out from Demeter as the last of the gray washed from her eyes and the color returned to her cheeks.

This was the mother I'd met in the visions. Less happy, more resolved.

She blinked and shook her head, as if she'd just had a dizzy spell. Her gaze darted around the meadow, then fell on us.

We tensed. She wasn't her dark self anymore, but that didn't make her any less dangerous.

Just less crazy.

"I suppose I am indebted to you, daughters of Melpomene." She looked at each of us in turn, but held my gaze longer. "You didn't give up. I will not give up on my daughter either."

The ground rumbled at our feet.

Demeter quirked her lips. "I'm afraid that though you stopped me from destroying the tree entirely, I damaged it enough to ignite my brother's wrath."

Tanzy's eyes glazed. "War comes."

Demeter nodded. "First, I will give you each a gift, for I will not owe a debt to the daughters of the Sirens who betrayed my daughter."

The three of us exchanged glances. I wasn't so sure we'd like these gifts.

"For you, Songwriter, I give you choice. Your wings will be visible only here in our world. You will be allowed to return to the human realm and to traverse between our two worlds at will."

Amity's wings shuddered, her cheeks pinkened. "I can go home?"

Demeter nodded. "You will soon redefine what home means to you, but yes, you may go home."

Amity squealed.

"To you, Maestro, I give you focus. Instead of all possibilities, at all times, you will see only those that matter most."

Tanzy beamed. "No more headaches?"

"No more headaches."

Tanzy skipped a little and stretched out her arms.

The ground rumbled again, more violently this time.

"And you, *Elpida*, what can I give to you? You have so many needs, so many desires." She pressed two fingers against the center of my forehead.

"My dad," I said, before she could make the decision for me. "I need you to save my dad."

She frowned. "He is on trial for disobeying the Council. I cannot save his life."

My heart grew heavy. I blinked back tears. "Then save his afterlife."

She pressed her lips together. "I will do my best. I'm sorry that I cannot do more." She bowed her head. "I must go. Hades approaches to collect his bride, and seeing me here will only infuriate him further."

"Too late," a dark voice hissed behind us.

We spun around. The tree twisted, and underneath its dying branches, Hades and Persephone appeared.

"The line has been crossed, the sides have been chosen." Hades, dark and delicious and utterly terrifying, screamed into the sky. At his side, Persephone cringed, and her crown of bones glowed eerily white against her forehead.

"War comes, brothers and sisters," Hades yelled into the sky, his mouth wide, his voice so loud it shook the ground. "Do you side with Goddess of Harvest and Fire and the Daughters of Air? Or do you side with the Keeper of the Titans, the dead, and the powers of the unknown and unexplored depths?"

The sky darkened. The air shook.

My stomach twisted.

Demeter growled, flicked her wrist, and a portal opened that led back to the human world.

"Go," she said to us. "You are no longer safe in this world. Hades has declared open war, and you are in his sights."

The ground itself lifted under our feet. Amity screamed. Tanzy's face went white. I grabbed onto them both.

We lost our footing and fell through the portal.

CHAPTER 46

The hot air of a Sedona evening hit us like an inferno. We rolled onto the dusty mesa, and our human friends and the priests jumped out of our way.

Dave trained Sully on us. Cloud crouched in attack pose. The priests pointed their staffs.

"Guys, guys, it's us. It's just us," I yelled, hands raised.

They froze.

It lasted for about a second before Dave dropped Sully, rushed Amity, wrapped his arms around her, and pulled her in for an R-rated kiss. Amity grabbed him right back, the ghost of her wings shimmering in the air. Not that Dave could see them.

"You stopped her?" Crannik stepped forward, his shoulders tight.

"We stopped her," I said with a mission-accomplished nod.

Cloud and Danica locked in a tight embrace. Crannik and the priests danced some kind of end-zone jig, made even more geeky with the addition of their staffs and hoodies. Might as well let them have a moment before we dropped the bad news.

Why was there always bad news?

"I'll let you tell them, Tanzy," I said and stepped to the back of the group.

Tanzy cleared her throat, tried to get their attention.

I took another look at this weird, cobbled together group of friends I'd collected. Crannik and his boys—who'd showed me that first impressions were often wrong. Dave and Amity—who'd taught me the past was heavy and shouldn't be allowed to weigh you down. Tanzy—who'd upped the weirdness and made me expand my comfort level.

And Danica and Cloud—my human friends, my best friends—who'd proved that true friends are always there, even when life sucked.

They were going to be super pissed.

Maybe someday they'd forgive me.

Maybe someday they'd understand.

Tanzy froze, looked over Crannik's shoulder. Her eyes went wide, seemed to swallow the world, and I knew she was seeing the future I'd just created. One she couldn't see before because I'd not made a plan. I'd not thought it through. I'd fantasized, I'd dreamed, but I hadn't made it real.

Until now.

I shoved my hand into my pocket. Grabbed one of Hestia's last three cookies, held tight to fate's thread tied to my heart, and shoved the inter-dimensional treat into my mouth.

Tanzy's screams followed me into the void and snapped silent as the void took over.

As I made my choice.

CHAPTER 47

My training room deep in Phorkys's fortress echoes color. With every panted breath, every drop of sweat, every swing of my sword, the colors shift. Blues, greens, reds.

Behind me, a thud. A gasp.

The room makes a leap from green to purple.

Not a color I'd seen here before.

I drop my sword. My heart squeezes tight. But I don't have to turn around to know…

She's here.

A NOTE FROM KRIS FARYN

Dear Reader,

Thank you for taking a chance on this series. I hope you have enjoyed Korrina's story!

If you did, I would be eternally grateful if you would write a review on Goodreads (even if it's only a sentence or two). Every review matters to authors and helps other readers discover the book.

Book 3 of the Siren's Call series: Song of Curses is out now!

I look forward to continuing Korrina's journey with you.

To Good Books and Living From Joy,

Kris

KORRINA WANTS TO KNOW - BOOK DISCUSSION

1. Things happened in this book. Major things. Which of my many trials and errors hit you in the feels? Was there one that you could relate to? If so, you bring the chips, I'll bring the salsa, and we'll commiserate.
2. Jared has...changed. What do you think he's struggling most with? Or do you think he's struggling at all? *gets out pad and pencil to take notes*
3. Would you have forgiven Luke? Has a friend ever betrayed you and then asked for a second chance?
4. What do you think about Amity and Tanzy? It seems I'm no longer 'the one,' but part of a larger whole. Do you think we're stronger together or apart? Why do you think 'the one' is such a common trope in books?
5. Demeter is essentially driven mad with grief—since she's the goddess of the harvest, her grief threatens many of my favorite things: bean burritos, coffee, chocolate, Cheetos. What is the one food you don't think you could live without? What lengths would you go to in order to save your favorite food?
6. Would you ever go skydiving? Why or why not?

7. One of the main things Demeter and I have in common is our grief. For her, it's the loss of her daughter, Persephone. For me, it's the loss of Jared, and eventually, my dad. Why do you think some people allow grief to destroy them, and others allow grief to motivate them? Should we be allowed to grieve at our own pace?

8. If you had to choose one of the Sirens' powers, which would you choose? The power to heal (that's me, baby), the power to write things into existence (Amity), or the power to see the future (Tanzy)?

9. Ania, I've discovered, is the darker half to my bright self. It's been super hard to accept her as part of me, rather than a stranger I have to fight, but I've found I'm stronger with her than without her. Does it seem strange to you that I have another half of me that is sentient? What would you do if part of yourself woke up and started talking to you?

10. Who is your favorite mythological character you've met so far in my world? I think my favorite might be Luke's ogre cousin. Not sure why. Or maybe Crannik —though is he technically human and not a creature? Or are humans creatures too? *thoughts I ponder*

11. The autumn equinox plays a huge part in this book, as it did in a lot of ancient cultures. Why do you think so many ceremonies were/are tied to the passing of the seasons?

12. The pomegranate tree is a symbol of life, regeneration, and marriage. And yet, Demeter wants to destroy it to presumably save her daughter, Persephone. I have so many questions about this. First, do you think Persephone knew that eating the pomegranate seeds would tie her to Hades? I mean, if it was a known thing that a pomegranate represents

marriage, it's not the biggest leap to think that Persephone ate the seeds intentionally. (He is extremely hot.) So is Demeter truly saving Persephone or is she trying to force her will on her daughter? Talk amongst yourselves.

13. Why do you think I chose to keep leaving to save Jared a secret from my friends? And how mad do you think they'll be?

KORRINA'S MYTHOLOGICAL CHEAT SHEET

Aglaope (ag-l-OW-pee)
In her own words, she is "the daughter of the Muse Melpomene, granddaughter of the Titaness Mnemosyne, blood of Gaia, and handmaiden to Goddess Persephone." No, I don't think she's stuck up. Nope, not at all. And I'm sure she loves her new nickname, Aggie. She's the OG of Tanzy's line, and they are considered the maestros of the song, mainly because they can see what happens next.

Molpe (mole-PEE)
Molpe is my gajillion-great Siren grandmother. We've gotten to know each other a little better, and I now believe she's not evil. Not sure about her sisters yet, but Molpe's cool. A bit too formal, but I'm good at loosening up ancient mythical creatures. Our Siren line carries the power to heal, and we are the passion behind the creation of music. Of course we are.

Peisinoe (pee-see-NO-ee)
Another one of Molpe's sisters and another one of my ancient great aunts. Her raven-like fathers reflect her shining personality. Peisinoe sent a shadow rat to chew on an invisible strand of fate connected to my stomach, placed there either by Persephone or a goddess cookie or Peisinoe herself. So...friend or foe? I still do not know.

Thelxiepeia (thel-ksee-EH-pee-ah)
Thelxiepeia is Molpe's sister, so that makes her my ancient great-aunt. She's also Amity's gajillion-great grandmother. Amity nicknamed her Thelma—as one does with ancient beings. Amity's line was "blessed with the ability to cast words as power," though I doubt Amity agrees with the word 'blessed.' Essentially, Amity and her line are songwriters.

GODS, GODDESSES, AND A TITAN(ESS)

The Council of the Gods
A tribunal of the Greek gods, led by the three Fates, who determine how the mythic world should interact with the real world. When I met with the Council—in a Chinese restaurant no less—Zeus, Poseidon, Hades, and Hestia held Council seats, with one empty seat saved for Demeter.

Demeter (dee-mEE-teer)
Back in *Song of Destiny*, I'd just thought Demeter, Mother of Persephone and Goddess of Agriculture, was cray-cray. But yeah, turns out we hadn't even scratched her surface. Though I get it, grief does things to a person. At least one good thing came of all this—I don't think Demeter hates Sirens as much as she used to, even though her curse still remains.

The Fates

So, I met Fate, or rather the Fates. At the Council of the Gods meeting in the Chinese restaurant. (Please tell me you find that as ridiculous as I do. I mean, we didn't even get a fortune cookie.) Three sisters whose figures change at any given moment. At times, they appeared beautiful, with long, cascading hair as white as the moon, and at other times they appeared as three hags, with missing teeth and curled, yellowed nails. Probably the most disturbing body image they chose to take on was that of a Frankenstein version of a Siren, with goose bodies and old hag heads in place of beaks. Shudder.

The Fates are goddesses who weave the threads of destiny together. Apparently they also hook them to your insides like tapeworms and attach them to other people who have influence on you or you on them.

Ask me how I know.

Hades (HAI-deez)

Hot. Hawt. Like, Legolas hawt. Also, super scary. Also, God of the Underworld and kidnapper of Persephone. By the way, I may have stolen a priceless, irreplaceable potion from him, and he will probably try to kill me at some point. He's part of the Council of the Gods, and I don't think he'll remember meeting me there at all.

Hermes (HUR-meez)

Though I haven't actually met Hermes, I heard him mentioned in a vision of Demeter and Phorkys, so I'm including him in this cheat sheet. He's known as the messenger of the gods and witnessed Persephone's kidnapping.

Hestia (eh-s-t-EE-aa)

Goddess of the Hearth, Hestia is basically the perfect home economics professor. She even sent Luke and me home with cookies. She seems friendly enough, but I've learned that you can't trust a goddess. She sits on the Council of the Gods with her three brothers, Zeus, Hades, and Poseidon, and her sister, Demeter.

Melpomene (mel-poh-mEN-ee)

Melpomene makes me sad. She used to be known as the Muse of singing and dancing, but she transformed into the Muse of tragedy. And well, that's sad. She's also the mother of the Sirens, so we're related.

Mnemosyne (mm-nee-mow-sEEn-ee)

A titaness. Specifically the titaness of memory, time, and tales. She's also the mother of the Muses, which makes her the grandmother of the Sirens, and the original owner of the scepter.

Persephone (pur-SEF-uh-nee)

Got kidnapped. Ate a pomegranate. Lives in the Underworld. Her husband, Hades—God of the Dead—is hot. Hot, but deadly. For half the year, Persephone lives above ground, which makes Demeter, her mom, happy, and so we have spring and summer. For the second half of the year, Persephone lives in the Underworld with Hades, and Demeter causes crops to wither and die —fall and winter.

Persephone believes that Molpe's sisters helped Hades kidnap her. She only trusts Molpe, which saved my life. But Persephone also doesn't seem to hate her position with Hades in the Underworld. Is this Stockholm syndrome, or is she actually in love with the God of the Dead? Which begs the question…—does Persephone need to be saved? Must explore this more…

Phorkys (fOR-keez)

Okay, seriously, who is this dude? His pictures look like a mashup of the leftovers from some Friday night lobster special. God of the deep and god of monsters, he's an ancient sea god who was dethroned by Poseidon. Oh, and the scepter belongs to him, which makes my life really complicated.

Poseidon (poh-SEE-duhn)

God of the ocean, father of Triton, grandfather of Ariel—who is a mermaid, not a Siren. There is a difference. He also sits on the Council of the Gods and has a resemblance to The Dude. That's all I got.

Zeus (zee-oos)

Zeus is the George Clooney of the skies. An obvious choice for the Council of the Gods, though he is a bit theatrical. As the king of the gods, I guess he's entitled to be dramatic whenever he pleases.

CREATURES

Chimera (KAI-mir-ah)

An indecisive mashup of a goat, a lion, and a serpent. I kicked one's butt back to the mythical side of the Veil in typical Korrina-fashion.

Cyclops (KEE-klohps)

One-eyed grandsons of Phorkys. We had a short meet-and-greet right before I sent them back to their side of the Veil in *Song of Destiny*.

Daimones Proseoous (day-MON-eez pro-see-OH-us)

I met these six sons of Poseidon six months ago, back in *Song of*

Destiny. They are essentially demonic, sea-ghost guns-for-hire. Poseidon banished them from his realm—they were cursed and, in their madness, attacked their own mother—and Phorkys must have taken them under his wing—er—claw after their banishment.

Echidna (eh-KEED-nah)

Snake from the waist down, woman from the waist up, and not a fan of wearing clothes. She does have a pretty awesome belly ring. Echidna is one of Phorkys's daughters, and she's known as the mother of monsters. I'm fairly certain we'll meet again.

Harpies (HAIR-peez)

These are also bird-women, but much smaller than Sirens, and not nearly as beautiful. They look like they were spliced with turkey vultures, but of course, I only got a quick glimpse. Their name means *snatcher* in Greek, and sometimes they're accused of snatching souls. Creepy.

Minotaur (meen-oh-TAR)

Disturbing monster. Man body. Bull head. His mom—Pasiphae, wife of Minos—had an affair with a white bull, got preggers, and birthed this thing. I wonder if mythological creatures have access to a good therapist.

Neri (nair-EE)

An interdimensional owl who claims she existed before time itself. She thinks she's right about everything, but I have some things to teach her as well. She says she's my spirit guide, my *pneuma*, and yes, she does guide me, and yes, she can yank my spirit out of my body, so yes, I guess she's my spirit guide.

PLACES

Anthemusa (an-the-MUSE-ah)
Island home of the Sirens, where they enjoy torturing other creatures.

The Grotto
Phorkys's special dungeon for those he hates most. We suspect my mother is kept there.

Tartarus/Underworld (TAR-tar-us)
Persephone's home away from home. Also, where mythicals go after death. Some humans who live behind the Veil go there as well. Like Guardians. My dad. He's hopefully in the Elysian Fields, if Demeter got there in time.

The Veil
A magical barrier that protects the human world from the mythical world.

The Void
An interdimensional space that sucks in lost souls and keeps them there for all eternity.

Vortices
Swirling centers of energy that are conducive to healing, meditation, and self-exploration. Or, you know, link to a goddess gone crazy across the Veil.

Cathedral Rock Vortex
A female vortex located in Sedona, Arizona. People are supposed to feel calm and comforted while there. We. Did. Not.

CEREMONIES

The Lesser Mysteries
Part of the Eleusinian Mysteries and the cult of Demeter and Persephone, each spring those who wanted to join the cult were invited to sacrifice a piglet to Demeter and Persephone. They then ritually purified themselves in the river Ilissos. I have no idea what that entailed.

The Greater Mysteries
Held in early fall in Athens, initiates who had been through the Lesser Mysteries ritual in the spring would walk the Sacred Way from Athens to Eleusis and reenact Demeter's search for Persephone. Many parts of the ritual are lost in history but, lucky me, I got to experience it firsthand. The point of the ritual is to learn how to hold peace while surrounded by the darkness of death—supposedly like Persephone does in the Underworld.

The Siren's Call Series

Song of Destiny

Song of Wings

Song of Curses

Free Novelette | The Nefertiti Curse

The Muse Island Series

Mark of the Gods (Book 1)

Power of the Song (Book 2)

Rise of the Storm (Book 3)

Curse of the Night (Book 4)

Book 5 ~ coming soon!

Muse Island Short Stories

Finn's Call

Gryla's Gift

ABOUT THE AUTHOR

Kris Faryn is known for her love of bean burritos, of traveling, and of her patooties at home, including the grown-up one and furry ones. She also loves baking, cooking, a good book, and a crackling fire.

Kris Faryn is a multi-award-winning author of Young Adult Fantasy books and Adult Suspense. Most importantly, Kris believes in turning dreams into realistic goals and that everyone has something special and unique to offer the world.

Get to know Kris Faryn at:

facebook.com/KrisFaryn

instagram.com/booksandfuzzysocks

bookbub.com/profile/kris-faryn

goodreads.com/krisfaryn

amazon.com/author/krisfaryn

patreon.com/KrisFaryn

Ingram Content Group UK Ltd.
Milton Keynes UK
UKHW010144110723
424906UK00005B/545